Cocaine and Carnivores

Ross Davies

COPYRIGHT

ACKNOWLEDGMENTS

It is about fucking time, am I right? It has been way too long since I published something, almost like long enough for people to wonder if I had just given up writing entirely. Well, I didn't(obviously), and I think you'll be as happy I didn't give up as I am, and I know you're going to love this story.

This is completely different than my other books for a grocery list of reasons, but the only one I would like to underline and emphasize the importance of is I lived as the character did. I researched most of the content too closely and nearly died in the process. I became an addict.

Whoopsie.

And I know I shouldn't depreciate my struggle, but fuck you, it is my birthday party, and I can depreciate if I want to. I was already an alcoholic, and I tried cocaine after saying no some many times and finally at thirty years old, I gave it the old college try, and ten years later a book came out.

Obviously, a bunch of other stuff happened but I don't have the time or energy to get into it. I don't recommend ever doing something that manifests as a personality or causes you to choose to be high rather than eat or sleep, but it is your life, do what you want. I'm still an addict and an alcoholic but I've never fallen so far as to hurt my family or trade my body to get high.

So that is a win, here is to making the best of a bad situation.

So, without further ado, here is my acceptance speech part and you can't play me off.

Thank you to my mum, brother Scott, and sister Mylan. Without you guys, I would've successfully exited life long ago. Thank you, Dad, as well, rest in peace Ace, still miss you and fuck you for dying.

To Pierre, my brother, my dumb to my dumber, my oldest friend and inspiration for Gabriel, without you I would be so much less. I can never thank you enough but I'm never going to stop trying.

Sean Martin, you're my fucking anchor dude, your honesty has kept me the good man I am even when I can't see that through all my darkness and deprecation. You're my compass.

Thank you to my group of Seven, especially Justin, just kidding, Kyle, Sean, Jake, Mike, Steve, Waylon -- you guys are my rock.

Eric, you saved my life more times than I can count, but seriously, thank you eternally for showing up and stopping me from really offing myself. You're excellent.

To Jesse, we both lost everything at the same time but found each other. I'll never forget our backyard talks or the kitchen parties. We punished ourselves for things out of our control but had each other in a time when we felt totally and completely alone, but because of you, I knew I wasn't. I love you, brother.

To Jesse and Leg, I can't thank you enough for helping me keep going through covid, reading to you guys is the only reason I kept writing. Sorry that we don't talk anymore but know it wasn't meaningless.

To every relationship I aided in fucking up while figuring out my shit, I'm sorry, but know each and every single one of you made me better. Really, I'm ashamed of my behavior, and I only hope that wherever you are is better than where we were.

Thank you to Dave Kirky for being my biggest fan. Dave, you're, to me, what a great man looks like. Selfless, providing, patient, and considerate. It will take me the rest of my life to be half the man you wake up as.

Big Erica, my brother Barry, thank you for every moment.

Trevor, my teacher, my brother, my fucking ball busting brother. Thank you for helping me stay humble and helping me see that you must laugh at yourself even when you want to cry.

Alex Cheese, dude, it is really like opening a can of sardines.

Skywalker, I'm still in denial, and I'm sorry I didn't do enough, and I hate that the last conversation we had was that one. I love you dude, and I miss you. Know that you brought so much joy to people that at your funeral you made enemies friends and friends became family. I don't know what I'm going to do without you but keep being the best version of the man you helped make.

This book is dedicated to Zach, Jesse, Bonnie and Alex...

I'm going to leave space there because during the process of just editing and formatting between 2023-2024, those names mentioned had their stories cut short far too soon from substances or suicide.

THE PROLOGUE

Look at you, reading a book, good for you. Wait. Don't put it down, keep reading, it's an awesome story. More importantly, you haven't heard this one...wait, sorry, read this one, because you're reading. This is more of a journal, a journal but not a journal. Don't think about it. Keep reading. This story is about motivation. Now, motives are like assholes—I know, I'm ripping that line off, but it fits—everyone has one, well, hopefully they have one because if not that would be weird, but it would fit with this story...not having an asshole would definitely fit in with this story.

What the fuck am I talking about...anyways...

These motivations can be called reasons. With reason you can justify doing anything. Man, people have been using "reasons" to get away with atrocities throughout time. For instance, Hitler...okay bad choice, but you get the point... really bad choice. Hitler was wrong, plain and simple, but to prove my point, he did what he did for a "reason", however disillusioned that "reason" was. And just for the record, I don't condone anything he did. But you get what I'm trying to say. Right?

So, if you had a reason or a motive, you could do just about anything and live with it. For this story, the motivation is drugs. Throughout time we have admired characters motivated by substance. Like these 20th century beauties: *Pop-eye* used spinach, *Mario* used magic mushrooms, and our "hero" uses—yes, uses—cocaine, alcohol, weed, speed, oxycodone...anything and everything that keeps him from being sober. Like those fictional characters, our "hero" will eventually use drugs to fight "evil".

And by evil, I mean supernatural creatures.

You see—well actually, you don't see, and that's the problem— the world is full of supernatural creatures, and you have been too blind to notice. By you, of course, I mean all of us. Humans have stopped paying attention to their surroundings, especially now, in our technology-driven, hyper-stimulated, social-media-based society.

We have become increasingly distracted and now with the addition of personal computers that barely leave our hands, it's no wonder no one knows that the supernatural exists. You—yes you, reading—have probably spent the most of today with your face buried in your stupid smartphone every free chance you had; to update your status, or post your shitty lunch on Instagram, or tweet something you think is more clever than it actually is. No offence— I'm kidding, all the offence. Keep that in mind the next time you're face profile stalking someone you haven't spoken to in a decade or hash tagging like an Uber-douchebag to what's trending.

With this in mind of course you have been completely oblivious to the bumps in the night being more than bumps, and I'm not talking about drugs.

Not yet, anyway. I'm talking about monstrous malevolence personified walking right by you on the street, and luckily it just walked by you instead of making you its next meal. You see, all those nightmarish monsters from legend are real and they do walk amongst us.

This is a story about someone so dumb and desperate that when they found out that monsters are real rather than fleeing and locking themselves in the closest panic room like a sane person, they instead, out of severe substance addiction sought out these evils and destroyed them. But not because he wanted good to conquer and triumph over evil, making evil its bitch...No, he did this just to fuel a fucking habit or better yet, eight of them.

CHAPTER 1

Our story starts in an apartment, mostly empty of things an apartment should have, but an apartment, nonetheless. Its contents include a bed, a lamp, and a lot of trash...oh and that man. The man you're looking at...sorry, the guy you're reading about, is Eddie Red. Or Eddie Read, like "read", the past tense of "reading" ...

You get it. Shit, sorry, moving on.

Eddie was never quite sure of the actual spelling because his parents never confirmed, or better yet, never settled on the spelling. His mom spelled it Read, and his dad spelt it like Red. And that was the basis of so many arguments. *I know you're sitting there and calling bullshit because at least for legal purposes, you need to have something on record, but they truly went out of their way to go against the system.* So eventually, when he was legally independent and emancipated from his parents completely, Eddie flipped a coin and decided. He just spells it like the color, like his dad did... *Anyway, I have digressed and should get back to the point. Let's move on.*

I refer to Eddie as a guy because being a man is something that takes work. Being a man comes with responsibilities and Eddie, well, Eddie has none. And if you don't think there is a difference or don't consider the importance of that transition, then you have no idea what the limbo of being a "guy" is like. It is a hellish and possibly extremely dangerous state where a boy has lost his innocence, and is thrust forward, learning as he goes, and he is lucky if he does more right than wrong and fully understands the difference between them. He is blessed if he impresses more than he embarrasses, and he will for certain embarrass himself at least a dozen times. And I don't mean embarrassing yourself by getting caught in a lie or being caught farting. I mean the kind of mortifying perverse shit that renders both parties from ever mentioning it.

Like, off the top of my head, when your mother catches you fucking a hollowed-out cucumber while watching scrambled porn channels. And before she can even speak or react, you cum. But you don't just ejaculate inside the poor vegetable that you gutted, no, you do something worse. While trying to hide what you were doing, you pull your stone solid, slimy fuck stick out as quick as you can from the recesses of that violated cucumber and now your mom gets to see your dick for the first time since she gave you baths.

Then it gets even worse; yes, something even more horrible happens when you pull out and flash your mom your cock, and you can't control it. (What's *even* worse is when you realize that even if you could control it— as fucked up as this sounds, and is, and the years of therapy you need and totally should seek after this event— you wouldn't. It just feels too damn good.)

So, when the cold air hits your dick, and you feel that temperature change, you explode, and burst fire your white life creating ink, outward and on. Your cock blasts, recoils, and blasts again, shooting jizz with such an intensity that it breeches the gap between the couch and television, building a stringy bridge.

This all happens while you're staring at your poor mother, so you avert your gaze toward the television, and watch the massive amount of your fresh milky fun juice cry clumpy tears down the screen. She does the same.

Now there is only shameful silence. And instead of her grilling you and shaming you further, she leaves. And you never speak of this.

That is just one example of many embarrassing moments one "guy" has endured. And that's just one of many off the top of my head and it isn't even close to the worst.

So, Eddie got stuck festering in the "guy" zone, and has remained there, even though he really ought to move forward because being a guy in your 30's, stuck in a mind state which is meant to be a temporary place between boyhood transition to manhood, is not okay.

Eddie is unconscious - not sleeping, he is out cold, and yes, there is a difference. You go to sleep, but you fall unconscious. This is the only way our pal Eddie ever finds rest: forced to it by exhaustion. He never intends on sleeping because he doesn't want to and hasn't slept properly in years. He doesn't because he is afraid to sleep and terrified to dream. Mortified of what waits behind his closed eyes. His method of not sleeping is to remain high until his body, and eventually his mind, gives out entirely.

The result: tangled in blankets, half-hanging off his bed, about to fall off.

If you wanted to you could say Eddie has seen better days and you'd be right, but those days seem almost ancient and forgotten, just like the lost city of Atlantis. Atlantis is supposedly fictional but knowing what I know now, maybe it's not. But it is ancient and according to legend was lost a very long, long time ago. Just like the days when Eddie was "okay". If you could flashback, and see those days, just like they do in the movies, it would go a little like this...

Eddie, young and innocent, his flesh barely a decade and unscathed by the years and damage it will one day scar from. He runs, freely sprinting across a large field of inch high, freshly cut, mostly green grass, a probable blend of red fescue and ryegrass. Its scent sticks in his nose, and forever keeps; whether he can describe it accurately, he will always know it. To him, it smells like summer. It smells like a sunny Saturday morning in the backyard of his parents' house. It smells like pretending to be a warrior and saving a trapped princess from a terrible dragon from a dark forest layer, all from the comforts of his imagination spreading its legs in that same backyard. The childhood imagination doing what it does best, making something out of nothing.

However, it also faintly carries with it the painful reminder from his elders that he should stop pretending all the time and know the difference between fact and fiction before he hurts himself.

He shrugs that last feeling and continues to run, immediately forgetting it; just like children do when given a check on a reality that they can't yet comprehend and should never have to. His feet bounce over the grass, gently crushing footprint shapes before the grass springs back up after his weight leaves it. This grass covers the backfield of his elementary school for as far as the eye can see but stops after the fence that encloses it, but at his age, it looks like this field goes on forever.

Eddie is ten years old here. And right now, ten-year-old Eddie is running from a gang of other children his age. But he doesn't seem in duress, no, he is smiling widely, his flawless white choppers spread wide with his tongue hanging tauntingly from between them. Eddie is faster than the wind that pulls back his hair.

They can't keep up. They all scream as he crosses an imaginary line, followed closely by another boy, and Eddie and the other boy celebrate, outwardly obnoxious, in their victory in the face of their peers. They revel in their winning and want the other children to know it, rubbing it in as deeply as they possibly can.

This is chickadee. Chickadee is a game where one person starts in the middle and tries to tag others that run from one side of the field to the other. Every tagged person stays in the middle and helps tag others until the last tagged person wins. Eddie and his partner are still untouched, the last ones standing, and have gone several rounds together untagged

That other boy is me, Eddie's best friend. Eddie smiles, and nods, and without words, I know what he wants to do. He wants me to win. He is going to sacrifice himself for me whether I want him to or not.

When the chickadee screams, we take off and the legion that intends to tag us rushes forward. We run right toward the horde of taggers, but Eddie taunts them and leads them away, because Eddie has a way to make anyone pay attention to him. Eddie has a power over people, a power to get under anyone's skin to the point where they can't ignore him. They all want to catch him, and because of this, I can make the other side untagged, so I can win.

Effortlessly and uncontested, I got to the other side, and as I catch my breath, I just watch them continue to chase him, completely unaware that even if they do catch him, it is already over. However pleasant this memory was, this is, in a way, when Eddie first fell in love with the chase. The chase was all he cared about regardless of the consequence. Know it or not, this was the first sign that Eddie was in real trouble...

How can I explain this? Oh yeah, it's easy Eddie is an addict. Not of anything, well actually, he sure does have his favorite vices like cocaine and alcohol, but he actually is addicted to anything that keeps him from being sober.

Eddie is rock bottom...actually, *fuck that,* Eddie is what is under the rock at rock bottom. *And before you challenge that, if rock bottom is the farthest one can fall, there is still a place under the rock at the bottom, you know, with all the moss and dirt, and Eddie is amongst all that...fuck, you get it...anyway.*

Presently, Eddie is about to fall off his bed and wake up.

A knock, loud and rhythmic, sends Eddie crashing to the ground. He grunts, coughs, and starts dragging himself across the garbage littering his floor. He dodges broken glass and half full bottles of unidentifiable liquids, crawls around balled-up used tissues (both happy and sad) and over piles of clothes that he can't recall—or could even if he wanted to—identify as clean or dirty. He pulls himself toward his blue plaid robe, which is definitely dirty, better yet, it is filthy— and throws it over himself, fighting to get each arm through. This robe is ancient and torn, missing the right sleeve completely but Eddie refuses to throw it out because it belonged to his grandfather, and it is all he has to remember him by. Eddie is what you could call sentimental, or more likely just mental.

He reaches for one of the many beer bottles that congest his bedroom floor; several groupings are packed together in different areas of his room, resembling caged cattle as though each cluster is a different herd.

He picks one at random, jamming it to his lips and swigging it back, gulping down what hopefully is beer, which he gambles on with ignorant optimism. He stops drinking suddenly, flinches, and takes a break from drinking it. He pulls his lips from the mouth of the bottle to remove a cigarette butt from his tongue and throws it aside and then finishes the bottle, unaffected by what is currently making you cringe.

He looks around and finds his target, an ashtray. He digs into it and finds a cigarette that isn't fully smoked. Even though it is nearly at the filter, it has enough tobacco left over to smoke. It's still good enough for a couple of puffs, and to Eddie, that's just fine.

Another knock, this time louder, reminds Eddie that someone is at the door. His head is pounding mercilessly from the hangover that doesn't have a beginning, middle, or foreseeable end. He grabs a bottle of pills that have had the prescription scratched off, pills he believes are some sort of extra strength opioid pain-relievers—*I say, pain-relievers, because the pain is never killed, it is just temporarily relieved.* He swallows two with another swig of that garbage beer to wash them down.

Eddie goes to stand, teetering for balance, coughing uncontrollably. He puts his feet into his old steel-toed boots that wait for him in a place—to Eddie's logic—where boots belong, and that is his kitchen. The boots are frayed desiccated husks of their once glorious shells, worn from wear and all of the tare; they come apart at the seam near the ankles and the leather covering the toes are gone exposing the hardened steel underneath—like lips pulled back over teeth.

He grabs his Ray-Bans—knock off Ray-Bans— and throws them on his face to guard his eyes from the falling light of dusk that burns through his blind-less windows.

The knock returns, again, and again. The one who knocks is impatient and not afraid to make that known.

"Yeah. Yeah. I'm coming. One second. Fuck," Eddie shouts from his "kitchen" which he crosses to get to the front door. Said "kitchen" is missing everything but the sink. No appliances. No dishes. No fridge. It is only called a "kitchen" because that is what it once was, and now is only an empty space, just another room.

He deviates and goes into the washroom and takes a piss. He shakes his dick messily over the toilet, and leaves. He travels through the empty space formally known as the kitchen and goes down the hall, passing his "living room", which, like the kitchen, is also just empty, unfilled space, to get to the front door. He unlocks the chain and the door and pulls it wide open.

"Yeah." He grunts, trying to focus on who stands in front of him.

Simon, Eddie's landlord stands there with a shocked and angry look plastering the five o'clock maw he calls a face. He was angry but is now just disgusted by Eddie and his open robed, full-frontal nudity. Eddie's man-bits still dangle and swing freely from the door opening motion. Eddie doesn't care, or rather doesn't know that he is naked and flashing this guy from his open blue plaid robe.

"Where is..." Simon looks from Eddie and his exposed man meat to a piece of paper and then continues. "Jane Summers?" Simon finishes his inquiry, trying his best to keep his eyes somewhere else, anywhere else, as long as they are not fixed on and captured by Eddie's dirty dangling junk.

"She isn't here...she's gone." Eddie sighs.

"She is two months late on rent and...wait...who're you?" Simon coughs, signaling Eddie, using his eyes that quickly dart to and from Eddie's dick, trying to considerately and not so subtly hint to Eddie that he should cover up.

Eddie looks down and smiles, laughs loudly, before closing his robe.

"Sorry. It's cold out here, isn't it? Sorry. I'm Eddie...her boy...sorry, her friend...I'm staying here for a while, so that makes me the one that is two months behind," Eddie says, tying his robe so it stays closed, adjusting his posture trying to hide the scene behind him from Simon.

"Alright, well, Eddie, either way, you, her, I don't care who lives here, but if the rent owed isn't paid in seventy-two hours, neither of you will be living here, understand?"

"Crystal clear like the waters of Lake Minnatonka." Eddie nods submissively in agreement. He just wants this scenario to end.

"Wait, Eddie? Her boyfriend? Shit, I didn't even recognize you..." Simon squints, examining Eddie.

"Nope, just her friend now. But hey, if I see her, I'll pass on the message. You have a fantastic day and take care." Eddie seethes sarcasm and disdain as he steps back and closes the door, nearly slamming it, just as Simon begins to respond but isn't given the chance.

Eddie walks into the empty "living room"—a place despite its title because let's be honest, no one really ever lives in that room—and he looks around, examining each outline once filled by things, traced by age, drawn by time and dust, marking the graves of long forgotten objects. He is haunted by what he sees, or more accurately, what he doesn't. He reluctantly remembers...

The past Eddie, not the ten-year-old one, but the Eddie from two years ago, stands in the same spot and revels in the sight set before him. He looks at a full living room. He gleefully and proudly examines each materialistic accomplishment, finding peace through each piece that completes the puzzle of ownership he had to seek. He has finally finished building a home with all the trinkets and treasures that make it one, accomplished, and now lives "the dream". He has a state of the art (meaning at the time the best you can get) high-definition TV with a 5.1 surround sound system, and cable package that comes with too many channels to watch. He has the "in" living room set—the red leather couch, and matching love seat, and side recliners with an onyx coffee table littered with oak coasters and joined by mini little onyx end tables— that is completed by an extravagant onyx steed in full rear posing as center piece. Eddie, currently, is completely certain that this room is void of any chance of fucking with the fashion sense and "Feng Shui" of the room.

He giggles, reactively; his entire body tenses up momentarily, responding to a kiss on the back of his neck, the area just before neck becomes skull. The kisser—a yet to be introduced character— laughs and cheers as she watches what she knows comes next, knowingly kissing that area because it always produces the same result. He turns shivering; his skin is goose flesh. He smiles, embracing her, and twirling her around before returning her to where she stood seconds ago. She smiles back. He turns, regarding their home once more before facing her. He looks at her lovingly and silently. What he says with his eyes is more than he could with all the words he knows, and she agrees speechlessly. She throws her arms around his neck and pulls him close. Their lips join, gently at first, and then they kiss hard. Connecting wetly, separating briefly, before returning roughly and passionately. Eddie loses himself in her lips, lifting her up, and heading for their bedroom, carrying her as she straddles him. As they kiss, he blindly navigates the hallway, and as they pass by all their memories trapped within picture frames that litter its walls, in this moment he could never believe that two years from now this place would be empty of all that once filled it, including her...

According to science, the olfactory sense has the strongest connection to memory. However, if you're like Eddie, and you can't smell much of anything anymore because of the damage you have done to yourself, and you purposely avoid thinking about the past, the moment when you accidently do, you are forced to remember things as though they happened yesterday.

Dust outlines act as markers for the barren spaces on the walls where paintings used to hang. And in turn, reminiscently, the same aged outlines help place the furniture that used to fill the empty room's wide-open space. This is times way of proving life, or in this case, that furnishing (life) once existed here.

But now this room, completely abandoned of those things, looks like it did before occupancy, and Eddie shakes, or better yet, shutters uncontrollably, from the memories of what it used to look like.

Everything Eddie could sell for drugs and booze, he did. And hell, if the kitchen sink weren't actually fixed to the counter and plumbing, he would've sold that too.

He feels the overwhelming and immediate urge to forget these memories, as fast as possible, and with that urge the answer comes in the way it always does - it is time to get high.

He opens his robe, freeing his bits, and goes into the bedroom. He moves his bed away to expose a large opening in the floorboards. He reaches inside of it and recovers a small wooden box made from some rich full wood, maybe oak that has been sanded smooth and polished to woodworked perfection. *I'm still unsure what kind of wood it is...fuck who cares...it's just a wooden box that he keeps his drugs in.*

He sits down crossed-legged and smiles widely because he truly feels like he just accomplished something. This is the root of his happiness, his destruction, and his delusion. This is Eddie's routine, and somehow even though it doesn't really work, it does. It keeps him alive.

He pulls one small bag with a dime-sized rock of cocaine from the box and shakes it vigorously in front of his face, gauging how much remains. He puts the bag on the top of the box and crushes the rock into powder inside the bag. He grabs a cocaine dusted silver platter once used for a fancy tea set that sits nearby and pours out a small pile. He takes a plastic card out of the box and a rolled up twenty-dollar bill. He breaks the small pile into lines. He cracks his neck with a full turn of his head before he plunges downward, stuffing the rolled-up bill inside his nose, and finally snorting a line through the bill, devouring it completely within a microsecond. He then inhales deeply, snorting, throwing his head back as far as it can go before, he freezes in that position.

A smile breaks across his maw shortly after, and slowly, indulgently, almost invisibly, the smile creeps wider and wider across his face. When it is as large as it can be, he puts the bill down and stands up in the same motion, flawlessly and fluently, and walks into the kitchen like nothing just happened.

Eddie paces back and forth in the emptiness of his apartment and to my observing misfortune he still isn't wearing underwear. He stops and turns and speaks, talking to no one, aloud, incoherently.

"You ever just look around?"

Eddie waits for a response, we both know he's not going to get but he continues, nonetheless.

"I mean, really look around, and if you look long enough you will see things that you never noticed before. Once you see these things that you now notice, you can never un-see them, no matter how hard you try not to. The harder you try not to look, the more you see, and the more you don't want to see, you will. The harder you don't look, the more you'll see what you don't want to look at. So why try not to look in the first place?"

Eddie tries to make sense of senselessness.

Eddie stands in the emptiness of his pathetic kitchen, his arms raised in protest, his eyes wide, and still, despite the insanity of it, he awaits an answer.

"Because you have to look...that's why! You need to look, and you need to see..."

Eddie walks back to his bedroom and sits down. He rerolls the twenty tightly and snorts another line, throwing his head back hard and inhaling until he can no longer.

"Phew. That's good...you know what I mean though, right?"

Eddie knows he is alone. He is truly just thinking. This is how he does it. He thinks aloud. Eddie doesn't know I'm watching, and he doesn't know one day you will be reading.

So, just to clear this up now, I was Eddie's best friend. I say was because I'm dead. Yeah, I've been dead for nearly two years. No, this isn't why Eddie is like this. I know my death did make it worse, but this life Eddie lives has been a long time in the making. Listen and please understand. I know it looks bad, and it is, actually it is worse than it looks. You're probably reading this and thinking how pathetic Eddie is and aesthetically speaking, you're right, his surface is ugly and probably beyond it, far deeper, it's even uglier, but give Eddie a chance.

I know I'm defending him but follow if you can and don't stop reading - there is hope for him, and because reading is a good thing, you have no choice, right? You started this and you need to finish it. That is what good people do, aren't you good people?

I know you're curious, but trust me, all be explained, not condoned, but explained...

Eddie continues talking to himself. Eddie continues ripping lines without concern that his supply is running out. He just smiles and snorts. He drinks the murky remnants of beer bottles and smokes the last of his already smoked cigarette butts. Dusk punched out some time ago and went home, leaving the night to take over. Eddie stares at that twenty and realizes this is the only money he has. His lips freeze with this realization and form something, not quite a smile, and not quite a frown, but something that slowly cements in the place of that beautiful smile of his.

He looks at his apartment and for the first time in days—hell, maybe even years—he realizes he is in trouble. Just this month, he lost his job and ran out of things to pawn. Eddie is finally out of options and that isn't something Eddie wants, and so, as he always does, he ignores what is and finds a way to continue what shouldn't be.

That reality is quickly forgotten and replaced by Eddie's high and desire to go out. He doesn't focus on the late rent and the situation that woke him. He doesn't even think about how he can't keep this way of life up. No, instead he focuses on the immediacy of his life and what he can do to better it.

Eddie kicks off his boots and drops his housecoat, exposing himself completely, and then searches through the mounds of dirty laundry that pour from two different laundry baskets and rescues one pair of seemingly clean boxer-briefs. He grabs pants—dark grey, not quite jeans and not quite dress—pants that he has worn for days on end. He throws on an off-white V-neck t-shirt and a dirty red and black plaid collar shirt. Boots go back on after he's done tucking his pants into his socks.

He smells himself and smugly looks toward the washroom. Throwing the light on, he stops, looks at the mess, and enters before turning to stare at himself. He nods in agreement. He smears Old-Spice deodorant, which is nearly exhausted, under each armpit, swiping each twice. He pours brute cologne into his palms and smacks it on his face and shirt.

Eddie feels, at least from his expression, satisfied. *I think he looks tired even behind those dark glasses and the bags they carry beneath them are at capacity, looking to burst at the seams if he continues carrying this burden, living this way.*

Eddie, however, is satisfied, content. He saunters across the desolate and dirty apartment and slides to his knees into the bedroom. He quickly snorts the last wide and only line he has left and doesn't know that is all he has. He pockets the twenty. Throws the box in the hole in the floor and hides the hole with the bed. He turns off his lamp; the apartment goes to the night. He navigates the darkness effortlessly, even avoiding the broken glass and beer bottle clusters as if there were a method to his garbage. When he reaches the front door, he takes off his Ray-Bans and pockets them.

He rescues his keys off a hook and...

Are you not at all curious as to whom I am? I know I said I'd explain but I can't keep talking about Eddie while you sit there...reading is good but...sit there, not knowing who is talking to you. Hell, I can't go on without explaining who I am. You know that I was his best friend but you don't know me and I believe you need to. My name is Gabriel and no I'm not a fucking angel. Listen, to each their own, but seriously, I'm dead. I haven't gone anywhere. I'm still here. Watching people. I chose to watch Eddie. Luckily, if I want, I don't have to just watch Eddie, I could watch the hot girl in 8A. I know, creepy, but honest. I'm dead and bored and Eddie was and will always be entertaining. Now what sucks about watching him? What really fucking sucks, being a dead guy, is watching your best friend "live", and considering how Eddie "lives", it is like watching him die.

When I say best friend, I should say brother, even when we don't share the same DNA. He is more of a brother—no offense—than the one I shared DNA with. Don't get me wrong people, I loved my brother. Eddie just knew me. Eddie, like my actual brother, was always there except—again, not hating my brother—he wasn't obligated to be there.

I've known Eddie before my brain could retain memory. Eddie and I didn't just grow up together. We learned together, grew together. This isn't going down the completely acceptable homosexual road, no, this is heterosexuality life partner personification. The connection I shared with Eddie is...sorry...was, an unbreakable bond. An indomitable reliance on one another, forever solidified and understood. We never had to explain it, confirm it.

This is why I watch Eddie. He doesn't blame himself for my death—*or at least I don't think he does, I can't read minds, I'm a ghost not a psychic...fuck*—and I don't blame him for it. He doesn't blame his habit on my death and I don't blame him for having this habit. Eddie was built to be on drugs and he finally found the one that he could live on.

Here I am, still not telling you who I am. I guess we will both have to wait to get into that because now Eddie is at Alexi's and what is about to happen is far too good not to explain.

CHAPTER 2

From a speaker embraced by a shiny steel ribcage, completely protected from harm, a voice demands answers. This voice will decide if Eddie can enter the building. It will unlock the large transparent thermoplastic polyurethane pane doors that are held solidly in place by the stainless-steel chromed doorframe. More importantly is who this voice belongs to...whom this belongs to...fuck whatever.

Eddie has luckily never had to fellate someone for drugs, but if his dealer forced him to because he can't pay and he already owes, well, it wouldn't be so bad because Eddie's drug dealer is a woman named Alexi. She does however put the man in woman. It isn't 'cause she is ugly; it is because she is physically superior to Eddie in every way. She is an ex-Olympic gold winning body-builder. She is Lithuanian. That country —*by the way, got its independence in 1990 and it never made the news, or at least I don't think it did, I don't remember*— has produced some of the world's strongest human beings. Seriously, look it up. She is beautiful but extremely solid, which, well, at least to Eddie and I, is unattractive. Plus, she can bench Eddie without breaking a sweat.

This isn't the girl Eddie wants or would ever bring home to meet the parents. Hell, Eddie hasn't seen his parents in forever so that is a bad example. She scares him slightly, and terrifies me, and I'm dead. He doesn't think about her sexually, and if he did, in my books he would be gay... *for the record, nothing wrong with that and I know I already hinted that it's fine but people are really sensitive, #relax.*

"Who is it?" The voice that can open the fortified entrance demands.

"The guy you love," Eddie spills out, projecting happiness and implicating harmlessness with his tone, almost like a white flag waving surrender but the one holding it smiles sincerely.

"I told you to call or text before coming. Always do that before coming."

"Do what before coming? Pull out? I always do that. You should always pull out before coming, Alexi, I hope you've been wearing condoms 'cause you'd make a horrible father."

A shriek buzz unlocks the doors.

Now while Eddie climbs the steps, I did tell you that Alexi was a woman, and what Eddie just did isn't cool. Eddie doesn't realize the mistake. Listen, I don't care how much fucking testosterone she's synthetically sucked down or injected. She is still a woman and women are sensitive. Women are much more sensitive than men. Well, at least according to biology they are— *Fuck, I sound so misogynistic. Hell, maybe I am, sorry—* need proof?

The way Alexi is going to react to Eddie's joke. To him, he is clever, and on his toes pretending to be on top of things when truly he is on the bottom. Remember: rock bottom. Now, protecting equality, her reaction could be solely based on the fact that Eddie owes her money and has for a while. Sure. It could easily be that. I still think women are sensitive, too sensitive, and I'm sticking to it. Hell, I'm dead because of one.

Eddie climbs the steps and gets to the front door, which is also extremely reinforced as far as doors go. He doesn't get to knock or talk. The door opens. He feels a sharpness keep his voice, as now, this pain, commands and completely eliminates his speech. He tries to cough but before he can forcefully exhale he is pulled inside and tossed weightlessly into an open closet full of racks of sharp shoes. The runners and functional footwear rest at the bottom, while the sea of unconventional, uncomfortable, sexy, sharp edged, unbelievably long heels are what comforts or, rather, un-comforts his fall.

Throat punched and tossed like a jacket, Eddie sits up trying to conceive of the sharp things that attempt to penetrate his flesh and stab at his balls. He doesn't get to say "ow". Nope. Her boot, yes, currently, she has boots just like Eddie's, newer and much sexier. But steel-toed and functional footwear, work footwear—all fucking terrain. That terrain in this case happens to be Eddie's swollen testicles and it's as if she grew up walking on them.

"Eddie. You fuck. You come here. Eddie I'm a goddess and have been so kind and you hurt me, Eddie, you are cruel. I'm not liking you Eddie, I'm not going to be nice anymore. I'm beautiful and kind and more than generous but here you are, fuck, Eddie, it isn't funny. You aren't funny..."

All the while, she digs her foot down. Eddie is in agony. Eddie is pain and torture and apology, truly, and probably only because her foot crushes his nuts, but right now, honestly, he's sorry.

"I'm fucking beautiful Eddie. I'm a goddess. I'm a woman. Flawless. Yes, Eddie, I'm flawless. Cut from unity—*Unity, the fuck does that mean?*— Eddie I'm what little men like you fear. Isn't that right?"

Eddie can't agree or disagree. Fire runs through his abdomen and makes him sick. Eddie is what sick feels like when it's about to vomit.

"I'm beautiful, right?" Alexi isn't asking Eddie anymore. She is still killing his sperm count but her attention is turned to the two guys sitting in the other room. These guys make Eddie look like a child. These guys are massive. These guys look like they are made of stone and steel and veins. The kind of size that one can achieve through vigorous and habitual work out smothered by synthetic stimulants. Rinse, and fucking repeat. Their hands look like they could crush nuts, and I don't mean the edible or testicular kind of nuts, I mean bolts. They just sit there and sincerely nod in agreement. They mean it when they nod, without doubt. You can hear every muscle in their tree trunk necks squeak in agreement actually.

"See. They know. They don't owe. They know the truth. Why are you here Eddie? When I take my foot off your dick and balls the reason you are here had better make me smile."

Eddie gets to speak with the release of his balls and the pain somehow, instantaneously - and I can only assume the pain's sudden absence directly caused by the amount of cocaine that numbs his system— is gone.

"First. Sorry. Truly. I'm sorry Alexi. Everyone in this room...wait...no, world, knows and will always know you're beautiful. Second, I'm sorry I didn't call or text but I was on my way to Maple St. pub and wanted to say hi. Actually, I get paid soon, and I wanted to say thanks for the patience and that I will have it within a couple days."

Eddie stands and tries to match her height but Alexi has inches on him. Eddie is six foot. Alexi is taller. Two inches taller. Eddie's eyebrows relax and that intoxicating smile of his slides into place. He's lying and even I believe him.

"You will have my money soon?"

He struts by as though his balls aren't swelling and like he feels just fine. As though he actually believes the shit he just spewed. The men watch him walk into the large and vast living room filled with expensive furniture, electronics, workout equipment, and their eyes watch his salivate over the only thing he notices. The center table that looks like it is cut from pure crystal and it easily could be, I'm no expert, so, I can't confirm. Eddie isn't looking at the table. Eddie is looking at the brilliant white residue and the long, countless white lines that sit, ready, willing, and desired to be cleaned from its flawless, transparent surface. His eyes make love to the brick sized chunk of untouched cocaine that sits, ready for separation, and scaling.

Eddie casually pushes between the titans, as though this is his house, wiggling in. Neither of them can comprehend his action nor understand his confidence. To them he is a soft, frail, junkie.

"See, Eddie, when I was hurting you for hurting me, I didn't make fun of you. I could've talked about your dick and balls. I could've said you have a tiny penis. Did I? No. Because I don't insult my friends."

"You'd be lying." Eddie smiles, comfort stains his teeth to a bright smile.

He looks at the two men who stare at him, glancing between them. He focuses on the one who sits on his left and looks at this man with the sincerest smile and wordlessly enquires about the smoke crushed behind his ear. The man doesn't even get to respond. In a fluent and hauntingly quick motion, Eddie snatches it away. He closes his teeth around the butt and looks away, pretending that he didn't just steal it.

Eddie lights the smoke turning for a second to show his gratitude for the gift that wasn't given. The man isn't angry; he just looks at Alexi, shocked and questioning Eddie's actions, and if he should respond. She nods at him, and then with another slightly different nod they get up and leave the room, walking up a spiral staircase and disappearing behind large black double doors.

"Nice guys." Eddie sits back lazily tossing his arms over the back of the couch while blowing a large smoke ring up at the ceiling.

Alexi sits down, kicking off her boots, she throws her perfectly toned stalks across Eddie's lap and slides back, staring up at the cathedral ceiling and Eddie's smoke ring that dissipated just before reaching it. The stalks, for the record, are her legs. Her legs are like tree trunks and muscularly sculpted and unbelievably long. If Alexi had tits and not perfectly chiseled pectorals, she'd be a bomb shell, I mean honest to—insert religious icon—she would be masturbation material because this is the kind of, sorry, would be the kind of girl you could only fantasize about and never touch, just saying—*yeah, I know what I said earlier, I changed my mind. Here I go contradicting myself. Be warned this might be a regular thing.*

"Anyhow, Alexi, how're you?"

"As always Eddie, busy, and good."

"Good. That is fantastic, almost fantastic as you look."

"Eddie. What do you want?"

"Alexi. Do you not want to know how I'm doing?"

Alexi somehow doesn't believe his reason for being here, despite that convincing smile he wears. I'm afraid for Eddie. Remember, dead guy here, but Eddie isn't and he has to deal with this.

"Eddie. You are here for something. You always are looking for something when you come. You always need something."

Eddie inhales deeply, attempting to hide that he is buying time. Time he is spending considering the next words that come out of his mouth. Why? Well, she has beaten the shit out of him. Yes, badly, and not once, but many times. *One of the reasons she frightens me. Eddie's empty apartment is largely because he loves drugs. He also loves not being assaulted. One of those two things that he loves is a reasonable desire. She never breaks his bones or does anything irreversible, physically at least, mentally, well, I'm not a shrink but again, being a guy, you don't want to say you got beat up by a girl. She never hits his face. She likes it too much and she doesn't want guys or anyone bruised coming to her apartment, or more importantly, leaving her apartment, noticeably injured.*

"That hurts Alexi. I'd like to think that you think I don't always just come here or see you because I want something. Most of the time, you're right, I come here for something, but not always."

She tilts her head; it rather eerily and suddenly clicks down and now faces Eddie. Her expression is only to be explained as void of humor and impossible to read. *I could say poker face, but this isn't a song.* Her eyes droop, as though closing to blink or shut, and then the unimpressed look that validates her sex overtakes what was.

"Eddie." She speaks, or rather, questions without questioning. *You know, the kind of question that doesn't ask: rhetorical. In my opinion and off-topic, the question-less question. I wish someone could've heard me say that out loud...anyway.*

Eddie sits motionless, preparing his next words, waiting, and completely enthralled by her seriousness. Eddie doesn't even flinch when her hand surprisingly and gently slides across his crotch, searching for what now fills her grasp: his dick. Eddie, enthralled, confused, aroused, and somehow at the same time, disgusted, still doesn't react. The cigarette ash, hanging patiently, finally collapses with its own weight and falls to his lap, inches from her hand. Still no reaction; no flinch. He doesn't even budge when that unwarranted but completely welcome over the pants hand job turns ugly as she stops stroking and starts squeezing. Testing her grip, proving her strength, and forcefully evacuating the blood from a perfectly good boner, my best friend Eddie is inhumanly cool. When she speaks, he flinches, and everything that should have hurt, does.

"You can't have anything until you pay me in full. Actually, because I do care, you can have three of those lines, and then, no more. You don't come here Eddie without my money. I'm not helping you after those three lines. That's it. You do those. You get out. If you come back without my money, I'll kill you, and no one will miss you and you know that. My money, Eddie. In full. No fronts. No favors. No hands outs. Nothing to talk about. Do those lines and leave."

She gets off him, doesn't look back, goes up the stairs and as soon as she disappears, those men come down the stairs. The cigarette had gone out, so he pockets it for later. Hurrying himself before those big men with guns reach the floor he now kneels on, with his twenty, the last of his physical wealth, he insufflates three lines and rises to his feet. He doesn't look at them. He doesn't run. He doesn't change. He just leaves, casually flattening his twenty-dollar bill with the intention of spending it.

Eddie knows, this is it, this is all he has, and all he is, at least I think he knows, but doesn't care how far he's fallen. I know for certain he doesn't feel anything right now. He should know and should feel how far he's fallen but maybe he doesn't realize it, despite how impossibly ignorant he'd have to be. Maybe...he chooses to fall and not think about what the bottom feels like. What it looks like, to me, or what he shows the world, is that he doesn't care. I don't know if he does or doesn't. Whether he is falling still, or he has reached rock bottom, I'm afraid for him, and I'm terrified that he isn't for himself, and doesn't care at all, either way.

CHAPTER 3

The bar: Maple Street Pub. This is Eddie's home away from home and really neither resembles a home. Here, however, Eddie feels just as comfortable as he does when he's in his empty apartment. He rolls the bill in his hand, gently smoothing out the creases with his palms and turning it from rolled to flat—*in order to make the bill appear it hadn't been used for drugs*—readying it for spending. He knows after this, he is broke. You wouldn't know it though. When he orders his first of three, maybe four pints, depending how cheap on the tip he feels like being, you really wouldn't be able to guess.

The cold glass filled with beer and topped by the perfect thin layer of foam greets his deception. He takes it in his hand and sips it, turning on his stool, looking at the bar and its occupants. He is studying them. He is looking for something, searching for someone who is high, or is going to get high. He counts the patrons and collects data. Watching carefully at the number of times each patron leaves to use the washroom. He collects frequency and absorbs each who fit his profile, cutting down the possibilities with age. He dismisses the elderly regulars who are truly just going to the washroom because their bladder doesn't allow them other options. The younger patrons are his targets.

Sadly, for Eddie, only one person fits the profile. Only one person is using or resembles using. A girl, mid-twenties, five-five maybe five-six, and much too sober for how many shots she's made disappear. She has visited the washroom way too many times and every time she returns, she is more alive than when she went in. She is using. Eddie wants to make friends.

This beautiful little blonde bombshell appears to be on a date. They don't look compatible. She doesn't stop talking, doesn't stop moving. She looks happy and carefree. He looks like somebody close to him just died. He is dark and broody. I get it. Girls dig that but this just looks wrong. He looks like he belongs on the cover of an emo music monthly magazine.

Everything he does is intense and out of place. Each expression that paints his melodramatic maw screams "look how dark my soul is" and people around him see what I see. Eddie doesn't care. He doesn't really want this girl but if the night goes that way, he wouldn't be against it, then again, he does believe in the "bro code". He doesn't want to mess up tall dark and handsome's chance, but then again. Eddie never turns down the chance at the bedroom dance because fuck does he ever "need" it right now. But what he really wants is to lick the white powder that she forgot to wipe off her nose from her last washroom trip. After ten minutes of her talking and him casting his gaze toward multiple directions in an attempt to look mysterious, she informs him that she needs to use the washroom and lies that the drinks continue to run right through her. Eddie downs his liquid courage and darts toward the washroom hallway and tries to get ahead of her, not to raise suspicion. He succeeds and he slows down when he gets into the hallway where the washrooms segregate. Eddie's timing is flawless as she whips around the corner, bumping into Eddie's chest.

"Oh my god. Sorry," she says, looking up, smiling.

Eddie smiles that unbelievably intoxicating and extremely out of place smile that few ever expect from a guy that looks like Eddie.

"No worries. Oh, you got something right there." Eddie replies, and in one smooth motion wipes the cocaine from her nose, gumming it.

"Umm…" The girl speaks, trembling from embarrassment, and slightly confused, not sure whether to freak out or laugh.

"We can keep it between us." Eddie smiles, turning toward the men's bathroom, reaching for the door.

"Hey. Do you want to join me?" The girl barks, surprising herself but retaining the confidence in her question.

Gracefully slow, Eddie turns, hiding his joy, and smoothly smiles while nodding in agreement. She beckons him to follow with her finger as she backs into the women's washroom. Eddie cutely looks from side to side as though he cares if anyone sees him go in. Eddie feigns the appearance that this is his first time going into the women's washroom at Maple Street Pub, exuding believable innocence and pretending to be nervous, he enters.

Eddie finds the girl in the middle stall, sitting on the tank of the toilet. Eddie begins to notice just how pretty she is. She wears a blue pencil skirt with a flowing white men's suit shirt over it that hangs open, barely concealing the red bra beneath it, tied by an enormous belt around her little waist. Eddie now can see the color of her underwear and he isn't complaining because she isn't wearing any. He laughs quietly as he enters closing and locking the door behind him. She has two lines already cut and laid out on the surface of the dark plastic toilet paper dispenser. She hands him a twenty-dollar bill that's been neatly rolled up and smiles, nodding toward the cocaine. He goes down and snorts the smaller looking line out of respect. He stands up quickly and pulls his head back inhaling hard, blindly handing her the bill.

"What's your name?" through the inhale Eddie asks.

She smiles and rerolls the twenty and responds,

"Christie. I've seen you here before. What's your name?"

She snorts the line and repeats Eddie's rituals—handing the bill back and forth, going line for line.

"I'm Eddie. You probably have seen me; I come here a lot. I've never seen you and I'd remember if I had."

She laughs. Goes into her purse and brings forth a bag of cocaine and pours out two more lines.

"Why's that Eddie?" she questions.

"You're hot. What's funny?" Eddie hides his eagerness for the bill to come back.

"Oh, the guy I'm with..."

"The stiff? What about him?"

She smiles and laughs and passes him the twenty.

"His name is Edward and he isn't a stiff," she responds with a hint of defense.

"He doesn't look like he's having fun, no offense." Eddie snorts a line almost mumbling his response.

"Looks can be deceiving, right?" she says, impatiently waiting for the bill.

"Spoken like a scholar. You are right babe; appearances are most definitely deceiving. Hell, look at me, you wouldn't know how awesome I am by looking at me...I know you were a combination of turned on and afraid out in that hall." Eddie smiles as he passes her that bill.

Her jaw drops hiding a mixed reaction of impressed and insulted, but quickly turns to a smile as Eddie shines his innocence through his relaxing brow and sickening grin. I'm always impressed by Eddie and now, so is she. She packs up her things and jumps down off the tank coming chest to chest with Eddie and stares up at him. He takes his index finger and collects the residual cocaine film from the toilet paper dispenser. It turns his fingerprint snow white and he brings it in front of her face. He offers and she smiles. She opens her mouth and he slowly rubs it clean off her gums. As he withdraws it, she closes her mouth around it and licks the tip. Eddie can't control his glee as he chuckles. She winks and walks around him,

"Hey, no goodbye kiss?" Eddie shrugs.

"Another time. Thanks Eddie, it was nice getting to know you." She smiles and turns.

"Thanks Christie," Eddie says sincerely as his defeated tone spills out, unhidden.

He waits alone in the stall and I'm not sure if he sees it or knows it, but all of this, the stall, the girl, his situation, is flawed and failing. It's hard to tell with Eddie. He should play poker; he has that face. One emotion completely hides the other and you actually can't tell what's going on behind those eyes.

Eddie gets to the exit and the door opens for him. A young plump woman stands shocked and smothered quickly by disgust. She came to relieve her bowels or bladder. She wasn't expecting Eddie. Eddie looks at the strange little symbol that identifies the washroom, like he doesn't know, and slowly he feigns intoxication.

"Shit. Ha! Wrong bathroom. Sorry," Eddie spits out slurring, trying to cement his lie.

He pushes past her. He recovers his swag in the hall out of sight. He returns to his stool and orders another pint, one of his last pints, and that fact is getting increasingly impossible to ignore.

I know that look smeared on Eddie's face. That look is realization and that souring impression ruins a perfectly good smile. That is the look he has avoided wearing and it begins with a beer count. He gets it. Finally, he gets it, and it has taken its sweet ass time to smack him in the face. He knows that after this pint, there is only one more before he is completely, and no pun intended, tapped out.

I'm going to sidetrack here because it seems relevant. No, sorry, it is relevant. If you do drugs, do not evaluate your life. Never, ever, do this. If you are high, do not come down with questions about your choices. You're high. You're not in any position to judge or ask if you need to change. Again, you're high, be high. Don't bring others down and don't bring yourself down. Drugs have to work through your system and you will eventually be sober, but for the love of—insert religious character of choice—do not be negative. You're high. High is euphoric. You did the drugs, you walked the road, and you wanted to be there. Deal with it. The only time to question your reality is if you're like Eddie, who is always high. I pray you're not and I'm not religious. Remember, I am a ghost, I know more about what comes next than you do.

Eddie and I used to get really tweaked and we'd help each other by stopping the serious talk. Anything of relative importance was quickly pushed and hidden under the metaphorical rug, which we would deal with when we were sober. Sadly Eddie, well, he isn't ever sober. I don't want to run on with the past, you and I both need to focus on Eddie right now. This is going to be good, hopefully. I am dead, not psychic.

Eddie stares down at the frothy truth. He sits attentively as though this cold pint speaks to him. He is high but he knows now. He leans back, adjusting his posture, clearing his throat. He prepares for the reality that his drugs can't hide. He looks past Ace, the bartender, and stares at a mirror. The reflection painfully looks back.

Fuck. We lost him. He shakes his head, as if he is clearing the thought, physically. Quick as it was there, it is gone, and Eddie is fine. He turns his focus, the short pathetic thing he calls an excuse of an attention span, to Christie, who now sits in front of that guy; you know the one, completely enthralled by his every unnecessarily dramatic expression.

Eddie looks past him and tries to get her attention. Nothing. She doesn't even know where she is, or at least it looks that way. Strangely, her life, that fire, the perkiness, is gone. The drugs and their stimulating side effects, void. This isn't the girl Eddie was within the washroom. Something, actually, everything about her is different. I see it, Eddie sees it, and you read it. Christie isn't home. Leave a message. Beep.

Eddie downs the last gulp of his pint. He shakes the change in his hand. It comes from within Eddie. He knows there is nothing left for him, defeated, he accepts that it's time to go. He looks at Ace. He looks at Christie. He looks around, searching for a hint of help. Desperation is his new scent, suddenly and sadly, masked by hopelessness. He dumps that remaining change on the bar despite it allowing for another pint and leaves Ace with a satisfactory tip. He doesn't care. He wants out. He fiends for his white lady. He prays he can muster enough from the empty bags at home but he knows that in the pit of his being, he is out. Powder-less and powerless. No more. Empty. Over. Finished. Fucked.

He smiles, still hiding the truth, thanking Ace; he turns and heads for the exit. Time slows, just like a movie cliché. Possibly it's me slowing down time for this moment. Why? I don't know what comes next but I hope it is a man who wants to be more than his habit. He wants to be more than a drug. He wants, no, desires change and, in this moment,, we should both beg that he realizes he needs to change.

Ok, so I have bad news. Eddie doesn't know we are here, obviously. He probably, at this point, would not care. Eddie does not give a fuck and he is not ready for change. He stops, turns, and walks toward Christie and the look alike from the movie series I will not name, and separates them momentarily, dividing them with his body and words, completely and purposely ignoring the guy.

"Hey, you want to get out of here?" Eddie spouts confidently, completely void of concern.

She doesn't even react, doesn't recognize his presence. She somehow stares through him, enthralled by the "man" behind him. I'm not quite sure what she sees in captain quiet and broody and I know Eddie doesn't know or care why she is with him. However, she is, completely with him. Eddie is like me, a ghost.

"Excuse me." The commander of intensity speaks up, his words flow magically between his questionably made up lips. I think he is wearing gloss or lipstick but I can't be...never mind, he is definitely wearing makeup—*nothing wrong with that mind you*. Eddie turns and captures the same stance but faces him. Eddie's brow raised in interest.

"Do you mind?" Same tone, unassertive, but received.

Eddie grabs the man's full beer, takes a mouthful, and rears back, gulping it down. Confusion now riddles Eddie's expression. The beer is warm, untouched and nearly flat. Eddie expresses disgust by sticking out his tongue and gagging as he swallows the gulp. He places the beer back and wipes his mouth.

"No, thank you, I don't mind. Oh? Ha! Sorry, I'm interrupting. How rude of me, I'm Eddie." Eddie smiles innocently and extends his open palm.

"I don't care who you are but you should leave." The man retorts, his eyes darken, and his expression exudes a seriousness Eddie can't comprehend. Eddie's palm remains lonely and unshaken, so Eddie gives up, and turns back to Christie.

He waves his hand in her face, trying to get a reaction, but either she isn't there or she chooses to completely ignore him. Eddie shrugs and returns to his stool. He signals Ace. Ace walks over smiling.

"You know that awesome tip I gave you Ace?" Eddie questions with the hint of preemptive apology.

Ace shakes his head barely offended and almost satisfied. He rolls his eyes and pours Eddie a pint.

"You'll get me another time, eh Eddie?" Ace drops the pint in front of Eddie and walks off.

Eddie sits up and calls at him.

"You're the man Ace. You know it," Eddie spouts, but his words are empty and barely heard.

Eddie sits back, takes a swig, and fights defeat. Eddie stares at his pint and he begins to shake. I'm not saying that you could sit there and watch the guy vibrate, but he is shaking. He is feeling something that many people feel when they do hard drugs and most people can't even recognize it is happening, but trust me, it is. Eddie happens to be one of the unlucky few that understands it. Let's call it hunger. A hunger that despite how much you feed it, it never truly gets full, insatiable.

This feeling, the insatiability, can only be explained, summed, or described in this moment as torment. Eddie wants more but what makes this feeling worse is that he knows he can't get any more. Eddie, luckily, if you can call it luck, knows that it will go away. He can wait it out. Sucks all the same but few understand the process and again, Eddie, for some reason, call it lucky or not, does. Another advantage to aid his excuses and continuance. I really don't know if he is lucky or not, if he has an advantage or not. It is simply perspective and I'm not even sure what side of the extremely jagged and nearly impossible to climb fence I stand on.

Eddie sweats, Eddie stares, Eddie jitters, and Eddie forces the thought away. The drugs slowly fade and Eddie starts to panic despite his strenuous effort not to. He can't escape. He downs gulp after gulp of the pint that hasn't left his hand and he stops at the last gulp to savor and assist the painful path he will now have to walk. He doesn't know where it will take him but it will not be somewhere he wants to go. Eddie is about to see himself and his situation for the first time in a long time. *I'm here Eddie. Please let this happen.* He just looks into the glass and sighs. There it is. He is about to take his last sip and start his trip down reality-street.

Eddie inhales his last gulp. He sits up and absorbs, collecting the images and surroundings he has ignored since his rejection. He pushes the empty pint glass forward while retaining believable success, as though he has won; conquered something. He hasn't. He moves from the stool; through the bar and the now shapeless crowd he pays no attention to.

CHAPTER 4

He hits the sidewalk and sparks a cigarette...*I'm not sure where he got that cigarette*. He looks at it, examines it, and inhales it slowly. He is coming down hard, crashing painfully, and he knows it. He shakes his head and draws at the ignited dart. He appears to have remembered something and I swear if this were a cartoon, that little idea bubble floating innocently above his head would be filled with pretty pictures. Eddie thinks he has drugs at home. He walks a couple steps, exhales hard, and stops like he is about to crash into someone or something. Nothing but the empty sidewalk and the empty way home Eddie.

He stands there questioning himself, nearly arguing out loud. This is when he gets distracted by a noise nearby; sounds like struggle. Eddie follows it ignorantly without regard for personal safety or any actual good "Samaritan" intention. He follows it to the back of the bar, the not quite alley, not quite parking lot, almost mimicking the completely cliché bad news scenario for countless nameless movies and there he finds...

Eddie stops, dumbly observing the beginnings of an assault. He leans in trying to focus and recognizes both the victim and attacker. The dramatic, tightly clad, pompous, grotesquely successful Edward stands above the apparently unconscious collapsed frame of Christie. He limply grips the pearl pommel handle of a straight razor that is slung open and reflectively sharp, glistening in the twilight.

The try-too-hard to be broody and mysterious Edward is going to cut poor Christie and neither Eddie nor I know why. Out of the many things Eddie could do, he chooses to help, but he isn't helping Christie. No. He isn't stopping Edward from making a big mistake. No. Eddie only considers the bag of cocaine that sits buried and lonely in her purse and if she goes it will be left unused and wasted, with no nose to snort it. Eddie imagines that Christie would be extremely grateful and would definitely offer it up as the first reward, the obvious one, if he were to save her. Of course, she would.

Eddie wants to help the cocaine whether he knows it or not, or even if he does, he doesn't see just how fucked up that is. He wants to help himself to it, and that is the only reason for involving himself. He knows there is only one option. Stop Edward, which, Eddie doesn't so much mind because Edward looks and has behaved like a gigantic vaginal cleansing tool and just for that, Eddie would gladly do anything that would piss him off.

Eddie moves in. He gets within a couple feet and suddenly finds a wall instead of Edward, quickly followed by the taste of his own blood. Edward appeared not to move; he was that quick, or more believably, Eddie is just that slow.

"Fuck." Eddie gets a word before Edward is already there again, unimaginably fast, and unfortunately for him, ridiculously strong. *Not such a good idea anymore, eh Eddie?*

Edward lifts Eddie off his feet, slamming him into a nearby wall, as though Eddie weighs nothing.

"Looks like I'll be dining for two." Edward smirks, freeing a hand from Eddie's collar but still, without any sign of fleeting strength, continues holding Eddie high above the ground, dangling him impossibly with only one hand. Everything about this feat of strength screams unnatural, whether those screams can make a sound or not.

"What?" Eddie chokes out a question.

"What do you mean, what?"

"Who says that?" Eddie responds attempting to distract Edward, delaying him from whatever he intends to do, and at the same time, ignoring the terror that now floods outward from within himself.

He fabricates and buys completely into a scenario where he isn't scared, not at all; instead he is battling shame from the embarrassment he will soon face from being beaten up by this joke of a man. Eddie convinces himself and wholeheartedly believes his lie; certain of it, and no longer challenges it. His delusion is reality.

Edward painfully tries to ignore Eddie, retaining his composure because all he wants to do, and soon will, is seriously harm him, before eventually killing him. But for reasons unsure, he can't help himself from responding to Eddie's question.

"What do you mean?"

"I mean, why would you throw some one-liner at me?"

"Because, I, I... It doesn't matter." Edward, frustrated, tosses Eddie like a cigarette into the opposite wall which is at least ten feet or so away.

Eddie hits that wall like it owes him money. He lifts himself and gets on all fours, clawing at the breath to stand but does not find it. Instead, he crawls toward Christie. No, wait, not toward Christie, but toward her large sack that she calls a purse and tears it open in a panic as Edward walks toward him. His hands get inside and immediately locate what they are searching for, the drugs, but as soon as he gets it in hand, Eddie is pulled backward. Edwards sharp claws that look almost like fake nails—the stereotypical kind that receptionist tend to have on—dig into him, tearing free stomach flesh, before he is tossed upward and then Edward grabs him out of the air, spinning him in place like a carousel before finally releasing him suddenly and violently, sending him flying in the opposite direction.

"What're you looking for? Her phone? Pepper spray?" Edward chuckles through a shit eating grin, as Eddie is launched through the loading bay of the Maple St pub. Eddie cuts right through the sheet metal collapsible door, landing loudly and painfully, finally stopping with the help of a two-four pyramid of unopened imported beer, that explodes on impact.

Eddie doesn't attend to the toppling beer cases that rain around him. He doesn't care that beer soaks his clothes or that he can taste blood. He isn't worried about the pompous douche monster outside. Instead, he spits blood, wipes his mouth, and opens the bag of cocaine, pouring a pile the size of his thumb on the back of his hand without skipping beat; he's as cool as cream. He snorts it off and licks the white coating that stains his skin. He closes the bag and stands up, throwing his head back, nasally inhaling until he cannot anymore.

Edward, confident Eddie is down, out, and hopefully dead, walks toward Christie. He opens the straight razor and leans down. Gently, he places the blade on her neck, hovering over the artery. He shuts his eyes while a smile pushes his lips apart exposing oddly large incisors, filed down, nearly flat. He tongues the dull end of one large canine, and it looks almost like he misses the point of it. *Get it?*

Edward tastes his own tongue as Eddie's unlaced steel toe makes its home under his chin. He topples backward but doesn't bleed and before he can react, Eddie is now the monkey on his back.

Eddie jams a broken bottle into Edward's chest as he jumps onto him. It cuts deep into his white, nearly pigment less skin. No blood. Edward, unflinching and calm, retaliates with his razor. The blade cuts cleanly into Eddie's cheek and almost finds the inside of his mouth; Eddie rolls off clutching the wound that spews blood. Before the broken bottle hits the ground and shatters, Edward is on Eddie, his mouth on Eddie's wound, gulping down what escapes.

Eddies eyes pop open wide. Disgust and confusion press deeply on his dimples. Eddie reactively tries to force the teenage heartthrob wannabe from his face but he can't. Edward is too strong. Eddie tries to slither free, desperately squirming but can't wiggle away from Edward and his hungry mouth. Eddie is helpless. Eddie's color fades, he feels weaker, and weaker. In one last feeble attempt Eddie pushes and to his surprise, Edward releases, agreeingly.

It isn't because Eddie finally found the strength or even the opportune moment, no, something in Edward's twisted expression tells the tale, the real tale. We all know this face, the same look, sick looks universally the same on all if us. Edward is going to hurl.

Now Eddie, surprised and overjoyed, knows what I know. When Edward first latched on, it felt as normal to him as eating, sleeping, or pissing. Edward seemed at home gulping down plasma, sucking back crimson. Now, in these short seconds before Eddie finds away to stop Edward, I notice, and Eddie notices that Edward is bleeding from the wound that didn't bleed when it was made. Edward is a vampire. And Eddie's blood made him sick.

Freeze-frame on Edward's face as his meal comes up. Eddie winds up with his boot and kicks out his teeth. Edward through the vomit carries a look of contempt as he watches them rain down on the pavement, resting in a pool of sick made entirely of blood. The only thing in Edwards stomach is blood. And he can't stop throwing up. Now, please look at Eddie, who realizes in this moment the truth about Edward, fighting the logic that tries its best to explain it but can't because that the truth of the matter is: Edward is a vampire.

Come on Eddie, do something...

As though he heard me, which is even more impossible than the existence of vampires or at least comparably impossible, Eddie runs to the wall right next to the loading bay and grabs the fire hose from its cage. He tugs the heavy nylon hose, swinging the fire engine red nozzle, making his way toward the puking vampire cliché. Ok, not cliché, well, modern vampire cliché.

Eddie lassos Edward by the neck and spins round after round of hose, choking him, making it into a giant noose. Eddie runs back and throws the release. Instantly the limp hose erects, solidifying as the water torridly rushes through it. Before Edward can move, before he even understands, the hose constricts and Edwards's body falls down, his head however doesn't join the rest of him. As Eddie spins the valve off, he watches in joy as the violent hose dances around, soaking everything nearby; it even pushes Christie back, rolling her over a couple times. He watches Edward's head roll toward his feet and he stops it by planting his right foot on it.

Eddie bursts into laughter. Loud, deep, hysterical, borderline crazy waves of laughter bellow out of him and echo in the emptiness of this almost empty alley. Eddie stops suddenly, lifts Edward's head, and shakes it.

"A fucking vampire. Holy fuck. A real fucking vampire, holy shitty fucking Christ, no way man, no way. A fucking vampire, a real fucking vampire!" Eddie yells in Edward's face.

Eddie begins to laugh again, this time it is warm and full of relief. He tosses Edward's head and accurately punts it across the alley.

He struts toward Edward's corpse and stops suddenly.

"Aren't you supposed to explode?" Eddie asks.

Who is he even talking to? I don't know.

"Let's see what you got..." Eddie whispers as he goes through the headless corpse's jacket, pants, and anything he has with a pocket. Cellphone. Eddie takes that. Keys. Eddie takes those. Lighter. Takes that too. Eddie goes stiff as his hand finds paper, a rolled-up wad of paper, but not just paper, money, and a fuck-load of it. Eddie doesn't count it, just pockets it, leaping to his feet.

Eddie takes out the bag of cocaine and feeds more on his hand, a small powdery ball, right between his thumb and index finger. He snorts it. He puts his index finger into the bag and rubs some cocaine on his gums. His finger comes back out covered in blood. The pain is there, he knows it hurts, but can't feel it.

He sighs and walks toward Christie. He stops in his tracks as he hears a noise, a strange noise. It sounds like sizzling bacon on a hot skillet. Eddie locates the source of the noise: Edward. Edward is sizzling. His body slowly appears to shrink. Eddie shakes his head and rubs his eyes. Edwards's body is gone and his clothes remain, empty. No blood. No sign that anyone had ever filled them, wore them. Edward has disappeared. Eddie looks around. No one is around. No one saw. No one in his or her right mind would believe this. He pockets the straight razor. He goes to Christie, kneeling down, and slowly shakes her trying to wake her.

She shudders but doesn't open her eyes.

"Hey!" Eddie screams.

She inhales powerfully and her eyes flick open. She sits up and slides backward, defensively and rightfully so.

"What the fuck?"

"What do you remember?" Through a soundless giggle, Eddie askes. Sitting down, readying himself for a listen, he crosses his legs.

"We did some bumps in the washroom." She struggles to remember.

"Bumps? Lady, we killed it off, I thought you overdosed. Scared the dick off me. Hey, you got a smoke?" Eddie spins a tale so effortless and convincing, that he believes it.

She nods and goes through her purse. She pulls out the pack and hands Eddie one. He snatches it and lights it quick. She sits there looking at her own unlit cigarette and her expression sours because Eddie hasn't offered her a light.

"Oh, sorry, ha-ha." Eddie lights her smoke.

"Why am I wet?" she whines, still grasping at her memory.

"I have that effect on women." Eddie smirks.

"Hardy har har...Seriously though?"

"I had to hose you, you weren't waking up."

"Hose me? Couldn't you have like, slapped me?"

"Don't hit women."

"Oh, what a gentleman. Fuck, I don't remember anything. I don't feel strung out either. You know where we can get more? I want to party some more." She says, trying to smile through her running make up.

"You sure that's a good idea?"

"Yeah, I'm down if you are."

"Give me your number, I'll go pick up and call you after." Eddie smiles, stands, and retrieves his new phone to enter her number.

Which he will never call or text her—asshole.

CHAPTER 5

When you discover that vampires are real, your first reaction no matter what it is, will almost certainly be saner than Eddie's. Eddie doesn't take his earnings or newfound knowledge anywhere productive. Eddie doesn't even recognize the significance of this event. Eddie does the only thing Eddie wants to do: get more drugs. Eddie runs down the street like a child chasing an ice cream truck. He doesn't slow or care how he looks. He sprints as though he is chasing something and for the sake of metaphors, he is, but it is not fucking ice cream.

Eddie hasn't checked to see how much money is in the wad of cash he took from the undead douchebag that attempted to kill Christie and end Eddie's "life", but he knows it's a large amount of money. It will probably pay off his debt and leave him with more than enough to get drugs and that is good enough for Eddie. Eddie, without reason, is just happy to be able to continue this so-called "life". He even imagines righting a few wrongs with this "new found fortune", even though, it is not found and in no way is it a fortune; however to Eddie, it truly is.

He tries to catch his breath before contacting Alexi because in the state he is in, she will ignore him. He has to seem in control. Appearances...few understand the power of appearances. By now, you know things are never ever as they appear but you don't understand what that means and you may never. For instance, when your inner darkness becomes your outer appearance, then, and only then will you know the importance of appearances. When you can no longer pretend you're not okay because people can see from your surface how much you're not okay. For instance, when your sickness seeps through your flesh and shows how you live on the inside and how far you're gone, but you have to get here, where Eddie is, and few can survive that journey.

He stops in front of the reflective surface of a store window and looks at himself. The store is a clothing store. The kind that supplies trendy clothes, clothes that are somehow popular now, much to the chagrin of every nineties kid who wore that shit against their will. He looks at himself, ignoring the oddly posed mannequins, and stares at his wounded face.

"Fucking kidding me?"

He asks as if I'm not the only one listening, pushing his dirty fingertips against the massive elongated incision on his cheek that vomits scarlet.

"Well, it is fixable," he says, reasoning with himself. And with this "reasoning" he pulls forth his Zippo and lights it. He stands there watching it burn. He sets it down, allowing it to heat. He removes the residue-filled baggie of cocaine he stole from Christie and tears it open, and then throws it in his mouth and chews the bag, licking out the remainder. When he cannot feel his teeth, he spits out the plastic husk, and rescues his ret hot Zippo. He closes it, extinguishing the licking flame, and then he opens the shell and thrusts the searing metal against his wound. It sticks to his face as it cauterizes one part of the wound closed. I can imagine the pain that Eddie does not feel. He is not done though because the wound is not closed. He sparks that Zippo and waits, sliding down with his back against the glass. When the flame flicks low he extinguishes it and presses the scorched and blackened end to the remainder of the unclosed wound and I bet if he could smell right now he'd smell his own flesh cooking,

He removes his phone to finds Alexi's number and enters it into his new phone because he can actually call from this new phone, unlike his own, which has been cut off for a couple of months. He considers calling but knows she won't answer an unfamiliar number, so instead, he writes her a text, and identifies himself.

Within seconds, she responds with, "Eddie...what?"

He fumbles with the unfamiliar keyboard and its foreign format.

"I have your funds, can I come by?"

"Shit." He frustratingly spews after a prematurely sent text.

He stares at the screen, as though his life depends on it—and when it comes to Eddie, I guess it does—waiting for a response.

"Come over."

Eddie shoots to his feet and dusts himself off. He forgets his face wound and the fresh first-degree burns he used to close it. He does not care about the fact that vampires exist and how monumental that fact is. He doesn't give it a second thought that he is lucky to be alive or that he is blessed by a second chance that some would even call a purpose, no, Eddie just wants drugs.

A few moments later...

He is at her door, calmly buzzing her apartment even though inside he feels like he has won the lottery and he wants to scream for joy. He is as cold as ice when the microphone signifies that someone is listening and he calmly and proudly announces his presence.

He wants to run up the spiraling staircase to her apartment but he calmly climbs each step with precise rhythm. He adjusts himself as he nears her door. He stops as a noise startles him, the phone in his pocket beeps out an annoying tone. It beeps repeatedly as he stumbles to wrench it from his pocket. He brings it to his face and squints. He is crashing and he knows it. It is a text from a person named Sebastian. He slides the small bar that unlocks the screen so he can read the text:

"Edward, we are meeting Thursday night...are you in?"

Eddie stares at the small text box and the keyboard. He considers that this may be another opportunity to cash in. Maybe this Sebastian is like Edward, undead and loaded. Instead of answering, he goes through the contacts on the phone. As he scrolls down the list, he realizes nobody on this list has a last name and some of the names are actually names of fictional vampire characters. Eddie smiles because to him this all seems too good to be true, even when, whether he knows it or not, he got fucking lucky taking down Edward. Eddie is quick to forget that Edward was kicking the shit out of him until he drank from Eddie's poisonous veins. That could be the only reason Eddie is still alive but our friend Eddie doesn't even consider this. This is a blessing to him and with that he answers,

Edward: "Sure, where do you want to meet?"

The strange text tone signifies Eddie's text went through. Another tone bellows,

Sebastian: "You know where."

Edward: "No, I don't."

Eddie ponders for a second. He wonders if this guy will know it isn't Edward. The tone goes off.

Sebastian: "It is where we always meet."

Edward: "I thought we were going to start meeting somewhere new, I don't feel comfortable there anymore."

Eddie bullshits as if it pays his bills. He doesn't know if this will work but it seems like the right thing to do.

Sebastian: "Good point...any suggestions as to where we should meet now?"

No...fucking...way.

Eddie echoes my sentiment and says in disbelief, "No fucking way."

Eddie giggles to himself while fumbling on the keypad.

Edward: "Maple St. Pub, Thursday night, 11:30?"

Eddie impatiently stares at the phone and almost pockets it but that little tone beeps off and he opens the phone to read the response.

Sebastian: "Ok brother. See you then. Stay from the light and feed in her blessing, her embrace, our Mother. Night."

Eddie stares at the text. He considers how to respond. He ponders the cryptic message and shrugs. He knows whenever people speak like that, the best thing to do is repeat it. He considers it to be like the twelve steps in Alcoholics Anonymous, the only thing that everyone in the group has to do is...

A: Say their name first and follow it with the admittance that they are an alcoholic.

B: Say some prayer from the bible, together synchronously. So, maybe, if these vampires meet up, maybe they have some sort of slogan or prayer.

Eddie again fumbles with the keyboard, learning it, and responds to Sebastian in turn,

Edward: "Till then brother. Stay from the light and feed in her blessing, her embrace, our Mother, the night."

Eddie stands there sweating; worried he has blown this even when he has no comprehension of what this is.

Sebastian: ":)"

Really? You have to be kidding me. A smiley face? If I were alive right now, I would piss myself.

Eddie laughs aloud and starts to climb the stairs. He responds in kind with a larger smiley, a colon and the capital d. Which looks like this: ":D"

Eddie has two days before the meeting with Sebastian and whoever else is going to be there. He might not come out so unscathed this time. Hell, he might not come out of it at all. But like all things Eddie, he doesn't think that far ahead.

He arrives at Alexi's door and looks himself over. He closes his shirt and wipes his mouth just to make sure no blood has caked around his lips. When he feels clean—even though he looks like he has had the shit kicked out of him, because he has—he knocks.

The door opens and Eddie is greeted by one of the juice monkeys from earlier, the one he stole the cigarette from. Eddie smiles widely and nods. The man stares at him, unimpressed, and steps aside, clearing the doorway so Eddie can enter. The door closes behind them and that gigantic bastard grabs Eddie and tosses him down the hallway toward the living room. Eddie stumbles to gain his balance but before he does he is caught by the other colossal meathead and before Eddie can react, he is lifted off his feet and dangled in the air. The one that tossed him runs up and throws a haymaker into Eddie's kidneys; Eddie goes limp. Surprisingly he does not scream out in pain from the crushing hit. The one holding him spins and tosses him across the room towards the large crystal table. Eddie limply slides across the floor smashing into it head first.

Eddie rolls on to his stomach and he comes face to legs with Alexi, who stands over him,

"What did I say Eddie?"

"That...fuck...if I came back without your money...you would kill me."

"And,"

"Alexi, babe, I have it...call off the dogs."

Alexi goes stiff with surprise and throws her hand up toward the encroaching monsters stopping their approach and calling off further assault. Her eyebrows flex strongly, pulling the flesh of her face tight, and she leans down, kneeling beside Eddie and she whispers in his ear,

"Bullshit."

Her thick accent hardens the statement, smothering her disbelief.

Eddie just smiles through the agony and digs into his pocket. He drags the wad of cash out clumsily, and as he does, bills drop freely. He hands it to her, and she struggles to cup her hands together to catch the raining bills. Her eyes bulge out, shocked in disbelief.

"Where the fuck..." she gasps interrupted mid-sentence by Eddie.

"No, Alexi, just don't. It doesn't matter. What does matter is that...what I owe...it's all there and more." Eddie coughs, attempting to sit up.

Alexi stands, walks backward, and falls onto her couch. She folds one stalk over the other and begins to count the money as though she is a machine made to do just that.

Eddie rises as the men walk toward him, offering an apologetic hand up. Eddie bravely—or stupidly— refuses their help and gives them a sour stare, almost in an attempt to antagonize them.

He walks around the large crystal table and falls next to Alexi. He cracks his neck turning to face her, and he smiles.

"So? Are we square?" Eddie coughs out.

"Darling. We are. I apologize but you must understand how unexpected this is. I didn't think I would see you again." She smiles a smile Eddie doesn't know; a smile that is refreshing and feminine, hell, a smile that actually makes Alexi pretty.

"Babe, you must tell me, where did you get this cake?" she cues questioningly, furthering her transformation from masculine to feminine.

"Alexi, why does it matter?" Eddie shrugs, sitting up, staring hungrily at what litters the crystalline surface of her table.

"Excuse me but I must protect my investments and you are now an investment. Usually, and no offense, but when someone like you stumbles on this much money someone has died..."

"Don't worry. They have been dead a while. I just collected." Eddie smiles.

"Like inheritance?"

"Yeah, just like inheritance. So, are we square? Take what I owe you and an extra two hundred just as an apology fee." Eddie stretches, digs in his pockets, before presenting more money and handing it off to Alexi like he doesn't have a care in the world. She accepts it, smiling a bright smile as she does, and laps it up from his hand with hers in a blink of an eye.

Alexi runs through the stack, takes what Eddie owes plus his gift to her, and hands him back the rest.

Eddie smiles that somehow—despite years of damage— pretty smile of his and he sits back, happily counting the stack. The final count is $4,400. He has more than enough to pay Jane's rent, live comfortably, and get sky-is-the-limit kind of high. Eddie couldn't be happier. Well, that isn't true, he is about to be. He greedily stares at the surface of the table and turns back to Alexi.

"I need an eight ball, a quarter of weed and ... do you sell weapons?"

Alexi gives him a hesitant look as though she wants to ignore the question and change the topic but within seconds reconsiders because she knows Eddie has a fortune and that she can capitalize on it because knowing Eddie, this won't last.

"Darling, wait here, relax and I'll be right back."

Alexi takes the staircase to her chambers to gather what was requested but a part of her feels terrible about furthering Eddie and his readily apparent self-destruction. Business or not, she still has a heart and Eddie owns a small space within it whether she wants to admit it or not because Eddie isn't just a client or junkie. Eddie is special, and I don't mean short bus special; Alexi recognizes him just like I do. This isn't the end for Eddie. This, right here, is a beginning; strange or seemingly wrong, this is the beginning of greatness. Alexi can see it or rather, feels it, and that is why she feels like Eddie is special. He's just in a bad place is all, a really long, seemingly never-ending self-perpetuating bad place, and she is questioning if the money is worth worsening his situation at the same time wondering if he is worth the loss of money to help him better himself. She reminds herself that this is still business, and don't get involved, despite the feelings she may have. She shakes them off because the risk isn't worth the current loss of reward.

Eddie leans forward, bill in hand, completely ignoring the monsters posing as men that observe him with anal-retentive attention, and snorts the remainder of cocaine from the crystalline surface like he owns it. He sits back with his head hanging oddly and a smile that breaches ear to ear, and freezes physically, allowing every little bit to be absorbed. He breaks the paralysis and turns to one of the giants and smiles that Eddie smile.

"Hey, sorry about the misunderstanding. Where are my manners, I'm Eddie...Eddie Red."

He extends an open hand and an intoxicating smile.

The first ogre looks to the other with a face that spells out the question: "What should I do?" and when his partner offers no answer, he just turns away, and does what feels right. He gently extends his enormous paw, warmly meeting Eddie's hand, and shakes it.

"I'm Tom, Tom Morrow. And that guy is Chester, Chester Day." He points to his friend, when anyone would be able to figure that out for themselves, but Tom and Chester aren't the sharpest tools in the shed, hell, between the both of them they're lucky to be even included in the shed as far as intelligence goes.

I know what you're thinking. Tom Morrow and Chester Day? Tomorrow and yesterday? Really? Yeah, really. These juice monkeys go by these names and I assure you, there is a reason. Tom Morrow comes first because you owe and he reminds you that you have till tomorrow to pay. Chester Day comes when you have already met Tom Morrow and you owed yesterday. Clever? Extremely. Functional? Yes, so much so that very few have actually met Chester Day. These are Alexi's dogs, and they work. They love Alexi. They're unwaveringly loyal. They do as they're told without question. And they come when they're called.

"Amazing to meet you guys...Oh, wow, where are my manners...want some?"

Eddie smiles, extending a bill. Extending an offer to take part in drugs he doesn't own yet. Tom and Chester quietly refuse with an almost synchronous headshake. Eddie shrugs and dives in, greedily inhaling the lines that remain. He falls back and sighs like he has just blown a load that has been working at releasing for a long time. His eyes slightly squint, pursing ever so slightly as they're about to close for slumber, but almost immediately pop back open. His body loses proper posture, and he relaxes, sliding down on the couch between the two monsters, and he settles in emulating confidently that he is welcomed to be this comfortable here. Eddie, welcomed or not, has made himself at home.

"Do you guys have any smokes? I'll pay for them?"

Chester sits up and extends a pack that has barely been picked at. Eddie welcomes it, drawing a crisp bill, and trades it without even a thought that this bill could get him four packs of these. Chester shrugs and accepts. Eddie pulls a cigarette and slowly puts it between his lips. He then offers a smoke to Chester and Tom, almost forcing them to take one by thrusting the pack at them. They both take one. Eddie removes his zippo and flicks open a fresh flame in one solid snap, lights their smokes before his own. He pauses with his first inhale,

"You guys would not believe the night I've had..."

He sits up and looks between them in a blink. Alexi walks down the spiral staircase so softly that Eddie, Tom, and Chester have no idea that she is returning.

"Okay, so, you guys will think I'm crazy but..."

"Darling, I have what you need. It is late and I'm tired..."Alexi says as she approaches the sofa that sits too many. She carries a backpack.

"You mean early?" Eddie interrupts, snorts loudly, sucking down the snot into his throat.

"Whatever babe, I'm tired, and I don't want to see sun-up." She sits down tossing Eddie the bag. "150 for the eight ball. 50 for the quarter. 500 for the piece. Are you okay with that darling?"

Eddie watches her sit without touching the bag that now finds home on his lap. You can tell just by looking at him that he wants to open the bag and examine the contents, but with a reservation that surprises us both, he remains motionless and cool.

"Better than okay Alexi, I'm solid."

She smiles sincerely and sees the Eddie she has always imagined, or more accurately, dreamed of. Honestly, I don't see what she sees, imagined or dreamed, but hey, I'm just an observer.

Eddie goes through the stack of bills and gives her 900 instead of 700. He smiles and rises. He begins to walk away but then agilely spins to face Alexi, Tom, and Chester.

"Tom, Chester, it was a pleasure to meet you...Alexi, you are as always, a treat. Have a great night guys, until next time."

Eddie leaves swinging the backpack as though he is leaving for the first day of school. Lost and living in his fantasy world that no one but Eddie understands.

That world that should've been irreversibly shattered and changed by the undeniable proof of vampires being real, in turn reactively forcing him to reconsider everything, and return to some sort of sanity, instead he remains unaffected. His entire reality as a whole, and everything within it, no matter what substance clouds it; should change, but doesn't at all. This is because Eddie is completely fucking—and there is no better way to describe it, Eddie is completely— "gonzo".

CHAPTER 6

Eddie walks through the dead hallways of his building and bides his time taking the stairs to the next floor. He stops suddenly, realizing his changed financial status, and backtracks to the first floor. He tiptoes his way to the landlord's lodging, pulling his fat stack of cash. He stops at the small black box marked "complaints" and steals the pen and paper from it. He writes a small note explaining that the money he will be sliding under his door is Jane's back-rent for the apartment that he "lives" in and he'll pay the rest owing within a week. He signs it *"Eddie"* and slips it under the door.

He sneaks off and giggles all the way as though he is being clever and that this, paying what he should have, has been his plan all along. He runs up the stairwell with no regard of the time, and the noise he makes, or consideration for whom he may disturb.

When he gets to his floor he changes pace. He changes from bull in a China shop gate to a ninja-like tiptoe and slowly creeps across the hallway. He stops several apartments before his own and listens. He can hear a tv blasting simulated gunfire. He changes posture and bangs on the door, assuming the role of authority figure even when no one can see this. The tv goes quiet and is replaced by the panicked vocal chords of several concerned tenants. He hears muffled footsteps and then a single cracking voice —raised octaves from its actual level—calling from behind the shut door.

"Who is it?"

"OCP. Open the door, we have had several noise complaints," Eddie barks, barely holding the stern tone, restraining himself from laughing and breaking character.

"One second," the voice responds trying to smother and hide an anxious terror that resonates in it, hanging like a freshly knotted noose.

Eddie hears the lock disengage, and he steps back, while still holding his thumb over the peephole.

The door comes open a crack and the man - if you can call this guy a man - changes his demeanor instantly relieved as he recognizes Eddie.

"Eddie...fuck...you scared the shit out of us."

"Jeffrey...someday, it'll be the OCP. I'm just preparing you." Eddie laughs through his warning and shows off a little smile.

"What do you want?"

"You know about vampires eh?"

"Eddie it is almost 5am..."

"And?"

"Yeah, I...well...yeah we know about vampires...why?"

"That is what I thought. Listen, tomorrow night, I'm coming by with pizza and you and the guys are going to school me about vampires, okay?"

"Twilight vampires or actual vampires?" he says as though he holds a degree in vampirism.

"Every kind."

Jeffery goes still, his brows rise like the wings of an eagle taking flight while he tries to figure out the situation. When he can't, they fall back down. And then only one brow lifts as his curiosity conquers his confusion.

"Why do you want to know?"

"I want to know...hypothetically, of course...how I would kill one with little to no effort."

"Yeah, but why?"

"I think I'm going to write a book about them... they're a hot topic, right?"

Eddie pulls that out of his ass and I have to respect him for it because no one asks questions when you say you're researching a book. Seriously, try it. Any topic is open when you start by saying you're going to write a book about it. It is a startling yet true fact; at least, in my experience.

"Okay, but remember to bring the pizza... and an open mind," Jeffrey replies.

"My mind is as open as the legs of stripper on a pole for a fat roll of bills, bud." Eddie, as usual, paints a picture with sly words no one needs to hear and no one needs to imagine but you have to give him points for creative flare.

Jeffrey smiles and appreciates Eddie's newfound interest in what should be fiction. He closes the door and runs to tell his roommates who all share the love of fiction and fantasy.

Let me start by saying that there is a healthy fascination with fiction and fantasy but when it becomes all that you know, and all that you talk about, you have a problem. Gamers for instance, the hard-core gamers are comparable to addicts in this regard. The only thing that matters to them is what they can immerse themselves in, what new way they can escape. They spend all of their money and time on the game they connect to—what sets them free—and that game becomes their life. They find games that render the same result as the last one and attach themselves. Gamers—not nerds—behave just like addicts. The technology entertainment industry has capitalized on this. Take World of Warcraft (copyright to them, trademark, and all that bullshit, because this may not even be here because of copyright infringement laws). For instance—which is so appropriate when using the word instance because they have a bunch of those that are a part of the problem I'm talking about. They continue to produce new content despite the fact that nothing actually changes and in order to play you must sacrifice the majority of your day. Somehow, they retain players with promise of something new but it's all the same shit. Just like drugs. Dealers talk of their product producing a new high, even though it is always the same, fast or slow, it is always the same. Drug addicts and gamers truly just chase the first taste, the first high. Just like a drug dealer appreciates a drug addict, the gaming industry appreciates a gamer. They appreciate people who will keep playing just for the title, for empty accolades, and even though they have no tangible reward, gamers will give up everything to complete them. Drugs and video games both leave you wanting more and no matter how much time and life you give them, you will never get anything real back...

Sorry if I just made you feel like shit for gaming. Gaming in moderation is good, just like anything in moderation. But if you know what I'm talking about then you should really reconsider things, like Eddie should.

Eddie gets to the end of the hall and opens the door to a place once called a home and enters. He throws on the light and sighs, shedding his dirty clothes before moving from the front door. Sadly, for me, Eddie is as he was born, naked and filthy. He goes into his jeans and pulls his cellphone out. He brings a number up, and begins to text it from his new phone that works. Okay people, you're about to hear about someone who—whether I like it or not—will be a part of this story. This person is Tessa. No, you don't get a last name because I don't know it. Tessa is all things toxic and wrong but beautiful and wondrous simultaneously. She cannot be explained or excused but she is addictive. She consumes you in a way that we know without doubt is bad, but we do it, or them, regardless. Just like a drug.

Eddie pushes the buttons as fast as he can without losing his words to the auto-correct.

"Hey, it's Eddie, I know it's been awhile but what're you doing?"

Seconds don't even get to pass before his new phone buzzes.

"I was just thinking about you... miss me? What's up?"

"Yes, can you come over?"

No response. Eddie nervously writes another message.

"I have a lot of blank pages that I need help filling, and I want to finish them as soon as possible."

This is code for I have a lot of drugs and I really need company. Time doesn't get a chance after this message is received.

"See you soon babe."

Eddie grins, laughs out loud, and kicks his boots off. He runs down the empty hallway and opens his fridge. It is empty except for a six-pack of beer. He removes one and cracks it. The sound of it opening is music—if music sounded like hissing and popping— to his ears and as he brings the opening of the can to his mouth, it pours over onto his bare chest as he gulps it down. He walks with the mostly finished beer into his washroom, going to where the medicine cabinet was until he tore it off the wall. He reaches into the hole in the wall where it used to be, searching through the dozen saffron bottles for the right pain medication. What Eddie lacks in furniture, possessions, food, and pretty much everything he should have, he "makes up for" with medication for nearly every aliment. His apartment is a functional drug store, that is, if he would ever share with anybody that actually needs something.

Eddie finds some oxy condone and takes one with a dry swallow. He puts them back, stopping at the fridge he grabs a fresh beer, and then enters his bedroom. Within a swig of the chilled suds, he picks up his notebook and reads through it. He stops on a forgotten passage and reads it aloud.

"He sits surrounded by empty beer cans and empty baggies in the middle of his living room even when he hasn't been doing any living here, or anywhere for that matter. He shakes and sweats in this circle of filth, sitting up on his knees staring at the light overhead. It takes him minutes to light a broken cigarette as tears fall softly and endlessly down his cheeks. 'I can't, I can't,' he repeats. 'Fucking light it,' he screams. 'Just fucking light it.' When that flame hits the end, he breathes in so deeply he coughs painfully. He cries, he laughs, and then he cries and laughs synchronously as he swings his arms toppling the cans nearby. He searches through the field of them for one with something in it, something cool to his dry mouth. But everything is empty, including himself.

This room is littered like his brain with things he doesn't want but thinks he needs, but all he needs is to clean house. He won't admit it, won't clean it. He reaches into the back of his pants. He pulls the weighted revolver out and brings it to look at it. He can't stay still. He mumbles and rambles. Shakes and jitters. 'She is gone,' he screams. 'Let her go, please fucking let her go,' he yells.

He puts the barrel in his mouth. He sucks in air and cries. When he exhales he squeezes so gently; restraint lives in that trigger finger. When the hammer snaps back and nothing happens he opens his eyes and grunts, coughing and balling new salty tears with the gun still sitting on his tongue. He squeezes again but this time quicker than before. Nothing. Again, and again until the barrel has made the rotation six times. He pulls the gun from his mouth bringing a string of saliva with it and looks at it. He opens the six-shell chamber and inside six bullets sit. He turns the gun, emptying them on his palm. The bullets are all intact. 'What the fuck,' he whispers. He throws them back into the gun and closes the chamber, spinning it closed.

He puts it back in his mouth, this time more angry than sad, and lacking restraint. He pulls. Solid snap back without fire. He pulls it from his mouth and drools, barely being able to lift the heavy pistol, and points it randomly without looking and pulls the trigger. His ears pop as the bullet rips from the barrel and smashes something made of glass. His ears ring as the small room provides perfect acoustics. He looks up hesitantly, tears slow, and his cheeks burn. He stares at what he shot, a picture of him and her, with a bullet hole that separates them and the glass that protected the picture, shattered.

'What the fuck,' he questions. He forces the gun into his mouth like unwanted fellatio and pulls the trigger, greeted by an empty click. He turns the gun back to the picture and fires. Another hole in the picture. He laughs, sadly at first, and uncontrollably in the next second. He fires again, and again, and again, cleanly cutting the picture into shards. He pulls the gun back quickly and jams it in his mouth and pulls... nothing. He replaces the chambers position to the last bullet and turns the gun back to the picture that is now more like a stain on the wall. Bang. The glass explodes and the frame falls. He stands and walks slowly toward the picture, toppling beer cans and bottles. He looks down at it, with an empty gun, and emptied of grief; he smiles a tired smile and says, 'It's time to clean up.'"

Eddie closes the notebook, briefly reliving that moment, and fighting the tears that well up, ready to run. He begins to consider the underlying message but before it sinks in and stays, a knock pulls him from reality and returns him to his fantasy.

He opens the door, holding his pants over his naked front, smiling wildly.

Tess hangs in the doorway and smiles.

"Aren't you a sight for sore eyes..." he smiles innocently.

Her smile is so subtle and small that you wouldn't see it unless you were as close as Eddie is now. Tess is beautiful as always; make-up, hair, clothes are all flawless. She is tall, mostly legs. She stands almost six feet, definitely six feet in heels.

Her hair is raven black, not too long, but not too short. It hangs behind her ears.

She looks like she was carved from milky marble and finished painted with a slight peach colored tint. Her mouth is pouty and pursing, trapped in that form.

Her lips are thick, succulent, and glistening as though she just applied gloss over the rose-red lipstick she is wearing. Her eyes, oh man, her eyes are deep arctic blue like a melting glacier with just the slightest tint of green—ancient and cold. Every part of her face is perfect, symmetrical perfection, just like she's a model pulled from a magazine. And then—last but worlds away from least—are her spectacular naughty bits. Her tits are big, but not too big, maybe C cups but they don't droop, instead firmly protrude looking like the dangerous tips of armed missile warheads. Her hips explode outwards from her hourglass torso, and bulge out into a big, bouncing, robust ass. Here is the kicker she looks better naked. Like when you're with a person and they look amazing dressed but when the clothes come off, nine times outta ten, you're disappointed. Like when you open a present that you were so excited for but when you unwrap it isn't what you thought it was because the wrapping tricked you. Yeah, you know what I mean. Well that is what I'm saying. With her it's different. As hot as she looked dressed, she looks much better naked.

"You going to invite me in or what?"

"Please come in."

She walks past Eddie, tearing his pants from his grasp, exposing him. She goes for the bedroom, removing her jacket, and sits down. Eddie follows her, right on her tail, and if he had one it would be wagging furiously. She sits down, removing her shoes that have heels longer than Eddie's flaccid dick. She sits up, arching her back while pushing out her chest to accentuate her cleavage before throwing her hair back before tilting her head back, looking him up and down.

"So, you have something for me?"

"Yeah baby, I have something and then some more."

"Oh yeah." She bites her bottom lip and then releases it; it springs back fuller and red and engorged. She spreads her legs causing her skirt to hike up exposing her uncovered moist fun bits, before she reaches out and takes hold of him. She digs her long vibrant claws into each of his naked cheeks and pulls him in.

Eddie stops her, lifts his index, signaling for her to hold on, and exits the room. He returns with the bag of goodies and a beer for her. She is now lying down, perched on her stomach, legs slowly kicking in the air behind her. Her clothes are gone. Eddie doesn't notice that she undressed at record speeds, he is distracted, and I understand why... hell, you do too, come on.

He sits down, reaching into the bag, and pulls out the drugs. She takes the bag hungrily, opening and pouring a large amount on Eddie's leg. She doesn't line it; she just snorts what doesn't fall off. She pulls her head back, inhaling, and shakes her head from side to side. She rubs her hand over her nose and brings it over her lips, licking off every bit of white residue. She then does the same on Eddie's leg. Her tongue cleans it completely. Without warning, she parts his legs, and ravenously vacuums his flaccid dick into her mouth. He grits his teeth, laughing.

Not sure if you know this, but drugs like this make you numb. Actually, with this drug, it can make you not just numb but temporarily unable to sustain an erection—like a bad joke and the punchline is even worse: it also makes you super horny. Shitty right? Yes and no. You see, with hard work, and constant attention you can circumvent that symptom and succeed at discovering the amazing yet terrible orgasm that cocaine produces. It is tantric sex for dummies and requires no self-control.

Now, with that in mind, Tess has the ability to override the natural way of this drug and Eddie is longer than her heels instantly, finding the back of her throat. Eddie winces as she touches her teeth against lower abdomen. Her canines scratch his sack and she gulps over and over again like she is swallowing something. Eddie has her hair in his hands and he is tugging. She doesn't come up for air, as though she doesn't need it. He swells, panting.

(If you want to continue being a pervert and continue reading this part, turn to page 167.)

CHAPTER 7

I want you to think about the first time you see—or in this case—read about a character. After a character's first appearance and you have no idea if you'll ever see—sorry, read about — this character again. But sometimes, some part of you just knows this character isn't going anywhere. Now if you have experienced this before, then you are about to again, or at least you should, because this character I'm about to introduce isn't going anywhere. So, deal with it.

As the morning sun rises over our quiet city, it fights to illuminate an alleyway already blanketed by blue and red blinking lights. Half a dozen cops close all access points with yellow tape, the kind that tells you not to cross, even though you always want to. Two cops not dressed in uniform stand around the empty clothes that Edward dissolved in and communicate only with sighs and shrugs. The one crouched directly over the empty clothes is that character I was talking about, that is Detective Calamus Shaw, and I know, Calamus is a weird name but it is his real name.

He looks up at his partner, Detective Dan Maurier, and then he looks briefly skyward before returning his tired, unimpressed peepers to his partner's weathered and wrinkled face.

"I know you don't care Danny because you're on the out, but if this keeps happening, my career is done."

"Cal, first, fuck you. And second, don't be so dramatic, this isn't the end for you. You just got to pay your dues and eventually you will be solving real homicides."

"Danny, how many is this now? Twelve or thirteen?"

Let me stop for a second and explain what should be obvious. Nobody investigates discarded clothing. There isn't a division that exists for the sole purpose of understanding why clothes become garbage or how they got there and where the person who left them went. No, nobody investigates garbage and how it got there. I know everyone at some point has seen a shoe and was like, "Where did the other shoe go?" or, "Why and how did a person lose a single shoe…" and the same goes for that dirty underwear you see lying in some gutter. You, like me, and everyone else that has seen that pair of grimy abandoned underwear, have pondered how and why, but you just move on and leave your imagination to wander. I know I have come up with several terrible stories for how they got there but I didn't start a task force.

With that in mind, they are investigating these clothes because of the property damages nearby and their presence resembles other crime scenes. Crime scenes where empty clothing has been found in laying perfect symmetry, like someone placed them to resemble where someone had died. Or in this case and those other similar cases, despite the impossibility of it, like someone disintegrated inside them, leaving them in a body shape. The latter explanation has never been considered, even when it is exactly what happened.

"This makes thirteen."

"I don't know why I'm even going to ask this, but were there any witnesses?"

Detective Maurier remains silent.

"Thought so. So, I guess we wait, yet again, till forensics gives us something."

Detective Maurier, being the conversationalist, he is, nods in agreement.

"Paperwork over breakfast?"

"Yup."

"Dan, do you know what I love about you?"

"What's that Cal?"

"You always know just exactly what to say."

Detective Shaw stands and painfully snaps straight up and cracks his back from crouching too long, and exits the scene with Detective Maurier.

Shaw is a Colin Farrell looking, straight out of a Hollywood movie stereotype homicide detective. He is tall, dark, handsome, unshaven, disheveled, and brooding. He always has his heart in the right place, usually on his sleeve, but is constantly getting into trouble for it. He is your run of the mill, carefree upstart who just wants to catch the bad guy. However, appealing or attractive the stereotype is in the movies or the books, in the real world, in the unseen or unknown grind that is police investigation, he doesn't belong. In most cities, in police precincts and law enforcing scenarios, he wouldn't belong and he sure as shit wouldn't last. Of course, in this case—his case—he will. Calamus Shaw worked his ass off like every other recruit but unlike every other recruit, Calamus Shaw single-handily arrested the worst serial killer our fine city has ever known. Now, because of that, he isn't going anywhere. Why? Public relations, that is why. You fire him and you have a nightmare knocking at your door twenty-four seven. The media made officer Shaw into a legend in less than four hours. You couldn't access any media channel without hearing about Calamus Shaw.

The serial killer Shaw nabbed was the 'Mall St. Mauler,' Heinrich GroBebose Wolf. His name translates to Heinrich "Big Bad" Wolf. He sodomized and murdered men, women, and children over a two-year period. Twenty-seven slain, and one survivor was his record. The survivor was never named to protect their privacy but rumor has it he was a seventeen-year-old boy.

Shaw caught him in the act, balls deep, Heinrich was destroying this poor kid. Because Shaw intervened, he prevented the death of that poor boy. Shaw was walking his beat, which fell into Mall St., and he heard the boy's cries and followed them. When he identified himself, Heinrich ran, and Shaw chased. As the story goes, Shaw chased Heinrich for two hours; through night till dawn he kept on Heinrich's tail, on foot, and according to Shaw's testimony, put several bullets into Heinrich but it didn't slow him down.

The story also says that after they had run outside the city limits into the country, Heinrich attacked Shaw, and even though Shaw was alone, he came out standing. He never had a chance to call for backup because he was running the entire time. Heinrich is a monster of a man, coming in at six-four and just shy of two hundred and fifty pounds, which literally dwarfs Shaw. But somehow Shaw beat him into submission barehanded and then called backup to pick up Heinrich. So, by morning, Shaw was a hero, and the Mall St. Mauler was safely behind bars.

Of course, there is more to that story, and you will get it, but not yet. Be patient. As I said, Shaw isn't going anywhere...

By noon, and after a dozen coffees, Shaw and Maurier are pursuing their first lead: DNA from the scene that matched someone in the criminal database. The DNA belongs to... drum roll please... Eddie Red, and they are now climbing the stairs of his apartment building. Eddie is unconscious and only has been for maybe two hours. He and Tess were going strong till the sun started to rise. That is usually when Eddie suddenly and without warning succumbs to exhaustion, whether he is wide-awake and balls deep inside someone, or he is just alone and high. That is his time, day in and day out, or should I say, night in and night out.

"Eddie fucking Red," Dan sighs.

"Know him?"

"Yeah, he is a pain in my hemorrhoid-ridden ass. The guy is a fucking waste of skin and he is always at the wrong place at the wrong time. Let me tell you though, this guy is a waste of time."

"He is all we have right now Danny."

"Nothing would be better than Eddie fucking Red."

Shaw knocks hard on Eddie's door. Nothing. Danny shakes his head, signaling Shaw to do it again. Shaw does, but this time much harder and for longer. Nothing. Danny smirks a smile that clearly says, "I told you so." Shaw ignores him and knocks again, but changes his firmness and adds a strange beat, tapping the door like a drum. They hear a loud crash followed by groaning. Seconds later, yelling,

"Who the fuck is it and what the shit do you want?"

"Mr. Red, my name is Detective Shaw, I need a moment of your..."

"Open the door Eddie, right fucking now. I'm not going to ask again you little shit. Drag your ass over here and open this door, now!" Detective Maurier screams through the door, pressing his face to it and turning a bright veiny red.

Eddie moves like he is on fire and he is at the door within seconds. He tears it open and smiles through his quick words,

"Danny! Long time? What can I do you for?"

Shaw and Maurier turn away, cringing at Eddie's full-frontal nude frame.

"Eddie, for fuck sakes, put your fuck fungus away and come back."

Eddie looks down at his exposed manhood and laughs, turning and disappearing into his apartment. He returns in jeans.

"What's up dicks?"

"Watch it!" Maurier barks.

"Sorry, Detectives... what can I do for you at this early hour?"

"It's noon shit for brains. We need to talk; you want to have this conversation in the hall or will you be so cruel enough and invite us into your shit hole?"

"Always the charmer Danny. Come on in?" Eddie steps aside, welcomingly.

Shaw and Danny walk into the "living" room and shudder at the cesspool that stagnates. Eddie pushes refuse from a makeshift chair which is built from empty twenty-four cases of beer and extends the offer to sit. Shaw and Maurier decline through crumpled expressions.

"Where were you last night and early this morning Eddie?"

"The bar, Maple St. Pub. Then home," Eddie replies, as though he has rehearsed the story several times.

"What happened to your face there? Looks painful." Shaw points at the wound on Eddie's cheek.

"Said the wrong thing to the wrong guy."

"Eddie, you wanna expand for us?"

"I was too friendly with somebody's girlfriend and he took me outside and taught me some respect. For the record though, she started it, I was just being polite. What's this all about anyways?"

"Found your blood at a crime scene and we are following up. You know, checking you out, and getting your story," Shaw calmly explains, watching Eddie with eagle eyed examination, trying to read him.

"Yeah, but what was the crime? You can't arrest me for getting my ass kicked and bleeding everywhere, can you?"

"No twat, we can't. But we can arrest you for destruction of property and interfering with an ongoing investigation." Maurier spits through his teeth and moves aggressively toward Eddie and stopping so they are face to face, uncomfortably close.

"Okay Danny, shit, relax... seriously. All I remember is getting my ass kicked and coming home."

"Alright, for the record, give me the details of what happened previous to, during, and after the fight."

"I hit on this guy's chick. She and I had a moment in the washroom, and then she went back to him after stopping whatever we had before it started. I didn't give up and we all left the bar, well, he dragged me out and she followed. He beat on me for a while in front of her..."

"Her name?"

"Cathy? No, wait, Christine... I don't remember; she was blonde, and hot. Anyways, he punched me a lot, kicked me a couple of times, and tossed me around. She eventually got him to stop and they left me there on all fours bleeding and broken taking any remaining dignity I had with them."

"His name?"

"Fuck if I know. I shook it off, cleaned myself up, and went home."

"Did you talk to anyone when you got home?"

"No... actually, wait, yeah, the gamer guys. I stopped by their place before here."

"Where do they live?"

"3B and Jeffrey is the one I talked to. It was early, he wasn't exactly happy that I stopped by, but he can tell you."

"Shaw, go talk to them, I'll stay here with Eddie while you collaborate his story."

Shaw looks at Danny, questioning him with a glance that signifies concern. Danny comforts Shaw with a look, dismissing his reservations about leaving them alone. They talk through glances and if eyes could speak, this is what theirs would say:

"Danny, are you going to press him?"

"No, just want to make sure he doesn't warn his buddies. Don't worry, I wouldn't risk getting his blood on me because he probably carries a bunch of diseases that I could catch.

From glances to vocals they continue the conversation.

"Alright. I will be quick."

"Be faster than quick. Be premature-ejaculate-quick."

Shaw laughs as he leaves.

"So, Danny, who's the fresh face? Your apprentice?" Eddie breaks the silence.

"Nope. Replacement. That is detective Calamus Shaw, you may have heard of him? Or have you gotten so bad that you can't even comprehend reality?"

Now, I know you're wondering why this guy is such a professional asshole towards Eddie, and whether it is personal or this guy just hates known junkies with a "criminal" background. To answer your question, it is both and more. Danny Maurier knew and cared for Eddie Red before he became the junkie he is. Danny Maurier was almost family to Eddie, but that was a long time ago. Danny Maurier is Jane Summers—Eddie's ex-fiancé's—uncle. He knows the whole story, and you will too, but hopefully, unlike him, you won't hate Eddie for it.

"The perfect fit to fill your shoes Danny," Eddie says sincerely, trying to retain eye contact but because of a buried shame looks away quickly.

"Can the cream Eddie, I like my life like I like my pie, without whipped cream."

"As you wish Danny. How're you though?"

"Well, still knocking on your door when I should be sipping drinks that would completely emasculate me on some beach with a name I couldn't pronounce even if I could remember what it was called in the first place. How do you think?"

"Gotcha." Eddie sighs loudly and purposely, rocking in one spot, trying to ignore the awkward silence that follows.

"How're you really?" Detective Maurier asks, with a warmness that is almost entirely alien of his constant cold demeanor.

"Cannot complain Danny, life is sparkling gold... just an absolute treasure..."

"Cut the shit Eddie. How much are you using?"

"Danny. Leave it."

"When are you going to face reality Eddie? This isn't life?"

"It is mine, and here I am, still standing. So why don't we just stick to business and leave our opinions and judgments to ourselves and stick to the facts."

"You stupid fucking..."

"Now, now Danny. Let's not fight."

Detective Maurier shakes his head and goes quiet, looking away.

Eddie goes to turn and head into the kitchen but Maurier stops him.

"Wait till Shaw gets back and then I'll fuck off but right now we are going to be quiet and stay still."

"Fine."

They stand in silence for minutes, until Danny makes a grunting noise and then growls as he spouts a question,

"Don't you want to know how she is or what she is doing?"

"No!" Eddie snaps reactively and furiously and he burns red through his pale skin. Danny gets a genuine emotional response and probably the first one Eddie has had in a long time because that question struck him like a snapping string on a badly tuned, Wal-Mart bought, guitar; cheap and worthless.

"She is happy now."

"Drop it," Eddie pleads through a watery curtain as he now faces reality and every single thing, he has avoided now floods back for recognition...

Meanwhile, Shaw knocks on 3B. The sound that was deafening from inside and carried into the hall disappears and is followed by a voice.

"Who is it?"

"OCP. Please open the door."

"Fuck off Eddie. Come back later. You said five."

"Sir, my name is Detective Shaw, and I need to ask you a couple questions regarding your neighbor. Please open the door."

Pattering of feet fly toward the door. The door opens and everyone that lives in 3B squishes inside the doorframe to see if the person who is at their door is the person they claimed to be. They all stare blankly at Shaw with open jaws.

"Hey guys which one of you is Jeffrey?"

"Me!" Jeffrey screams in that slightly higher voice than he didn't intend to share but excitement released it without his control.

"You're detective Shaw!" Jeffrey pushes the others back and salutes him.

"You sir are a hero and the media didn't fully encompass the reality of your achievements, nor did they properly capture your striking charisma. It is an honor." Jeffrey bows.

"Fuck. What the... Jeffrey. Thank you, but stand up. I'm just a guy..."

"The guy who beat the shit outta the mauler and walked away unscathed," Eric chirps from behind, correcting Shaw.

"Guys. Seriously. Thank you. But I need your help."

"Anything!" the entire apartment shouts.

"Was Eddie Red here early this morning?"

"Yes he was, and impersonating an officer of the OCP, to make things worse."

"Nobody likes a rat Jeffrey. What time was he here?" Shaw says quietly.

"Around five this morning."

"What did he want?"

"He wanted help with research for his book."

"What research?"

"The easiest and most effective way to kill a vampire. Hypothetically of course."

"Of course. So, you don't find it strange that Mr. Red shows up at five am asking about vampires?"

"Well, no, I mean Eddie doesn't sleep normal hours and neither do we but Eddie gets high a lot and when we do talk to him, it is never about something serious, or real."

"Eddie gets high a lot eh? On what? Do you all get high together?"

"No sir, we don't get high." Jeffrey protests. (*Which I know is bullshit. They smoke weed. Sure, they don't get high like Eddie does, but they do get high.*)

"What does Eddie do when he gets high?"

"I don't know... guys?" They all shake their heads, implying a shared lack of knowledge.

"Would you say you are friends with Eddie?"

They all look at each other and then Jeffrey speaks,

"Well, no, but Eddie is a good guy. He keeps this place pretty safe and before he started getting high all the time, he was a really stand-up guy. The kind of guy who was always nice and kind and never complained."

"What do you mean safe?"

"Well before Eddie and Jane moved in there were guys that used to hang around, gang members, and they used to hassle, steal from, and attack tenants. They robbed us a lot, like not our apartment, but like when they caught us outside. It was terrible and the police didn't deter them. But after Eddie moved in it stopped. Him and Gabe just talked to them, and they left everyone alone. Eddie and Gabe got rid of them, with words. They didn't threaten them. They just convinced them somehow to leave and they did. Eddie and Gabe have a way with words, well Eddie still does, and Gabe did. "

"Gabe did?"

"Yeah Gabe died years ago. That's when Eddie got into it, the drugs."

"How'd he die?"

"A horrible accident."

"What happened?"

"Well, Eddie has his own version. But he got hit by a train."

"Alright, well, thank you for your time and the OCP appreciates the cooperation. If you remember anything pertaining to last night feel free to contact me, here is my card. But guys, please keep it professional."

"Yes sir, thank you sir, and glad we could help."

They salute Shaw as he walks away and pays them no attention. However, what they don't know is that Shaw doesn't feel like he wasted time. No, Shaw is actually interested in their story, despite what should be dismissed and left as irrelevant. When looking at this case, Shaw sees something else. Shaw sees this because Shaw has seen things that don't fit into our known reality. Ever since Heinrich, Shaw has altered his perspective completely because Heinrich wasn't just a man that night, and that is why Shaw never called backup because he couldn't believe his own eyes let alone convince someone else of what he started chasing.

Shaw knocks and Maurier answers.

"So?"

"His story checks out."

"I told you Eddie wasn't worth the time."

"Mind if I talk to him?"

"Why?"

"Humor me and start the car."

"Fine, but you're buying tonight, and doing the paper on this."

"Deal."

Shaw walks in as Maurier leaves without a word. Eddie leans against the frame of the room that connects his "living" room to his kitchen.

"So, you're the hero cop."

"Vampires?"

"What?"

"You're writing a book about vampires?"

"Yeah... so?"

"Well, say I have an open mind, and say that I think it is strange that you show up at five in the morning to ask your neighbor's about the easiest way to kill a vampire. Say, if for some reason, I had a hunch that you aren't doing research and that you actually wanted as much information on how to kill a vampire because they are real and you want to kill them, what would you say? Hypothetically, of course?"

Eddie is sick and speechless, scrambling to read this stranger, and omit that what happened wasn't just a trip and he did luckily kill a vampire. He chokes and excuses himself with a wave of his hand as he runs to the washroom holding back vomit as he faces the possibility that this isn't all real, but someone else knows or at least visits the concept that it could be, and that this person is a sober cop.

Eddie spews the liquid from his stomach and it burns on its way up and out. It is empty of food and full of mucus, chemical, and bile. He hangs limply on the seat as Shaw walks up behind him.

"I know that everything told in stories, told in nightmares, is very real. I have known for a while. I faced a werewolf; an honest-to-god, flesh and blood, teeth and hair, werewolf. And I beat it. I learned in that moment not only that nightmares were real, but also that they enjoyed sodomizing people to death. Yeah, werewolves, or at least the one I encountered, fuck their prey to death and eat them, well, eat most of them. Now, I don't know if vampires are real, but I have found empty clothes in the shape of a person and sometimes the clothes had a hole in them, just over where the heart would be. Then there are the people drained of all their blood leaving an empty corpse behind. Every case is unsolved and ignored, but if vampires were real, they would fit the profile and it would explain everything. Before Heinrich, before seeing him change from a wolf-thing to a man, this would all be an unexplained mystery. After that night, and witnessing fiction become fact, I am open to something else entirely. So, Eddie, am I crazy? Or did you just make a new friend?"

Eddie hurls again, repeatedly without break, and then he gasps for air, whimpering for the end to his sickness. It comes, only for a moment, but long enough for him to speak two words.

"Not... crazy."

Eddie dry heaves, gulping as much air as he can between heaves, and then painfully finds thick bile surging up his esophagus, burning its way out. Finally, his sickness ends and with it he hyperventilates, greedily eating all of the unobstructed oxygen but over-does it and loses consciousness.

"Thought so. We will be in touch; I'll leave my card."

I know how convenient this appears and I know you might be questioning it, but don't. How can strangers from polar opposite worlds immediately trust each other without reason? That is how it happens, that is trust in reality. Trust isn't solid or visible or something that has a set of fixed rules. Why or how you trust is like life, it is all about perspective. It is situational. Whether gained over time, or immediately earned, trust is all the same. It varies person to person, as with everything. So, stop putting so much value in the rules of trust, fuck. You don't have to be naïve but don't be paranoid, sometimes you just have to trust strangers to do the right thing, and hell it might surprise you when they do.

Now, beyond that, I want you to consider every horror movie you have seen, and all you have learned. If said horror comes true and without any doubt that said horror isn't fiction but fact, how could you not accept it?

Because in fiction, literature or film, it is as though humans have never heard of vampires, werewolves, zombies, etc. In the fiction world, humanity is a virgin to the supernatural. But you aren't. It is pounded into you from an early age and you are made aware—whether you like it or not—of the variations and differences between everything supernatural. Every country has folklore, myth, fiction, or religious sect, and they all have their own take on the supernatural, and even you, yes YOU, probably know a bunch. So, in this case, logically, you know what you know now. And being previously prepared by the variations of said horror by those many channels—but in no way easily accept them as part of your new balanced reality—would do everything in your power to learn the difference between the fact and fiction of them. What works against them and what won't. Because in this case, Eddie's case, if not your own case, separating what is, from what is made up, can and will make the difference between life and death. Just like with every lie, somewhere exists a truth, and just like that, you are born and instinctually driven to discover the difference between them.

CHAPTER 8

The smell of pizza wafts through the hall as Eddie struts down it, juggling a twelve pack of Beck's—the one with alcohol, not that near-beer shit—and a large cheese pizza. He stops at 3B, composes himself, and then knocks. He spent most of the day sick and trying to sleep off the damage he did to himself the night before. Normally Eddie wouldn't have an issue with the day after, but the visit from Shaw and Maurier threw off his whole routine and kicked him into a state of reality he wasn't ready to even consider considering. The reality check, however needed, is now undeniable. He can't go back to his self-loathing and self-destructive cycle even if he wanted to because even fiction is tired of remaining fiction, and it is out for blood, literally. Sure, Eddie has his motives for venturing down this new path. On the surface they appear only to be fueled by his habit. But now there is more to it, more that he can't ignore; something has unlocked deep inside him and encouraged new motivation. Whether he starts this journey for all the wrong reasons, doesn't mean that nothing good will come from it. Sometimes opportunity doesn't knock. Sometimes you have to decapitate it, watch it melt, realize what it is-----—even though it can't be- what it is—then take its money and start searching for other opportunities just like it.

"Eddie?"

Eddie blinks, comes to, and realizes that Jeffrey has been standing there in the open doorway trying to get his attention.

"Hey boss! Sorry, I zoned out. My bad. Can I come in?"

"Please do, the guys are waiting in the living room." He moves out of the way letting Eddie enter and signals for him to head to the living room. He was going to ask Eddie to remove his footwear but after noticing Eddie is barefoot, he stops himself.

Eddie walks down the hallway, looking from decorative picture to picture. Each frame doesn't hold photos of family or of any of the occupants, but rather they are awards from winning gaming conventions. Each certificate bares their gaming team name: "The 4 Hearse-men". Eddie doesn't have time to count all of the certificates but he gathers, based on sheer volume, that they are really good at what they do. They are professional gamers.

Eddie enters the living room and stops in the doorway to take in the sight before him: a multiple screen TV that spans an entire wall. Eddie doesn't know how many inches it is, and I don't either because I can't measure it, but I'm certain that you can't buy this stock; this is custom made and extremely expensive. In front of it are four recliner chairs, each perfectly positioned so that whoever sits in each can see their part of the TV. Three of four of them have an occupant. The chairs swivel around and face the hallway to greet Eddie; they turn in such a way that each of them looks like villains in a Bond movie.

"Hello Mr. Bond," Eddie says, smiling.

Each of the roommates carries the same reactive expression to Eddie's greeting and that is: confusion, because none of them get the joke.

Eddie ignores this and turns to Jeffrey, roughly handing him the pizza box. He then moves to the unoccupied couch and falls into it with the twelve pack still in hand. He sits up and extends a beer to each of the roommates and one at a time they all decline. Eddie shrugs and removes one, placing the case on the floor at his feet.

"I'm Eddie. I've met Jeffrey, but I don't think I've met the rest of you guys... have I?" He looks at Jeffrey, and Jeffrey shakes his head.

"This is Eric." Jeffrey points to the one on Eddie's right, Jeffery's left.

Eric is tall, maybe in his early thirties, and is much darker than his whiter housemates. Eddie can't place his ethnicity, but he doesn't waste time trying to figure it out because skin color isn't important, right? Eric has short-cropped black hair that hasn't seen a shower in what looks like days, and his eyes are even darker, but not as dirty. Physically, he is in good shape, but he looks worn out and smoked out. His eyes are bloodshot, and it doesn't seem to bother him, because he isn't tired, he is either really high or really burnt out. He wears a sedated wide smile, the kind that can only be achieved through chain-smoking joints.

"This is Gary." Jeffery points to the guy in the middle.

Gary, also tall, and probably also in his thirties, sits up straight and extends his hand, shaking Eddie's and nearly crushing it. He doesn't just sit up straight; he suddenly has perfect posture and attempts to prove it. He is in shape, more so than Eric, but only at first glance. He is in freakishly good shape at first glance. He looks like he was sculpted from stone, cut perfectly, and he has a nearly impossible fat-to-body-weight ratio that everyone who labors for could only dream of. But if you look closer, he hides something, some physical aliment that has plagued him for his entire life. Some disease that forced him to wear a back brace during puberty to help his spine grow straight and stopped him from joining the "popular" crowd because he was noticeably different. This stopped him from a "normal" upbringing and separated him because of his special needs, which helped him find video games, and this life. This slight physical difference caused his parents to be way too protective. They babied him too much, for too long, and they made it so forcibly apparent how special he was — without ever considering how much worse it made his life or how he felt — those other kids bullied him. Because of this, Gary spent every moment after elementary school and high school, changing himself, refusing his fate. Through rigorous exercise and self-awareness—obsessive self-awareness—he has learned to disguise his physical aliment almost perfectly. *I know all of this of course, because I'm a ghost, don't question my knowledge.*

"And this Ger…, sorry, this is Trudie." Jeffery corrects himself after nearly calling the occupant of the third chair, a very timid and withdrawn girl, by what I can only assume is her given name. A name that from the glance she gave Jeffrey is a name she never wants to speak aloud.

Trudie is a petite girl and way too skinny, if you ask me. She is probably in her twenties but it's hard to tell exactly how old she is. You know the type, looks young, but could be a lot older but could also be younger. She hides. I am good at reading people, and so is Eddie, but this girl is a mystery. Forget that I didn't know she lived here because I've never seen her before, but she is so withdrawn that she could probably walk right by you, and you would never even notice her. She is pretty much a ghost, and that is saying something, because, you know, I know what it's like to be one. She has dark hair that hides her face and even if she didn't have all that hair covering it like a blanket, she wouldn't let you see it. What I can only assume is that she is this way because she wants to be. She wants to be left alone. She doesn't look like one of those Goth kids, cloaked in black, but if you saw her, you'd get that vibe. The: "life is so painful, and I hate everything" vibe. She doesn't even try to greet Eddie, she just spins to look at Jeffrey to correct him, and then disappears, hidden behind that crazy comfortable looking chair.

Then there is Jeffrey. Jeffrey looks and acts just like every gamer stereotype. He is overweight and out of shape. He is greasy in all ways: skin, hair, and clothes. He wears clothes that don't fit right. He talks like he is important and knows everything. He tries way too hard, at everything, even at the things he is terrible at… like social interaction and anything that requires physical exertion. He is a nerd, through and through. The kind of nerd that other nerds make jokes about. Not that there is a scale of how nerdy someone is, because everyone is a bit nerdy, and nowadays, that actually makes you cool. But Jeffrey is that super awkward, micro-managing, control freak. He is that unbelievably and unnecessarily pompous know-it-all, with absolutely no regard for social interaction kind of nerd that created the stereotype.

Actually because of people like him, so many suffered for so long. However, no one deserves to be bullied. Even the people like Jeffrey who make you want to make fun of them. It is never okay, and hopefully, by the time you read this, you won't know what I'm talking about.

"So, the '4 Hearse-men' eh, what's that all about?" Eddie blurts out, breaking the extremely long and uncomfortable lingering silence.

"It is our clan," Trudie says quietly, almost whispering. If it wasn't already silent in the room, Eddie wouldn't have heard that.

"Clan?" Eddie shrugs, snapping open his beer.

They all sigh loudly, judging Eddie through his ignorance.

"Yes. Clan. It is our clan title. A clan is a group of people who game together, and in our case, "pwn" together," Jeffrey explains.

When he says "pwn" it sounds like *p own*. Maybe you know what P stands for, because Eddie and I sure don't. I get the own part. Which I assume means they school people.

"Oh, so you guys like 'school' people when you play against them?" Eddie is ahead of me.

"Yes. If by 'school people' you mean they don't stand a chance, then yes, we 'school people'. Jeffrey answers coolly and actually mimes quotations with his fingers when he says school people. What a fucking guy.

Eddie, being Eddie, either doesn't notice or doesn't care that Jeffrey is being brutally condescending. Instead, he absorbs every word of Jeffrey's dribble and, intentionally or not, mimics sincere interest in it. I honestly can't tell if Eddie is bullshitting or not, so that means neither can Jeffrey, and you can be sure as shit of that.

Eddie swigs his beer and crosses his right leg over his left, exhaling softly. He tries to imply that he wants to change the conversation, and before he has to overplay it, he pipes up.

"Guys. Dig in. I brought the pizza for you."

Jeffrey exits into the kitchen, fumbles around loudly, and returns with plates. He distributes them and sits down next to Eddie, opening the pizza box. He removes a slice and passes the box on. Everyone pulls a slice, cheese limply stretching with each piece, like an umbilical cord waiting to be severed. Eddie refuses the pizza, chugging his beer back, and reaches for another one: his dinner.

Eddie isn't hungry; he ate his one meal for the day earlier when picking up the pizza he promised the occupants of 3B. That meal consisted of part of a panzerotti (which is a giant pizza pocket according to Eddie) and a quarter of a chocolate bar. Eddie rarely eats much unless he is sober and he is coming off a bender, far too sick and exhausted to start another one. When that happens, he eats anything and everything he can get his hands on or that he can afford. I like to refer to those situations as his "pre-hibernation" feasts. He eats, and eats, and eats, right up until he sleeps, and when he sleeps it is for nearly twelve hours at a time. I think it is how his body copes with the lack of daily nutrition and required sleep. Anyhow...

"So..." Eddie sits up, his posture straightening. "About what I asked for?" Eddie cuts right to business.

Jeffrey puts down his plate and dusts himself off, smiling awkwardly. He lifts his hand, signaling with his index for Eddie to wait, and he scurries away. Eddie chuckles, looking at the others for an explanation for Jeffrey and his motives, but they ignore Eddie, giving nothing as they devour their food. Jeffrey returns with a beige file folder and proudly presents it to Eddie.

"We have compiled a comprehensive and thorough guide to vampires as per your request. Any and all information pertaining to the subject of vampires that you can research online will be in that file. It includes documentation of vampire related fiction as well as cultural variations of the myth, compensating for geographical variations of course. If they are, or they are like vampires, they are in there. Needless to say, all of the information that we compiled was found through searching for what we know as the 'pop culture vampire mold'."

Eddie didn't catch all of that sales pitch, but he plays it off like he did. He opens the file and begins to browse through the stack of papers. I have to say, I'm impressed, because this file looks like an official document. It is a research masterpiece, divided into numbered sections separated by color-coded tabs, with a built-in easy to follow index.

"Wow, guys, I have to say, I wasn't expecting this kind of detail. Thank you. I'm speechless."

"Well, if you're going to do something, do it right the first time," Trudie squeaks up.

"I owe you guys more than pizza. What can I do for you, name it?" Eddie says, closing the heavy folder.

"Honorable mentions if you publish whatever you're using that for," Gary says without turning around to look at Eddie, as he is now lost in the screen in front of him.

"Okay, done, but how about something I can do presently? Like something I can do now?"

"Another large pizza." Jeffrey smiles.

"Another large three topping pizza," Eric chimes in.

"Done. I'll make the call." Eddie laughs, digging for his phone.

Eddie goes to open his phone and sees a new text message from Sebastian. *Just in case you forgot who Sebastian is, he is the "guy" from the dead vampire's phone that Eddie texted and made plans with.* Eddie doesn't read it but makes a mental note that he will later. He calls the pizza place and orders the pizza they want, and when they ask him how he'll be paying, he proudly says in his coolest and deepest voice: "with cash".

Eddie browses the file while he waits to pay for a pizza, he isn't capable of eating in his current state. I could go on and on about what is in that file, but I won't and Eddie sure isn't reading it word for word, but he is absorbing all the regular ways to kill a vampire.

I don't need to list them, do I? I mean, come on, you should know them or at least most of them. Stake in the heart? Cutting off the head? Those are like the two most common and consistent methods for killing a vampire. Whatever, I'm not doing the list right now, but I will later. *Or I might not.*

Eddie knows that one of those killing methods—removing the head – works. Tried, tested, and true. However, according to this research, the most popular method, "the stake through the heart method" for destroying a vampire, is something he needs to try.

A knock rouses Eddie from his thoughts to reality.

"Pizza. No one gets up. I'll get it."

No one but him flinched at that noise. He answers the door and before him stands a middle-aged man holding out a large pizza.

"Twenty-five fifty."

Eddie raises his eyebrows, staring beyond the man, just over his shoulder. Eddie is looking at someone else.

"Brought a friend?"

The pizza guy turns and looks, and then looks back at Eddie confused. He doesn't see the man behind him that Eddie sees, because he can't.

"What do you mean?" He looks back again.

"Nothing. Here, keeps the change," Eddie says, passing him thirty dollars, and taking the pizza.

"Thanks."

The pizza guy turns and walks right through the man he doesn't see. Yes, through. Not past. Not around. The pizza guy walks right through the mystery man. Eddie stands there speechless. The pizza guy passed through the other guy like he wasn't there, but Eddie can see him.

"Eddie?" Jeffrey calls him from within the apartment.

Eddie turns to tell him it's just the pizza guy and when Eddie turns back to the mystery man, he is gone. The pizza guy turns the corner, out of sight. The other man is nowhere in sight, vanished in stale air. Eddie shakes his head, trying to dismiss the mystery man as delusion, that he is just too high. That is when fear decides to take a bear hug hold of Eddie. That is when terror goes in raw and dry and without warning. Because this is when the terrible and cold very real truth hits him: Eddie isn't high. Eddie is sober.

With that, Eddie soundlessly mouths, "what the fuck" and closes the door in front of him. Turning on the spot he walks back toward the living room with the pizza currency in hand. He places it on the table, dropping it. Almost crawling across it, he reaches over the table and awkwardly yet successfully rescues the research file and his now three-pack of Becks before standing straight up.

Jeffrey, Gary, Eric, and Trudie have stopped what they are doing suddenly and now pay him their full attention. They all share the same eerie experience, and they know it without having to confirm with one another. Something just happened. Whether they know what it is or not, they felt it happen.

I know you're wondering what ACTUALLY happened, just like they are. I'm talking about the mystery man and I know you're like, "Yeah, I know that, but what the fuck was that?" Actually, you should be asking who that was, but let's not get mixed up with semantics. That wasn't a delusion. That wasn't just Eddie seeing something.

That was Eddie seeing and acknowledging something he shouldn't be able to. But because he did, it became real, and it stained him with a lingering presence that they all felt. Just like when you feel like you're being watched or that you just saw something out of the corner of your eye but when you look for the source you can't find it and you instantly dismiss it as paranoia.

Well, if you were able to actually witness—like Eddie just did and will again— what is actually responsible for those feelings, then it wouldn't be just paranoia.

It isn't your imagination playing tricks on you. Because the moment you really see it, when it becomes corporeal and you touch it, it will never be just part of your imagination again.

Hell, want to know something that is more terrifying than that idea? What if it was never your imagination playing tricks in the first place? It was always real and waiting to be. And the only reason it wasn't real was because your imagination instinctually protected you from these ideas. What if it was just your imagination that made it a figment? And now suddenly, your imagination gone, it is real, and it can hurt you. Scary thought, right?

"Eddie?"

The words hit Eddie like a good slap in the face, pulling him back to reality and bringing the color back to his ghost white face.

"Yeah, sorry, I have to go. Thanks again guys. Enjoy the pizza. I'll be in touch. I'll have my people call your people and all that noise." With that Eddie and his beer abruptly exit, leaving Jeffrey, Gary, Eric, and Trudie staring at each other cluelessly.

CHAPTER 9

A large glass window slowly shudders. A bit at first but then begins to bend and shake. Like it is breathing. Its wide transparent surface violently ripples from the commotion just behind it. It changes, tensing, and warping outward. Then the solid surface cracks, one single crack. Then another. Then another. And then it bursts into thousands little tiny pieces of window that spew forth from the now empty portal. With the broken window and its tiny little pieces follows Eddie, unconscious, in mid-air. He hits the sidewalk and slides to a stop. He is out cold, in the cold. A hockey mask falls off in the impact, revealing a large wound that spans his forehead.

It spills sanguine over his face, running down the side of it, filling his right ear. If he was conscious, he wouldn't be able to hear out of it. Then again, being able to hear perfectly is the least of his problems at the moment.

Red, blue, and white lights pulse toward him, growing closer. An armada of police, ambulances, and fire response vehicles speed toward the scene. Responding to a 9-1-1 call that sounded a little like this:

"9-1-1, what is your emergency?"

People screaming and the pulsing sounds of a club's overpowering bass subwoofers nearly drown the caller's voice out completely.

"Please... you must help us, help him, he is all alone... holy shit... fuck... fuck... fuck... did he just... WHOA that guy is still alive? That can't be... he cannot be alive after that, wait, now he is down again... they aren't human..."

"Sir, please calm down, I need you to tell me what is going..."

The 9-1-1 operator goes quiet when she hears a blood curdling scream, followed by a sick popping noise, quickly followed by a wet thud and people screaming louder.

"Sir? Are you still there?"

"Yes ma'am. He tore the head right off. Popped it from his shoulders like popping the yellow head from a dandelion. Fuck, holy fuck. He just took his head right off."

"I'm sorry sir, did you say someone just decapitated someone?"

"Yes ma'am, they aren't men, they are... they aren't human, they are... this man can't take them all on."

The man screams so loudly that it cracks up the microphone to static making him sound like a robot and then the call is cut off.

The operator slides across the floor and screams into the dispatch radio. She directs all available units to the origin of the call; a club called The Board Room...

Two hours before the massacre at The Board Room...

Eddie walks down the street toward the Maple St. Pub carrying a duffle bag full of things he thinks he needs. Things that the file told him would kill vampires. He is lit and smiling wide; biding his time. The night is young as the sun just ducks behind the skyscrapers, lightly throwing its glow across a quickly darkening city. The city is alive as people are either heading home or heading out to embrace the night. If they knew what Eddie knew, anyone with half a mind—Eddie obviously would be lucky to have half a mind—would be going home. The night, already unsafe, is much worse now with the existence of the supernatural.

Eddie goes toward the danger, toward Sebastian, his next payroll. Eddie doesn't even consider for a moment that he might've just got lucky when he killed the last one. No, Eddie has one thing on his mind: finding a way to stay high as long as he can. He seriously believes this is easy money.

He corners Banker and Fourth Street and is only a block from the Maple St. Pub when his new phone buzzes away in his pocket. He stops abruptly on the sidewalk, blocking people from getting by, and digs it out of his pocket with his tongue hanging out of his mouth. He pulls it to his face and flips it open, squinting at the light that stabs his pupils to pins.

Message: "Meet up is a The Board Room now L sorry Edward."

"Fuck," Eddie breathes out, letting his lungs hang on to the word until the last letter sounds like a hard click rather than a k.

"That is all the way down, downtown," he says out loud. People stare at him while he talks to himself and he ignores them.

Eddie shrugs, spins on the spot, and struts in the direction of The Board Room.

Four hours before the massacre at The Board Room...

Eddie stands in "Home Is In the Hardware", filling his cart with the most random items in the store. In his cart there are three pieces of two by four and three wooden baseball bats. Below them there is a hockey mask, football shoulder pads, a neck guard, and chest piece. Now he stands in front of a huge display of axes. Large fire axes, wood chopping axes, and hand held hatchets. He scans them and pulls the reference file from his bag and flips through it. He reads a section that discusses the decapitation of vampires and along with his experience this reference pushes him to buy a hatchet. He flips back through the pages and reads the section on wooden stakes as he shuffles between the two-by-fours and the baseball bats. He keeps picturing a stake to the heart being a vampire eating too much steak, which leads to heart disease, which leads to death. He laughs out loud.

He grabs a hatchet. Black handle, gun metal black, and swings it in his hand to feel its weight. Satisfied, he tosses it in his cart.

He wheels his cart to the check-out and waits.

"Eddie?"

His skin stretches and then shudders, covered with goose flesh—*side note, why is it called that? Because as far as I know, geese have a shitload of feathers and you can't even see their flesh... anyhow*—and he goes stiff. He slowly pivots and turns slightly, just enough to look back at the person who called his name.

"Eddie, is that you?"

"Hey Jane..."

He swallows so roughly that the sandpaper an isle over cringes at the coarseness of it.

"...How're you?"

"You look..."

She pauses and forces herself to hide her actual reaction and facial expression. She recovers brilliantly; her performance deserves that little golden statue that actors covet.

" You look so... you look good. How're you?"

Liar. He looks like shit on a good day. He's worse than you have ever seen him look, and you fucking know it.

"I'm good Jane. Just doing some shopping." Eddie grabs the hatchet and flips it in his hand, while wearing that smile that she knows all too well, and then casually drops it back in his cart.

Jane is Eddie's ex, but not just any ex, the ex. She is the girl who got away, the one who left him, heartbroken and falling apart, the same one he still tries to forget. Eddie loved her before all the drugs. Before he lost me. Before he initially fell apart. Jane knew Eddie as an off-balanced and nearly incapable of having a serious relationship kind of guy. But she has never met the drug addict that stands before her. The Eddie she knew back then was worlds away from the broken man that stands before her now. She thought the Eddie she knew was bad. But she didn't watch him suffer alone with loss, hers and mine. She didn't watch him slowly lose humanity and become only addiction. She left well before things got really bad. Eddie loved her like nobody has ever loved anything or anyone and probably will ever love anything or anyone as deeply again.

Eddie had what you could and should call "a hard upbringing". According to medicine, Eddie was broken and needed medication just to function in society. Because of this, Eddie didn't grow properly and was never comfortable being just Eddie. He was forced to take pills that promised to make him better but only made him worse.

Eddie spent his entire adolescence, teenage, and young adult life convinced that he couldn't be without medication and constantly tried to get better while being completely overmedicated - actually, more accurately - sedated. One day when Eddie could decide for himself, legally speaking, he chose to be without the medication he supposedly needed, and for a while, despite terrible withdrawals, it worked. Sadly, his independence from substances didn't last because he never learned to be himself without the help of a drug.

He struggled for years, self-medicating with booze and weed, but only to the point where he still felt like he was in control. It worked for him, at least if only to get by, but he was still incapable of making genuine connections with others because he didn't have a genuine self to connect with. Without substance, he wasn't there.

So he got by making fleeting connections, until Jane. And then Jane changed everything. I know what you're thinking. How were Eddie and I so close if he couldn't make genuine connections?

Well, smartass, that is because Eddie and I were friends before all the substances. We met as children. So, my friendship with him, our bond, wasn't affected. We shared a pure connection. Something Eddie was unable to reproduce after the drugs stole him with the only other person he connected to before all that which was Jane.

When he met her, he did his best to continue his system. He tried to have a brief connection with her but she wasn't having that, and somehow, she connected conduits in him that had been severed and helped him build a new connection. With her love she started to repair him, and together they began to fix something that modern medicine, psychiatry, pharmacology, and overpriced but useful psychology, for years, had failed to do. He immediately gave up drinking and smoking weed, which were his only vices at the time. At the time they kept him sane but like all deep problems, it was only a matter of time before he had to face them.

But with her help, he did, and he did so healthy and sober. She brought out the man she fell in love with, the man she saw inside screaming to be himself, the man she saw when no one else did. She succeeded brilliantly in freeing the true Eddie from the dark recesses of the broken Eddie. Then the intended "paragon" Eddie was born, and he slowly erased every former quality, good or bad of the old Eddie, until there was only the new.

Sadly, in the process he lost several important qualities that made him the man she fell in love with. Excited and at the same time terrified of this brand-new person, she let the new Eddie revel. She waited for reciprocation. She stood by, waiting to be acknowledged for believing in him, and yearned for the love he could give unburdened by the pain and sedation of his previous situation. She waited for the new Eddie to do everything he was now capable of and to love her like the old Eddie was only partly able to. But that old Eddie loved her, truly, and flawlessly.

The old Eddie, however broken, loved her completely and purely. The love the old Eddie gave to her was more than enough because that love was the entirety of love that Eddie possessed. That love was unfiltered, genuine, absolutely natural, and totally limitless. Growing exponentially, infinitely, growing beyond any measurement that exists presently or ever will.

Jane truly only wanted what was best for Eddie and that is why she tried so hard to change him in the first place. But Jane's only fault was thinking that if Eddie could love himself more, he could love the world around him more, love her more. Which he couldn't do because something that is infinite can't be more infinite.

The new Eddie was without the capacity to consider anyone but himself. The new Eddie was unrealistically happy, never serious, and always evasive about anything to do with problems, or even tomorrow. The past didn't matter anymore, nor did the future. It was only right now that mattered, and if the current situation wasn't satisfying, it wasn't for Eddie. He was fun to be around. He was the life of every party. He was the perfect person to help you forget about reality. But the moment you tried to get serious, he was gone; you couldn't get in or even get a real response. He was impenetrable. He started living life to the absolute fullest, daily, as though tomorrow was the end of existence.

So, when Jane realized that what she had helped create— better yet, release—was an egomaniacal, emotionally distant, self-serving monster, she folded. She stopped trying because he didn't need her. The thing about Eddie was, and still is, is that he doesn't have a medium. There was never a middle ground. Eddie was born absolutely incapable of achieving any kind of balance. The "just right" Eddie was a goal he always tried to score but never could. Eddie was cursed with hot or cold reactions, only polar extremes; only one tap could be turned at a time. He only understood day or night. There was no dawn or dusk. You get the point by now, and if you don't, well you're as hopeless as Eddie.

It isn't Jane's fault that he is like this now, for the record. Of course, it isn't. But she didn't help his case any. He made it clear before they got together that he had issues, but no, she wanted in. And just when she got in, at a time that was so crucial for her to stay, she cut her losses and jumped ship. I don't blame her; I just wish she knew the power she held over him.

When people say better late than never, they have never nor will ever understand just how stupid that saying is...

"Eddie?"

Eddie shakes his head and looks at her, trying to not see her as he used to, but still does and always will, without trying to, which to him is the physical embodiment of everything beautiful.

"Yeah, sorry, went somewhere in my head. So, what're you doing here? You look great."

Eddie ignores the guy just behind her because he knows who he is and because he does, he erases him from existence.

"We're just grabbing some camping supplies for the weekend. How 'bout you? What's up with the chaos that is your cart?"

"Oh, this junk? It's for a project. I know, random, but everything here is necessary... hey, by the way, I ran into your uncle a couple days ago. Great guy. He is nearly retired, right?"

"Yeah, he is done next month."

"That is great. Anyhow, I'm strapped for time. It was so great seeing you." Eddie swallows dryly through that sentence, keeping a composure I didn't think he possessed.

Eddie spins his cart and starts to head off but is stopped with a question.

"Eddie, are you okay?"

Eddie doesn't turn. He just sighs. He closes his eyes, takes a very deep breath, and starts to push his cart toward the cash acting like he didn't hear her question. He fights the urge to turn and tell her how not good he is doing. But he swallows and keeps his pride in his pocket, right over his heart, hiding his feelings and he pushes on, never looking back.

T-minus minutes to the massacre at the Board Room...

Eddie walks past a long line of people trying to get into the Board Room. He skips the line and heads right for the bouncer. He carries a duffle bag full of the goodies he bought at the hardware store slung over his shoulder and because of this bag he sticks out like a sore thumb attached to a well-manicured hand; completely out of place. People carrying or wearing next to nothing compose the line of people he bypasses. They all throw him hateful glances as he ignores the democratic policy of the line. But Eddie doesn't pay any attention to the people, the rules, or anything but getting past the bouncer. He walks right up to the bouncer and tries to walk by but he is immediately thrown back.

"Where do you think you're going hotshot?" the bouncer chirps Eddie condescendingly.

"I'm on the guest list," Eddie sneers, and moves forward.

The bouncer throws him back again.

"There isn't a guest list."

"I'm a friend of Sebastian's."

"Oh yeah?"

"Yeah."

"Prove it."

Eddie stands there gaping, grasping for proof, and suddenly he blurts out the first thing that comes to mind.

"Stay from the light and feed in her blessing, her embrace, our mother: night."

Eddie smiles awkwardly and his mouth begins to gap, paralyzed by his statement. The bouncer stares at him blankly and for a moment Eddie thinks he has just spewed gibberish and worsened his case for immediate admittance but the bouncer, without change in expression, steps aside, beckoning Eddie to enter.

Eddie is still frozen solid and hasn't caught up with the current situation. He is shocked that worked. But as quick as Eddie spewed what should've been gibberish but wasn't, he comes to and enters, playing off dumb luck for intention.

He walks through the open door and leaves the night behind, entering a club that is darker inside than the night outside. He can barely see anything as he pushes his way past human obstructions lit only by the split-second bright flash of a strobe light. What's worse than the periods of seizure-inducing strobe light and darkness is the volume of the "music". It isn't music, it is digitalized beats that have no timing or rhythm and are so loud that it chemically triggers a physical defensive response. They called it Dubstep—*who are they? I don't fucking know. Them. Shit. You should know that expression...*

If you don't know what Dubstep is, then it died, and let it rest in peace with its terrible ancestors: techno, house, and trance. Dubstep is the bastard child that you couldn't bear to kill at birth when you realized how terribly unnatural it was, so instead you kept it chained to a wall in a secret room of your basement.

So, Eddie, void of two crucial senses: sight and sound, navigate directionless through the swelling and shifting masses of bodies that congest this club looking for someone he doesn't know and wouldn't recognize even if he could see him.

Suddenly Eddie can see, through a dull red glow that ravages his pupils.

He is standing in a large room full of convulsing sweaty bodies that grind into each other to the chaotic and deafening sound. The ceilings of the club are covered in mirrors reflecting the red pulsing lights that seem to emulate the rhythm of the music, meaning they fire off sporadically. He squints, takes a second to adjust, and looks back at the darkness he came from. He scans the room and sees detached booths that could hypothetically hold secret meetings. He sees a group of people at the only occupied booth and decides that those people, who are shrouded in darkness and separated from the rest of the club, must be the people that Edward would've met if he could've.

Eddie readjusts his duffle bag, shouldering it. He looks for an easy way to the booth but realizes that the only way is through the "dance floor" so he tightens his grip on the bag and pushes his way through.

He forces his way through the ignorant and sedated flesh. He pushes, dodges, and screams at the top of his lungs, announcing his path. In the end, the only thing that works is force, and he becomes it. He just wades through the human weeds and muck that make up this marsh of a "dance floor".

When he reaches the other side, he pulls from the crowd as easily as a newborn being pushed from its mother: labored. He looks as though he is spat from their ranks as he stumbles forward, but quickly he regains his balance. Then he takes the steps that lead up to the booth, climbing cautiously.

This is the terrible moment where Eddie realizes that if this is the meeting Sebastian is at, he is extremely outnumbered. Eddie quickly swallows that chicken-shit feeling and buries it with the rest of the very rational fears he should've paid more attention to.

Each step he takes feels like he is walking through mud, slow and tedious. In his head, he hears that "Ew Watcha Say" song, but he doesn't know why because it isn't playing and he hasn't heard it in forever. It seems appropriate, with his tortoise like pace. He sings a name under his breath: "Jason Derulo." He breaks his lips for a wide smile and looks from under his brow at the large group that fill the booth. Each look similar to the next in the regard of pigment, pale and painted with makeup; the expensive animal-tested kind, proven through pain. They wear only shades and not colors.

Eddie takes the stolen mobile out and texts Sebastian just to be sure that he is with this group and if he is, Eddie wants to know what he looks like…

Eddie: "I'm here."

Seconds later the stolen cell phones buzzes from a received text.

Sebastian: "We're in a booth in the back."

Eddie looks up at the booth, trying to identify Sebastian, but the red glow of the dancing lights makes it nearly impossible. So Eddie sends another text and watches the booths like a car crash; with his eyes fixed and unable to look away.

Eddie: "Be there soon brother."

Then he sees Sebastian, open his cellphone, respond and close it. Eddie immediately receives the response.

Sebastian: "Sounds good J"

By the way, every time Sebastian sends the smiley face emoticon, it has little fangs, just so you know… fucking twenty-first century vampires' man…

Eddie turns and hunts down the washroom to prepare for this encounter. When he finds the door in the red glow, he uses his shoulder to open it, almost throwing himself into it without regard for anyone that could be behind it.

The brightly lit washroom has his pupils in pins. He grunts loudly in disgust at the overwhelming decadence of the club washroom, brightly lit by buzzing white halogens that are intended to sober the drunks from their daze. The walls are jade, or at least this is jade green to Eddie. The stalls are matte black and there are so many Eddie loses count.

The washroom has a terrible reek about it. Somewhere between the ammonia smell of freshly flushed urine and the acrid stench of caked vomit, but strangely neither overpowers the other. He looks at the urinals from the reflection and watches as a twenty-something, wet behind the ears guy pisses next to the urinal rather than pissing in it. Eddie utters, "Really?" under his breath as he stumbles toward the sinks.

He throws down his duffle bag on the red granite countertop and zips the bag open, exposing the goodies inside. He looks up at the mirror and jumps back from his reflection, scrambling for his nerves, which he seems to have left outside the club in that long line. He ignores the people behind him and their illicit behavior as he begins to remove his belongings from the bag. He pulls the football shoulder pads over his shirt, and straps them down. He makes a robotic "ta-ting-took-cha" noise, doing his best to mimic that he is a transformer from the cartoons.

He stops equipping himself briefly to drink from the tap, even though as clean as it looks it's probably filthier than the floor of this washroom. He splashes water in his face and uses it to slick back his hair. He grabs some coke, spills it on his hand, and snorts it ravenously. He takes a huge pull of his flask to chase it and the whiskey burns his throat, before pulling the hockey mask over his head. He puts each hockey mitt on and turns them at the wrist before closing and opening his hands, feeling out their encumbrance and mobility—or the lack thereof. All the while in his head he imagines a video clip montage with each piece he equips, rock music playing in the background and progressively growing more epic and louder.

Finally, just before he removes the hatchet and baseball bat from the bag, a drunken frat boy breaks his concentration with a question, slurred and intoxicated, almost nonsensical.

"Is this some sort of art performance?"

Eddie looks up at the mirror, looking at the drunken frat boy through its reflection, and smiles wickedly before nodding the mask to fall down, shielding his face, and finally answering.

"It is whatever you want it to be but what happens next, happened, and you were there when it happened, therefore you get to tell the story any way you want."

The frat boy rocks back and forth silently, but struggles to comprehend Eddie's response. He stops moving altogether, frowns, shakes his head like he is trying to dry his hair and then lunges forward for the bathroom exit. Eddie turns toward the door, takes several rapid breaths, and then charges out the bathroom door into the dark and red glow of the club.

Let the massacre at the Board Room begin. And try to remember it's just business…

Eddie bolts across the dance floor with hatchet and bat in hand, running off the thunderous palpitation of his furious chest engine. Blood surges through him and energizes him like a freshly charged car battery, ready to go. He hits those stairs to the booth before the first scream drowns the droning pulse of the sub woofers. Just like a record being scratched and ending a song far too soon, summoning the complete and total attention of everyone in the room, so does the music stop and everyone starts to scream at what happens next. Eddie takes flight off the final step, flying into the group of what he knows to be vampires, and catches the closest one completely off guard with his hatchet. The axe blade makes a clean path through the vampire's neck, severing its head from the rest of its body, and this happens before Eddie's feet find the floor waiting beneath them. Blood geysers upward from the fresh stump that the vampire once called his neck as his head rolls away toward the scattering people who congest the dance floor, inciting complete chaos. When the other vampires feel the crimson shower splatter down on them like a flash rainfall, they move reactively.

Two immediately scatter from the party, leaping from the booth over the divider, landing on the dance floor, and disappear into the herd of fleeing club goers that congest the exit. The remaining three with their heads still attached stay behind and rush Eddie. One of them catches Eddie's hatchet-wielding arm and relieves him of the hatchet before feeling the full force of Eddie's boot collide with his chest repelling him backward. And the other reaches Eddie just in time to meet his bat-wielding arm—the one he knows as Sebastian—and this is an introduction that gives a new meaning to first impressions.

The bat splits on impact with Sebastian's jaw, shattering explosively and loudly. So loudly in fact, it does so cacophonously. A noise so terrible, it is cringe-worthy regardless if you knew what caused the sound or not. It just sounds so big and horrific. The sound of the bat's separation, and how I described it, barely—in terms at least descriptively— offers so little comfort in just how barbaric the impact actually was. So, for the sake of credit being due, I'll attempt to elaborate just how vicious it was… The noise created by the union of Sebastian's jaw and the bat was inorganic, or better yet, it was completely alien: a sound existing beyond our comprehension. Because if you heard it, like me, you wouldn't be able to explain it or want to try because it just doesn't make sense.

One piece of the bat remains whole inside Eddie's two-handed grasp, resembling the classic wooden stake. While the other half of the bat shatters—freshly liberated and explorative— that part he still holds is nothing more than a broken club end while the other half flies free in the opposite direction of the initial impact, completely emancipated, before landing and clearing a nearby table of glasses destroying them, splintering them into shards of different shapes and sizes.

Eddie's hands sting from the vibration. His victims jaw—or what's left of it— has seen better days cause it is still there and sickly droops, barely hanging from the threads of flesh that it dangles from. His lower jaw looks like a nut sack full of broken bones.

Fear overwhelms Eddie, fresh and different, because this "new" fear comes in the form of questions. Questions he shouldn't ask because he should already know the answer to them before going through with this. He takes a second to doubt, allowing the possibility of this entire operation to be a mistake. What if the whole vampire thing was just delusions? And if they are just manic manifestations and he has finally lost it, making him a murderer?

He regrets everything, from start to finish, and even feels remorse for assaulting them entirely. That is, until the one with the sagging hanging jaw retaliates without restraint. Sebastian does so completely unaffected by his gruesome injury, swiping viciously at Eddie, now armed with a straight razor. A straight razor just like the first vampire Eddie killed. Or destroyed. You know that Edward Douchebag that Eddie decapitated with a fire hose. Eddie knows this is real.

Eddie, liberated from his mental purgatory, barely gets those bulky hockey mitts up in time to defend himself. Just in the literal knick of time as little chunks are cut and torn from them. The stuffing is violently ravaged from them through each swipe, and with every pass less and less is left; bleeding white cotton candy from the newly formed gashes. Eddie defensively steps backward, keeping his mitts up, continuing to defend himself from each forward slash that turns them from the once solid mitts to the mere ribbons that are left over.

To make matters worse, while Eddie walks defensively backward, he unknowingly walks right into a trap and gets caught. Arms belonging to a faceless aggressor catch him and welcome him and constrict powerfully. Immediately trying through suffocation to kill him. Completely immobilizing, hugging him in a sweet, seemingly inescapable embrace.

You know the kind I'm referring to: the bear hug. Regardless of researched and sourced definition. The bear hug is never what it seems. It sounds a lot friendly then it is, even though, when you actually think about it...It would end terribly. Somehow still, genius and inept alike, immediately arrive at the same place. They associate positive scenarios and always romanticized and entirely ignore the literal situation completely all together.

If a bear, an actual, wild bear "hugged" you, however cute—and deeply misinformed and dangerous the attempt would definitely be— still sounds playful, but isn't. No matter how much your mind is screaming at you, presenting you with inarguable facts, facts you accept as absolute, without a shadow of a doubt, you instinctually know the truth. It isn't safe and you know bears are dangerous...good for you, because they fucking are.

Imagination wanted to argue. A real hug from a bear would always render negative outcome. It would be physically harmful, brutal, and even if one were to survive it, it would be certainly painful. And unless successfully escaped, always fatal.

So, after all, when you really think about the name, it isn't friendly but for some reason when I hear bear hug, I never immediately associate it with terror, when I should...maybe that's just me. Moving on...

Eddie's arms are now pinned against his body, completely useless. He is left defenseless through pinned appendages. He is trapped, embraced by an unknown foe. He looks up through the fenced visor of his mask and can only watch what comes.

He sees the blade before it strikes and gets to know the blade and everything about it before it does. As though time halts completely, he gets to watch frame for frame as it slowly restarts— like it or not— he witnesses every detail.

Just like one of those slow-motion comedy video clips that are hilarious because you get to watch what you know what is going to happen, savoring every delayed second before it finally does, and is even more awesome when it finally does. This isn't one of those times. It isn't awesome, farthest thing from it. Eddie lives a slow-motion clip that he never wanted to watch or share, and within those minutes, which seemed like an eternity, he learns everything about that blade, right down to the last microscopic detail.

Things Eddie never wanted to know and didn't need to learn. Much like most of his high school classes, the blade and its finite details, Eddie didn't need to ever learn. Wasted brain cells better saved for something, anything else.

Because, as the straight razor makes contact it slides harmlessly across his mask, only scratching it, doing no actual harm.

Before Eddie falls completely and irreversibly into "I'm completely fucked" mode and gives up, he reacts, returning to this situation, and intends to come out of it victorious.

He throws his head back swiftly and violently, catching the person "bear-hugging" him in the bridge of the nose, collapsing it, sanguineous. When his arms feel freedom, he doesn't waste a second, not even the slightest split of one. He jumps forward, burying the severed remains of the baseball bat-now-stake into the chest of Sebastian, with the seesawing jaw.

What happens after he does that nearly paralyzes Eddie. After being impaled, Sebastian instantly seizes up. He immediately morphs from alive—vampire or not—to a fucking inanimate object. In the same instance that the wood penetrates his sternum, piercing his heart, he changes completely. As though he was never a real boy in the first place, just a magically animated statue feigning life no longer. As though he was always just a statue, awaiting his inevitable return to what he is, just an object living a lie on borrowed time...

He's petrified; turned to stone. Instantaneously, when the makeshift stake hits his would-be heart, he becomes a concrete statue, just like the legends of medusa's glance. He is a lawn ornament.

The Sebastian statue topples over, absolutely lifeless with the majority of baseball bat freshly buried in his cement chest. The wooden hilt of the bat that protrudes out of the statue's rock-solid chest, somehow, is the only thing that looks out of place now, as insane as that sounds, it is unchanged.

Eddie looks back within a regular blink of his tired lids over his left shoulder. Just to catch up with the condition of the "bear-hugger".

The unnamed vampire has recovered from the head butt and is donning his own straight razor. Eddie knows he won't reach his hatchet in time. Lurching forward he reaches and catches the bat handle stopping the Sebastian statue mid-fall. He tears the buried bat-now-stake free.

Again, Eddie can't believe his eyes because as he retrieves the bat turned stake from where he buried it—from the recesses of Sebastian's solidified chest—the chest inexplicably returns to flesh from its stone-like state; alive again. From lawn decoration instantly to living flesh, Sebastian returns.

He returns to "life" so quickly that his recovery rate could only be described as inhumanly fast, because it is, and you and I both know it. I guess in this case, he hastily returns to what he was, not alive, but again undead.

Eddie makes a split-second decision, choosing to rebury the stake and take his chances against the other one, instead of fighting two functional vampires.

Eddie returns the bat—now stake, thoughtlessly and effortlessly.

Sebastian changes instantly back to stone and falls, petrified, with the bat buried to the hilt in his chest.

Eddie turns back just in time to see the blade coming for his face. He ducks, and with all his human strength, spears the attacking vampire off and over the stage, landing on the dance floor... closer to his lost hatchet, tackling him like there was a reason he chose football equipment.

This one springs on top of him closing his hands around his throat. He tries to move but the man lifts him by his neck, and then quickly smashes him backward, cracking his mask against the floor. He hears it break from the impact. This creature's sheer strength has the mask's integrity crumbling. The mask was designed to withstand severe pressure and high impact hits and blows but not from an assault from a supernaturally strong monster, no, the mask wasn't tested and approved to withstand that. *I don't think that made it to the testing phase.*

Eddie reaches out, desperately trying to retrieve his hatchet, but every time his hand even gets close, it is immediately pulled back as he is tossed back against the floor.

Eddie is being choked out by the vampire he speared on to the dance floor, and now he is overpowered and being strangled, and crushed against the floor. Just as the darkness pulls over his eyes because he has run out of oxygen completely, he tastes air. His air pipe is suddenly, and more surprisingly, unrestricted, and he laps down the air greedily never questioning it.

His attacker, releases him, tearing his mask is off and exposes his face. Intent on feeding on Eddie, and Eddie inhales rapidly as he comes back to consciousness, chasing every bit of oxygen. Every single second he can breathe, makes every single difference between living and dying.

His attacker, momentarily distracted, ignores Eddie as he goes inside his jacket for something—probably a straight razor, because they all seem to have one— giving Eddie time…

Time to breathe. Time to think. This gives Eddie time that he absolutely doesn't deserve and shouldn't get. He makes the absolute best of it.

Eddie remains still, patiently. He is now armed and doesn't move, he just sucks in air, retrieving his strength, but he does so incognito. Eddie feigns helplessness. Eddie knows that if he wants to overcome this enemy, he has to be patient, continuing the façade, because if the "creature" thought any differently or had any suspicion otherwise, Eddie would already be dead.

Living is about lying...

The beast of a man (but isn't a man) finally locates his weapon, and guess what? It is a straight razor, but this one is personalized.

His is longer by the blade length and crueler looking than the last; its hilt is crudely manufactured metal. This straight razor looks cold and mad. The blade is chipped and dull. Almost like the blade's edge is a broken maw of razor-sharp serrated shark teeth.

He flicks it open completely, locking it straight, and swings his massive arm backward readying to cut it across Eddies neck. He visualizes through the cut, freeing Eddie's artery of its crimson treasure, the untapped river locked within it, flowing freely. He pictures himself hungrily eating it up as Eddie bleeds out, pawing helplessly at life. He imagines what is about to be, and instead of acting on it, he takes a moment and reflects.

He is lost, imaginatively. He holds that arm high, locked and held in place while he daydreams the outcome of the intended follow through. The creature revels in it briefly, greedily so, and that would be the second of two mistakes that shouldn't have been made...

One: Underestimating Eddie.

Two: Even though Eddie needs no help harming himself and fucking himself over inevitably and worse of when left to his own, you chose to get involved.

Eddie is pinned, watching the beast sit atop him, salivating. Eddie reacts, and he does so mimicking the speed of light, or at least that is how fast he appears to react. However impossible, it appears as though he moves at the rate of a lightning strike to the human eye; it's over before you realize it's happened.

From stillness to happenstance, Eddie's retaliation is already over, yesterdays news, printed on tomorrows paper. That is just how fast he moves.

Eddie swings, swiping upward, connecting hatchet edge to target, and leaving the other-side of the creature's neck. Eddie is already one step ahead.

Eddie had already imagined it, saw it, and knew it would happen...

Eddie's hatchet cleaves cleanly and clears through so powerfully that the crunching noise that follows through its path, removing the creature's head from his body, resonates so loudly it echoes sickly in the emptiness of the club.

Fresh scarlet from the creature's freshly formed stump of an orifice sprays out plasma— almost comically in frequency—like a torrent waterfall over Eddie and blankets his face in dark coagulated sanguine.

Eddie reactively turns his head in an attempt to avoid this unwanted scarlet shower, all while trying to breathe, gulping down fresh air, throwing the convulsing corpse on top of him aside. He pulls himself away from the headless creature and he goes to stand, watching its body melt away inside its clothes. Eddie loses himself, forgetting time, and ignores everything else as he focuses on the now, enthralled by it.

Eddie suddenly snaps out of it and comes to terms with his situation and how dire it really is. He needs to bail. He quickly accepts this, returning to whatever sanity that remains. He has only moments to collect the belongings of his battle and flee with whatever spoils he can before the cops arrive. No one would believe his story. Eddie just needs to go.

Eddie moves, scrambling...

CHAPTER 10

The first thing Eddie does after shaking off the shock is retrieving his mask and he dons it, pulling it over his head, hiding his identity. He scrambles to collect the treasures (the money) left behind in the lifeless husks of the destroyed and decaying vampires that now only resemble nothing more than a pile of dirty laundry.

After ransacking the clothing of the (very) recently deceased, Eddie pockets their spoils and books it for the front entrance, or in his case, the thing he knows as the entrance. Before he leaves, he takes each of their straight razors. He takes a second to recognize that they are all different from one another.

He sprints through the darkness toward the way he entered, now far richer, weighed down by those very same heavy packed pockets. Those heavy pockets—before tonight were empty but now overflow—encumbered by money collected from those who never existed for real, at least technically have never existed. By all accounts Eddie hasn't done anything wrong and that is the only reason he hasn't gone mad after his kill spree.

Just before Eddie's hand finds the bar that will dislocate the mechanism that opens the door and frees him completely to the world beyond it, abolishing him completely of the crimes he never committed because they don't technically exist, something stops him entirely.

Eddie is unable to flee from the scene. He is captured by a presence that he doesn't currently understand, nor ever will understand, and it hinders his retreat.

"Stop."

Eddie doesn't hear the order because it was never spoken vocally. His ears have no business here. The order comes to him like an instinct...

Fuck that, forget resemblances, it mimics instinct flawlessly.

Eddie obeys chemically. He doesn't move. He remains frozen, paralyzed, subconsciously awaiting further instruction despite the desperation to leave the scene he felt only moments prior. What he knew he needed to do seconds ago is now ignored completely and he waits subserviently for what to do next.

"Turn around."

Eddie obeys, not knowing why, or caring. Just like when you know you're alone but you feel like someone's watching you, you feed the psychosis, even though you recognize it for what it is, you do it anyways just to be sure. Eddie does the same.

Eddie looks back at the dark hallway behind him and he sees nothing. But what Eddie doesn't see is the very thing giving instinctual orders, there in the dark and looking back at him.

This will be the first time that you and Eddie witness the true "antagonist" of the story. But that definition doesn't even scratch the surface. Sure, literally, this entity is the "bad guy". However, even the most vile and evil "bad guys" or "antagonists" that have ever existed couldn't comprehend just how terribly monstrousness this "thing" is, and if they encountered it they would all immediately experience a crisis of identity. This thing is so evil, so diabolical, and so completely despicable that definitions avoid it.

It exists on a level that bad doesn't understand. Bad tries to understand it and pretends to be it and as soon as bad realizes it will never get close, it passes it off to vile.

Vile has a mid-life crisis because of it and buys a convertible and tries to find itself through a late in life soul search, but instead gives up, settles down, has a family, and seeks therapy.

And all the while as this happens, without wasting time pure evil immediately gives up its title and just quits the business altogether, legally changing its name out of disgust of the discovery of said entity. It recognizes that it'll never compare to it and seeks protective custody in fear of it. Evil accepts its new identity immediately and learns it thoroughly, so it will never be found.

So just in case after all that, you still don't get just how villainous this antagonist is... this motherfucker is the absolute worst of the worst.

You can't find anything "badder."

From the darkness, a formless, faceless "thing" shambles toward Eddie. Eddie can't see it properly. Like watching a scrambled channel constantly changing in static, but knowing deep down that there is a solid image behind it. Maybe it—this unspeakable and incomprehensible evil thing— won't let itself be seen, or maybe Eddie is just unable to see it because in doing so it would forever damage him, and instead chooses not to.

"Abandon this path. This isn't the answer you seek, so end it, and you can persist your parasitic existence otherwise. However, if you continue to interfere with us, I guarantee there will be consequences born from this that you haven't considered and won't be able to live with. Know this... this is the only warning you will get, and one you do not deserve. I won't repeat myself."

Eddie hears this like he has headphones jammed in his ears, buried deeply and blasting fully.

Before he has a chance to speak—hoping to insult whomever just spoke through sarcasm and disdain— he doesn't; he doesn't even have a chance to move, not even a microsecond grace period to process the warning before he is thrown violently backwards by an attacker that he can't see or even feel the physical force of.

He hits the window so hard that he is already knocked unconscious before he goes through it. But he doesn't go through the window with the first impact. No, instead, like a pendulum, Eddie's unconscious body is pulled toward the darkness and then launched back at the window again, levitating impossibly the entire time. No strings or wires; this isn't show business. This is supernatural.

Eddie is suspended in thin air, frozen in place with his appendages dangling like an unattended marionette. He is left unconscious, levitating off the ground by some unnatural force, and before you could have the chance to figure out this is no magic trick, he is tossed through the window on to the sidewalk.

You now know how Eddie woke up on that sidewalk.

CHAPTER 11

Ten minutes after Eddie woke up on the sidewalk...

"Shaw, pick up, fuck."

Eddie pleas between the unanswered chimes of yet another missed call to Detective Shaw. Eddie huddles over Sebastian's corpse, hidden behind a midnight blue dumpster in the alley of the club that is now completely surrounded by cops, first responders, and anyone nearby that followed.

Eddie had woken and immediately went back into the club, without a moment's waste, void of would-be rational thought, and ignoring completely what threatened and rendered him unconscious so effortlessly in the first place. Eddie did the first thing that came to mind...

He went back for the very impaled body of one known vampire (Sebastian) that he had seen die, resurrect, and die again via baseball bat-turned-wooden stake, and dragged said corpse out the back exit of the establishment.

At this point in the story, I don't know about you, but I'm not sure if this proves just how dumb Eddie is or just how smart he is.

"Hello?"

"Shaw!"

Eddie screams joyfully and loudly, his voice echoing like a bass drum in a tiny room. He covers his mouth immediately and regretfully, as though by that motion, it would change the volume already achieved.

"Shaw, it's Eddie, I'm in trouble. I need your help," Eddie whispers.

"Eddie?" Shaw questions because he doesn't know to whom he is talking.

"Eddie Red. Nightmares are real. You made me lose my lunch, literally. And that lunch I lost was all I had eaten in days..."

"Eddie! Yeah, yeah... sorry. What's up?"

"What're you up to?"

"Working."

"Does that involve a club? A possible homicide at a club?"

Shaw doesn't respond. Eddie bites his tongue, trying to remain calm.

"Eddie, what's up? Why did you call?"

Shaw slows his car, coming around the corner and seeing the blinding strobe of lights that congest the street in front of the "Board room" and as he pulls closer, he hears the echo through the speaker of his cell phone.

Shaw slams on the breaks. He already knows.

"Eddie..."

"Shaw, listen, I need your help. Nightmares are real, and I have actual proof, solid undeniable proof... you need to get me out of here. You've gotta see it first hand, no one else will believe it. You know what it's like to hope you're insane, know you aren't, but know for sure if you told the truth it wouldn't matter in the slightest because proof or not nobody wants to know what we do. Please... I need your help..."

Eddie stops whispering because he hears the same echo. He rises from behind the dumpster and sees Shaw and his car blocking the alley. Eddie smiles widely, relieved. His smile is so hauntingly and unnaturally wide that his teeth resemble tiny stained mirrors. Even if a slight glimmer of light did exist in the absolute dark of the alley then that light would be, and is, amplified so brightly that it is impossible to ignore.

"Eddie. Listen. Don't talk. I am going to pull into the alley and you're going to get into the trunk and close it. Then I am going to pull out and park. You are going to stay in the trunk, silent, no matter how long you wait. You won't move, speak, fart, or sneeze. Deal?"

"Yeah but..."

"No ifs, ands, or buts. Agree to these terms or I will personally and gladly arrest you."

"Deal..."

It takes every ounce of willpower Eddie has to remain quiet. Shaw pulls up, and the trunk of his unmarked Crown Victoria springs open wide. Eddie lifts Sebastian and dives in with him. He struggles with Sebastian's rigidity. Moving and bending his frozen appendages like an action figure, shaping him into the preferred pose before closing the trunk. Eddie is fixated on attempting to achieve some level of comfort, while remaining absolutely silent because his freedom depends on it, all while trying to come to terms and not lose his shit because he is in fact trapped inside the trunk of a cop car, the worst thing though is being stuck indefinitely next to a corpse— that is only a corpse because of wooden stake in its chest...

Detective Dan Maurier struggles to exit his unmarked car. His age naturally factors into his physical capabilities, but he is slowed by something else, and that is his complete lack of luster for his job. He knows that he is already retired and rightfully so, but he has to just physically show up and be present on paper for the few hours remaining that he is required to serve. So to make it legit on paper, he follows suit.

Dan feels his age, and instead of worrying about it, he welcomes the reality of it. He accepts that he is no longer able to physically "do" it anymore and that he is truly—just like the iconic movie line—"too old for this shit". He is at call, and even with his frailty from age, instead of freaking out about it he has never been more content with anything in his life because after tonight, it doesn't matter, this will be his last shift.

Dan finally is on his feet standing upright and already exhausted. He pushes forward, shuffling with the minimal effort necessary to get him where he wants to arrive at, the front door. Not any front door, but the front door of a house he knows all too well. All the while during his ascent he unconsciously, and vocally, grumbles in protest. Complaining, breathlessly, he objects through incoherent mumbles that solidify his discontent.

He is responding to a domestic dispute that he has responded to so many times before. But he took the call because he knows the situation, and it has always been easy to resolve, and he has resolved this issue for the last decade.

Dan has spent every Friday for the last ten years resolving the same thing between one Mr. and Mrs. Patterson. It has always been the same fight, and has never escalated where a police presence was ever actually required. But despite that, and countless fines laid and paid in full. Without break, the Patterson's have kept to the same routine, regardless of cost, reality, and anything resembling sense.

A therapist would be cheaper in this case. Regardless, Dan has answered this call, and always has because it has always been safe.

Dan's heavy frame creeks with every step as climbs the crumbling stairs he has walked so many times before, but this time he forces himself to be more careful than usual. His bowling ball bald head already rains sweat clouding his vision as little droplets trickle over those thick grey untrimmed bushes he calls brows and the sweaty little tears burn his faded blue eyes. A lower button on his faded stained off-white shirt pops off releasing his gut to the cold air and the button ricochets off a step disappearing, he curses aloud, in a mumble, and with that he slows his ascent. Dan isn't taking chances on anything, especially not avoidable dangers like accident-prone staircases. He does this because he doesn't want to get hurt and could be liable for it because he didn't take precautions to avoid it and this would somehow interfere with his retirement. Dan does everything to avoid anything that would hinder him and his well-earned retirement.

Dan reaches the front door, looking back at the crumbling cement staircase, and takes a moment to evaluate his surroundings. A weed invested lawn surrounds the walkway at either side. Some weeds larger than others appear like protruding tombstones in a dilapidated grave yard. The yard is covered in refuse however well-hidden the trash is by the long uncut grass, it's still visible with a closer look. He decides proudly and silently decides that if this was his walkway and yard that he could easily fix it. He smiles, appreciating his retirement and all the free time it will give him, looking forward to all the home repair possibilities it offers.

He looks at his watch and is overjoyed with the reality that this might just be the last call he ever takes because in just a few mere hours (three and a half, and counting), he is done. Paid and done.

Dan doesn't get a chance to knock, the door opens before his fist finds home on the old badly painted door and its cracking teal paint. Instead of the grizzled and intoxicated Mr. or Mrs. Patterson that normally would greet him, screaming blame at him, castigating the other, he is instead greeted by only the darkness of an empty doorway. Even worse is the realization that this call isn't the call he expected to answer. No, this was a call he should've ignored entirely.

Everything is too calm and still. When Dan hears the voice, he knows it's over.

"Hello Dan."

Before Dan Maurier has the chance to comprehend the situation or even try to… and much before his body has time to react instinctively to protect itself, even if his age would allow it, it is entirely too late.

Delayed, Dan's hand draws his pistol and fires from the hip, wastefully squeezing out several rounds that find no target.

Dan topples backward, clutching at his throat. The wound that spans across it is impossible to contain because the blade that made it was so sharp, it's surgical; carrying a clean path through while completely severing the carotid artery. Hot crimson jets out and paints the direction of the blades journey, leaving a thick hot path of scarlet on the front of the house.

Dan is dead before his body gives out and falls backward. His corpse ragdolls, sprawling down the same stairs he in life took the time to carefully climb, and now in death impersonate the ever so popular whatever year-trademarked toy: the "slinky". Slinking each step, he stops finally, and remains motionless at the base of the stairs.

From the darkness of the doorway a man comes forth, gracefully sauntering down the steps, slowly closing a straight razor. He leans over Dan's body and removes his cellphone and pockets it. He rests the straight razor in Dan's hand before folding his dead hands over his chest, crossing them over his heart. He stands straight up, looking up at a flickering street light above, and then disappears into the night between its blinks. Leaving Dan to be the first homicide of several discovered here...

CHAPTER 12

In the dark red light of the trunk Eddie fights the urge to freak out and scream. He is completely fed up with being crammed in this trunk, regardless of the consequences he would have had to face if he'd been caught at the scene. Shaw did save him from the scenario but with every passing moment, he appreciates the rescue less and less until he barely does at all. He has lost all concept of time and doesn't know how long he has already spent spooning a real vampire that is rendered temporarily comatose by a wound that is only a wound because it is kept open. If that broken bat were to be removed, this vampire would return instantly, completely pissed off, and its first act would be to immediately kill Eddie. And to make matters even worse for Eddie, he is almost completely sober.

Just before Eddie reaches his capacity to wait any more and rescues his arm to bang on the trunk to demand release, the trunk opens and he is blinded by the night.

As his eyes adjust in focus, he recognizes Shaw who is now standing over him, smoking a freshly lit cigarette and shaking his head in disappointment.

"Start talking."

Eddie, still upset by being imprisoned within the trunk goes to speak, trying to sit up, but his expression annoys Shaw so badly that he closes the trunk violently, forcing Eddie back, trapping him once again.

The metal connects with Eddie, knocking him prone, disabling him concussively. The blow to the head extinguishes any energy Eddie held, smothering his fire before it was flame. Shaw's blow to the skull makes Eddie revisit the situation that Shaw rescued him from, returning him to the fresh hell he just escaped. Eddie shakes the blow, trying to hear the muffled question from beyond the trunk that Shaw has just asked.

"Before I let you out, you're only going to explain everything in absolute detail as to what happened and nothing else, right?"

Eddie grunts in agreement.

"Or I'm going to keep you in here. Get it?"

Eddie grunts louder.

"Good."

The trunk opens and Eddie sits up, holding his tongue. Shaw moves back, giving Eddie room to stretch, but remains close enough to slam the trunk closed on him if he wanted to. And that is when Shaw sees the corpse and he goes white as a ghost. Eddie silently looks around before looking at Shaw but when he does, he immediately realizes how bad this looks and goes to speak. Shaw slides back and draws his firearm, training it on Eddie as fast as lightning striking ground, between a blink.

"Eddie what the fuck? What the fuck have you done? What have I done..." Shaw screams through closed teeth.

"Shaw, whoa, calm down. I know this looks bad. Hell, it looks really bad. Now that I think of it this looks super fucking bad but..." Eddie says, looking down, shaking his skull from side to side. Eddie goes to look at Shaw and as he does Shaw's finger slides over the trigger of his Glock 22.

"Eddie raise your hands above your head and lock your fingers behind it. Slowly, I mean tortoise-setting slow because I will add new holes to that empty fucking head of yours if you don't. Do it right now and don't say another fucking word."

Eddie does exactly what Shaw asks but he does it even slower; he moves at sloth-setting.

"Now slowly, but faster than that, get out of the trunk."

Eddie does, rising slowly, and starts stepping out of the trunk but his legs are asleep, and as he realizes this, he loses his balance and falls flat on his face onto the wet asphalt, hard.

"Ow..." He says out of the corner of his mouth because somehow his hands didn't move from behind his head to catch his fall and he hasn't tried to get up.

Shaw laughs out loud to his own surprise but quickly gains composure.

Eddie begins to rise, pushing himself up with his knees feeling his pants act as a sponge, drinking up the little puddle beneath him. Eddie, filthy and now standing straight up at attention, awaits Shaw's next orders.

"Now turn around, drop back to your knees, and keep your fingers interlocked."

Eddie's expression sours.

"Seriously? I just stood up."

"Now!" Shaw insists.

Eddie closes his eyes, obviously disgruntled, and sighs in discontent but submits to Shaw's request eventually. He turns on the spot like a sad carousel, turning his back to Shaw. Eddie looks down at the contorted corpse formally known as Sebastian, locking on his dead glossy gaze, and within it Eddie knows how to diffuse this situation instantly.

Shaw approaches, holstering his weapon before he removes his handcuffs. He reaches toward Eddie's right wrist intending to cuff it, but before he can, Eddie is gone. Eddie bolts forward, just escaping Shaw's imminent reach and the first wrist-constricting embrace of cuffs, that if latched to completion would be the absolute end of Eddie's quest to prove his sanity altogether. Shaw reactively drops the cuffs and instinctually reaches for his sidearm as his training takes over, but consciously chooses to keep it holstered. Shaw lets his curiosity dictate his next actions—and let's be honest, at this point it couldn't actually get worse by doing so— to see what Eddie does next.

He is pretty much fucked either way.

Eddie grabs the bat handle and tears it out of Sebastian's chest. A coagulated mess follows. Sinew and crimson decorate the stump. The gore grows incrementally darker the closer it gets to the broken stub's end. The makeshift stake now resembles a dipstick, but instead of oil, it is drenched by blood.

Eddie spins face to face with an armed Shaw, proudly donning the bloody broken baseball bat. Ignoring altogether how reckless and stupid his actions were; or maybe not even realizing just how much worse he is making it. Regardless of whichever is the less stupid justification he chooses; he lucks out because Shaw humors him and awaits Eddie's logic to expose itself and hopes that will exonerate everything.

Shaw remains still, waiting for something to happen that would completely justify, and legitimize, his involvement with this insanity. His hand rests on the handle of his undrawn weapon, impatiently. But the seconds flick away, as does his confidence, and is quickly replaced by regret and an insatiable desire to do whatever it takes by the books to save himself from this career-ending mistake. Even though if nothing happens, it is already over and he is an accomplice to a mad man. He draws his weapon and points it at Eddie, scrambling to regain control.

"Wait! Just give it a second."

Shaw lowers his weapon, looking beyond Eddie. Shaw knows that it couldn't do any further harm, 'cause he is already fucked.

Eddie looks from Shaw to the corpse. He is sure of what follows and how Shaw will witness what he did and how it will fix everything. However, and quite unfortunately, the corpse doesn't move. Eddie begins to sweat. He suddenly questions his own sanity. Nothing is happening. And it doesn't seem like it is going to.

Those seconds that pass while Eddie waits for something to happen feel like years, and those seconds that feel like years become passing minutes and each one feels like a century, and when five minutes have gone by, Eddie feels like he has watched all of existence be born and die, leaving him watching powerlessly from an empty space, left in the nothingness to just witness time and time again. As though everything that has happened or will, has already happened and he is now realizing that all of it passed him by and as it did it took Shaw with it.

Crushed beyond disrepair, Eddie has finally tasted the consequence of impulsivity and is seeing everything as it is, for the first time. Eddie is receptive and vulnerable, lacking completely the defense mechanisms that he spent his entire existence creating to prevent him entirely from just this. He is completely naked now. His mental armor is disintegrated and now he is wholly susceptible to every last thing it once defended him from. It all comes crashing and charging in. Everything he evaded for years rapes and rips him, leaving wounds that will never heal.

Eddie is stone cold sober now and reality leaves a very bad taste in his mouth.

All those once powerful and immovable walls that stood for so long break synchronously—harmoniously so, in perfect union, like the repetitive over-practiced climax of a symphonic crescendo — and like a failing dam, everything held behind it comes rushing through its crumbling pieces all at once...

Doesn't matter how many kings' horses, or all the men ridding them there are, in this current moment, Eddie can't be put back together again...

Was this all bullshit? Was it all just the delusions of an addict trying to justify his actions? Did he just murder a bunch of people, hiding behind irrational mania, and was just now coming to terms with that horrible reality?

Eddie releases the bat, defeated, and offers his hands to Shaw, forgetting hope and questioning if he ever had any. He brings his wrists to touch, flush, and he awaits chains. He shuffles and approaches Shaw as passively as he possibly can, leaving no room to interpret his advance as anything but what it is: surrender.

Shaw ignores Eddie and how much he sincerely needs to surrender, and is. He only pays attention to the corpse, still hopeful—fuck that, praying— that something, anything, will happen.

But time ticks on and fades away. The remaining thing, the only thing that changes, and that thing that time carries away with it, is the necessity to accept what needs to be done, and do, and eventually Shaw, however reluctantly, does: obliging Eddie, arresting him.

Eddie hangs his head fearing the judgmental gaze that Shaw most certainly casts his way. He feels the embrace of galvanized reinforced steel on his wrists. That tight embrace, however welcomed, now coldly mutates into an unfriendly chokehold as they lock around them. A fate-cementing grip that brings only a feeling of a grim reality that Eddie never wanted anything to do with.

"I'm sorry," Eddie whispers.

Shaw shakes his head, ignoring Eddie.

He goes to lead him toward the back door of the squad car while rehearsing Eddie's rights, which sound like verses from religious scripture—routinely recited but empty now because he no longer believes in the power they are intended to possess— but he stops, freezing in stride and speech within a single observation. Shaw sees something peripherally, and as soon as he does, everything changes. By catching it, everything is okay and not at all okay at the same time.

"Why did you stop?" Eddie weakly mumbles, completely unaware of what Shaw saw and how important it is that he did.

He flips back, like a god fearing idiot that was baptized late in life, believing he is truly reborn, and nothing before right now matters, just because someone told him it doesn't. He blindly believes his innocence.

Sebastian is sitting up. Alive again, even though he cannot be, acting and moving as though he is. Sebastian is examining his surroundings, squirming around in the trunk, even though he was a corpse for the last hour with a baseball bat impaled where his heart should be. But that doesn't appear to bother him at all. When he sees the damage to his chest, he looks annoyed instead of terrified, as he should be. No, this fucking guy instead just stares down at the sinkhole wound disappointingly, now that his chest has a cup holder sized hole in it. He appears to grow upset by this and visibly so, shrugging as though he is about to start a temper tantrum.

Shaw says nothing. He just watches, encapsulated fully by the awe of what immediately follows. He observes fiction and is overwhelmed, stunned, as fiction becomes absolute—couldn't argue otherwise, even if you wanted to—fact.

The blank space that is Sebastian's gaping chest wound fills instantly, completely regenerating as though it was never there and it does in a blink of an eye. But within that blink, Shaw sees Sebastian's cavity first repair the blackened pulmonary device that wasn't beating to begin with, as it suddenly is a heart, still not beating but a heart once more. Then the bones that make the cage that it is kept in, return, constructively trapping it once more. Then follows the muscle, reforming and overlapping the bones, dressing the ribs with a bright stringy red coat. Finally, a layer of milky white skin appears and conceals everything below it. And Shaw knows that everything about this is anything but natural...

Sebastian has resurrected, but he does so without chocolate, bunnies, or any sign of faith or purpose. Whatever brought him back and whatever he is, it isn't good.

Shaw acts, pushing off Edie, and dives to retrieve the bat. Once Shaw has it in hand, he instantly, accurately, and violently returns it to the place Eddie removed it from.

Shaw drives the bat into Sebastian's freshly reconstituted chest, driven solely by instinct, without thought, hesitation, or consideration. As though Sebastian's second coming never happened and even though it did, was obviously never meant to; all that was left to do was to undo what was done...

For the record, all the while, Eddie and his inexplicably flawless clairvoyance, even though completely unaware of it, is again right. It's like he lost a magical rabbit's foot that grants wishes up his ass and blacked out, forgetting it was ever lodged there. Eddie is saved completely. Whether he knows it yet or not, he is. Eddie doesn't know just how important this moment is to Shaw. Because Shaw is visibly accepting that what just happened, happened. That returning the undead spawn is real, exonerating both himself and Eddie of any crimes that they didn't commit because Eddie wasn't lying and Shaw wasn't wrong in trusting.

Fucking un-be-lieve-able

Shaw releases his white-knuckle grip on the bats handle. He missed by only millimeters from where Eddie initially impaled it. Sebastian, mute and completely confused, doesn't even get the chance to speak, let alone understand the situation, before he is returned to the catatonic-like state he just recuperated from.

Shaw goes to Eddie, shaking him by his shoulders while at the same time lifting him to his feet.

"Okay Eddie, start talking. And if I feel like you're bullshitting me at all, so help me, I'll fucking put you back in this trunk."

Eddie nods vigorously in agreement. He begins to thaw from the cold illusion that he was only crazy and that nothing he witnessed was real. Eddie slowly warms and realizes that he isn't a delusional, murderous drug addict. Accepting what he always had known. He is a drug addict that has found a way to legally continue and pay for his habit without hurting anyone in the process.

This was what Eddie wanted in the first place, and however unhealthy the choice, it is his, and he is okay with it.

Eddie tells Shaw everything that happened in the club. Eddie fills Shaw in as though he is reading from the page of a stenographer. He recounts the events just as they happened and never embellishes at all. He recollects word for word, second by second, moment after moment, as to what occurred. Leaving no detail out, however small or unimportant. He tells all. He does this to prove his sanity, and attention to detail, and how infallible his memory is therefore proving its validity. In turn, by doing this, he attempts to prove how inarguable the case, in accordance with the law, would be.

Shaw stops him just before Eddie tells him, or has the chance to tell him, about the unspeakable thing that tossed him out the window. Shaw has heard enough, convinced, and doesn't require more courtroom rhetoric.

"Alright, Eddie, What's next?"

"Well, just to add salt to a jury."

"Don't you mean insult to injury?"

"Yeah, what the fuck ever. Help me get this guy into my apartment and we can get answers that only he can give. Okay?"

Shaw nods in agreement while removing the cuffs from Eddie.

Shaw asks, "So what now?" with a shrug. Eddie smiles that fucking annoying smile, and responds through body language in kind, "Just help me carry the body upstairs."

CHAPTER 13

"Just drop him, here is good." Eddie struggles grasping for breath, almost asthmatic.

"Keep it down, seriously. Let's just lower him in," Shaw snaps back, turning beat red in color. His pigment alteration stems not from exasperation but from his obvious disdain of Eddie's relaxed and carefree demeanor.

"Drop him, he'll be fine," Eddie responds, sneering.

"FINE!" Shaw screams through a whisper while releasing his grip. As he does, Eddie thoughtlessly follows his lead.

A single sound, so loud, and made that much worse by the surprising volume that it creates upon impact; that sounds resonates and fills the hallowed emptiness of Eddie's apartment. That sound grows, sickly birthing another, echoing uncontrollably, growing and seeming to repeat without end.

What is that sound, you ask?

That is the ensuing sound when you drop a "dead body" into a bathtub made of old metal, made worse acoustically because it resonated from an empty apartment with no furniture or belongings to muffle it. And that ringing sound is worsened because Eddie and Shaw just spent the last however many minutes, or even an hour—and they pray it isn't more than an hour— trying to silently get it here... which now seems like a complete waste. But it isn't.

That sound becomes the bell telling them that school has started and they have a lot to learn, and they both realize that synchronously. Within a shared stare and a tandem dry swallow — their Adam's apples feel more like throat dumb-bells] — they accept that they can never go back. There is no point of return and there never was in this scenario.

"Eddie. What now?" Shaw asks through his teeth because he can't unclench his jaw. His words are empty of thought and instead form a question through reflex, almost like he is a parrot repeating what it just heard. He is too focused on the body in front of him. Shaw just stares at the twisted corpse in the tub, unable to process the fact that it could be a real vampire, a mobile and deadly monster at any moment by merely removing the obstruction in its chest.

"Well... honestly? I..." Eddie starts to mumble a response but leaves during its composition. He leaves Shaw and the truth behind in the washroom.

Eddie goes to his stash, ignoring completely the cop in his apartment, and forgetting everything that said cop did for him.

Eddie you've got to be fucking kidding me... You're despicable...

Eddie sits on his shitty stained excuse for a bed that barely passes as a mattress, and busts out a line of cocaine that is Hollywood big—unnecessary.

As Eddie fumbles with his drugs, Shaw's phone rings, startling him, and causing him to drop his bag. It hits the ground, kicking up a mushroom cloud of white powder. Eddie grunts out a sigh, disapproving and angered. He tries to collect anything he can, savoring every grain he can recover.

In the next room, Shaw is broken from his trance and answers his phone.

"Talk to me."

Eddie tries to listen in as he rescues what he can, licking the residue off the floor pathetically. He tries to ignore how expensive that fumble was. He stops suddenly as he realizes Shaw has gone as white as the powder he tries to ravenously lap up. Shaw stands silently; his expression changes with every word that falls from the other end of the phone.

"What?" Shaw yelps, noticeably injured by whatever news he is receiving. "When… when did this… okay, where? Tell me where!"

Shaw storms out of the washroom and heads for the door, trying desperately to hold it together when he looks at any moment like he is about to collapse.

Eddie runs after him.

"Yeah, I understand, I'll be there soon… I don't care… Touch nothing! You hear me?" Shaw hangs up his phone like he is trying to break it. He turns to Eddie with tears pooling in his lids but Shaw is so angry they are afraid to fall.

"Um… are you…" Eddie stops his question because he knows the answer and feels stupid for even thinking to ask it, as the answer is so obvious it may as well be a neon sign above Shaw's head.

"It's Dan. He's dead."

CHAPTER 14

Shaw's car careens around the corner of 32nd and Main at a dangerously gravity-defying angle, his tires barely connecting with the pavement, freshly wet from the cold rain that now drools with the break of dawn. Eddie's face finds the window with that turn and he dizzily shakes off the pain.

Shaw's expression is as solid as his skin: so tightly pulled back, it looks as though at any time it will peel back from his face completely, exposing tightly clenched sinew and muscle.

Shaw drives with such precision and speed, as though his driving could prevent the events that have already occurred. He hasn't said a word since spilling the bad news and Eddie hasn't had the balls or the bravery to question him further.

The car jerks to a stop suddenly and violently. Shaw disappears from the driver seat so quickly Eddie checks to see if he put the car into park. Shaw ducks under the bright yellow "do not cross" tape, flashing his badge and moving toward the forensic team without speaking a single word.

All the while Eddie sits watching from the passenger seat, the hallow thud of raindrops on the windshield become his only company. The pattering echo is like thunder booming inside a glass jar. Eddie feels just as trapped. He observes, shivering in his seat.

He watches as Shaw collects information and gets the low-down on this very dark event. Shaw's expression grows visibly worse with every word. And finally, when they lift the sheet exposing Dan—his partner, his mentor—lying under it, Shaw turns as white as the sheet and collapses through the hands that go to catch him.

Eddie suddenly spots something that makes his stomach sink and forces him out of the car, running toward Shaw. He saw something that makes him forget for the moment that Dan is dead, completely putting aside his past and keeping him from the grief of his loss, if only temporarily.

He sees it in the hands of a member of the forensic team. It is locked and sealed in a Ziploc evidence bag being carried away. Sealed away in plastic is an ornate straight razor, freshly soaked and marinating in blood, and Eddie already knows to whom that blood belongs.

Under the tape Eddie goes, pushing past raindrops and the grabbing hands of officers trying to stop him. Eddie moves toward Shaw and in doing so he incites a swarm of chaos carrying badges and guns, birthing a maelstrom of unnecessary mayhem. He gets within earshot of Shaw before they tackle him to the cold ground below but even through the bedlam, he shouts something that wakens Shaw from his coma-like state, resurrecting him to immediate reaction.

"Let him go!" Shaw screams, killing the chaos through command.

They release Eddie and he runs to Shaw.

"I know who did this," Eddie repeats.

"Eddie, how can you? Do you even know what happened here?"

"Well, no... not entirely. I know Dan is dead... fuck... Dan is dead... hell, that is just a god damn... fucking..."

"Eddie!?"

"Right... sorry," Eddie says, pausing, his eyes frozen on the corpse at his feet that he knows is Dan before shaking his head and continuing.

"Your boy over there." Eddie points at the faceless forensic worker who is collecting more evidence. "He found something... a straight razor... right?"

Shaw goes whiter than he already is; his face twists, souring with confusion.

"Yeah... yeah, but how did you... Eddie... what does it mean?"

"I've seen it before... well, not that one that one specifically but one that looks..." Eddie begins to babble.

"Eddie! Get to the point. What does it mean?"

Eddie gets really close to Shaw and whispers. "They all carry one, I can show you. I mean it isn't the same one, but it looks kind of like the other ones. I think they all carry one. They must, I mean, that would make sense wouldn't it. Oh hell, it can't just be a coincidence. Not one is the same and maybe each has their own meaning like a rank. Like seniority or something. Hell, maybe like the military. The more decorative the more decorated..."

Shaw tries for a second to ignore just how annoying talking to someone who is lit out of their mind is and how incomprehensible their ramblings can be and listen to Eddie.

For the record, when someone is really high, they just babble, never really getting to the point they initially started to make, but I promise there is always a point somewhere. There is always a method to the rambling madness of an addict; you just have to help them get there if you can.

"Eddie!" Shaw shouts sternly, interrupting him, forcing him to come down from his run-on thought marathon and return to a reality he can recognize as acceptable conversation.

"Shaw, every one of those things I've encountered carries a straight razor..."

Shaw looks to his coworkers, who all look at him and this strung-out junkie, and Shaw realizes this isn't the time or the place for this conversation.

"Thank you... Eddie, is it? We appreciate your cooperation and we need every bit of help the public has to offer. So how 'bout we discuss it back at the station? I'll take you there personally after I finish up here. So, go wait for me in my car," he says pointing towards the car Eddie is already very familiar with. "I have to finish up here and then we can sit down and go over your witness statement."

Eddie immediately realizes that this isn't the place for him or this conversation either and plays along with Shaw. Apologizing, he returns to his car.

As the sun rises and this new day begins, Eddie watches from the passenger seat, coming down completely, and watching the hours on the dashboard and their evil green glow slowly morph from one number to the next. But the numbers take their sweet fucking time to change and Eddie does everything he can to avoid looking at the clock. He actually shouts "Come on!" after thinking he has spent enough time looking away and he is infuriated when he looks back to see that only three minutes have passed. After several hours of this torture, Eddie, now sober, falls effortlessly into solemn slumber, curled up in that passenger seat. He snores loudly and comfortably in a deep sleep, completely unconscious for what might be the first time in days.

Meanwhile, Shaw goes over the scene meticulously, spending as much time as needed to figure out the events that transpired here that led to the deaths of Detective Dan Maurier and the homeowners.

His notes are as follows:

· No sign of forced entry –suspect must've been someone homeowners knew? No. No. Doesn't fit.

· No prints other than homeowners and Dan's. Including footprints, or marks, or scuffs of any kind... also doesn't make sense.

· No fibrous material. No spit, blood, or semen. House is clean, too clean.

· Strange - windows were open, screens all intact, and haven't been tampered with... why were windows open? It's fall...

Shaw closes his notepad, rising from crouching to standing tall, and cracks his back briefly before fully realizing that where he currently stands is in fact inside, dead center, dead smack in the iris core, of the room that witnessed everything that took place the night before.

The living room is the epicenter of all the bad things that became, birthing and nurturing them, growing to become all the horrors that now live on, unhappily ever after. This is where everything started last night. The primordial ooze, in this case, the alpha to Dan's eventual omega. This was the place where the beginning of the end became.

Shaw, somehow, just knows it started here. But he'll never know just exactly what went on and may never know.

Shaw somehow is always at the wrong place at the right time, it's like his supernatural gift.

Shaw lets out a defeated exhale and shuts his eyes for a second, taking a moment to gather himself before speaking with the detective leading this investigation.

The lead is a veteran on the force, pulling the same number of years Dan had under his belt. Julius Black and Dan didn't see eye to eye on anything and Dan never told Shaw why.

Shaw never prodded him but they had history and it seemed as pleasant as war crimes.

But today, Black seemed hurt by Dan's demise. And this wasn't the Hollywood stereotype that all cops, no matter their history, have each other's backs, because cops are people too and some people just don't like each other.

But people are people, and death always shakes everybody by the ankles the very same way before dropping them head first into the river Styx, not to drown them but to scare them, reminding them that they're eventually next to drown in it when their time comes.

"Black."

"Shaw. Sorry about Dan." Black doesn't look down at Shaw. Having half a foot on him, Black is the height and weight of a professional defensive linebacker but he is out of shape, his skin is leathered and drooping. His gut is distended and filled with cheap cold cuts and dollar coffee. His hair has thinned back to the very edge of his crown and silvered almost completely grey, chasing away the raven roots he groomed years ago still slick with grease that they discontinued in the 60's.

"Yeah, thanks, if you hear anything..."

"I'll let you know."

Shaw nods, Black nods, and Shaw heads out into the cold rain pulling his leather jacket over his head to shield himself while sprinting toward his car.

CHAPTER 15

This is where the story may get a little weird... Yeah, I know it already is pretty weird, but you'll see.

"Eddie."

Eddie tosses and turns in the passenger seat of Shaw's car still very unconscious. He hears someone call his name, just a distant whisper from somewhere else, somewhere far away.

"Eddie. Open your eyes."

Eddie's body convulses at the request, stirring momentarily as if to wake before settling to a still, calming naturally to slumber's embrace.

"Eddie. Follow my voice."

Eddie's mind has reached REM sleep, what is commonly known as the dream state. And he complies, dreaming away.

Fun fact about REM sleep, despite muscle paralysis males still somehow achieve erections... just so you know...

In this dream, Eddie stands on a train platform wearing nothing but his ragged black combat boots and soiled white boxer briefs. It is raining here too, but he doesn't feel it. He looks around scanning the crowd that passes him by. Everyone is faceless. They're all formless blobs. That is until he sees me, Gabriel, standing on the other side of the platform. Unlike everyone else here, my face has characteristics and he instantly notices that and recognizes me.

"Gabriel!" he shouts in a tone containing elements of both joy and disbelief, but as loud as he shouts his voice is muffled by the sound of the oncoming train. But I hear him even from the great beyond.

Because you see here, somehow, I can make contact with him. This is the weird part that I failed to mention earlier and probably is super important... sorry, my bad. I don't know why but this is the place where the dead can contact the living. The dream world is at the crossroads. Now the fuck of it is that few living people will remember, let alone believe anything they experience in a dream to be real or important. Usually people forget or ignore their dreams, because that is what living people know as fact: that dreams are just dreams. They mean nothing. That isn't true to the dead at fucking all. Dreams are the only conduit that the dead have to the living. Dreams are our only chance after life for us to say anything, share anything, because after life... shit, I forgot I can't tell you that either. Sorry.

Isn't it just a total shit deal for the dead? I mean fuck, we're dead and if that isn't bad enough, it gets worse. Even though the dead are remembered, the only place where we can say anything at all to those we love, and miss is the one place the living always forgets. Doesn't that just suck complete fuck? Anyhow, back to Eddie.

I stand there, waving, and then I beckon him over.

He sprints toward me and leaps, completely ignoring the speeding murder machine that flies toward us on the track he bounds across. It races by, barely missing him, and he lands in a crouched position right at my feet. Shivering because he thinks he should be cold, he just looks up at me, smiling that stupid Eddie smile.

"Eddie. Listen. I don't have long."

I really don't. I don't know the rules, but I can only make brief contact with him. Still haven't figured out the finer details of this oh so shitty deal.

"Gab, I'm so sorry, I should've..."

"Eddie. Shut up and listen. You need to question the guy in your tub. But you'll need to do a couple things, specific things to be able to..."

"I'm so sorry Gab... God damn it... It should've been me. I should've been the one that went, the one that..." Eddie begins to sob, reaching for me and I instantly recoil.

Yeah, if he touches me this connection immediately breaks and again, I know what you're thinking, and I don't know why that is, so just fucking drop it.

"Eddie! I don't blame you. I love you. But you need to shut up and just listen to me and retain this, this is important, remember this. Write it down as soon as you wake. Repeat it over and over again so you retain it. Do whatever you need to do. Eddie hear me and carry this out."

Eddie wipes the snotty mess from his nose like an injured child and nods compliantly even though visibly confused; he looks like he knows this is important, letting me know he understands.

"You'll need to keep him submersed in salt water. It doesn't matter what kind of salt, don't get caught up in what kind of salt, but it has to be salt water. That way he can't become incorporeal and escape when you remove the stake. Also, for good measure, if you can get yourself some iron bonds, bind him with them but it has to be actual iron. Eddie, do you understand"

Eddie turns his head like a confused dog.

"Iron hand cuffs, like in the westerns. Get a pair if you can and chain that fucker down. That'll keep him where he is."

Eddie nods like he is head banging to metal music and this doesn't fill me with a whole lot of confidence, but I continue anyway.

"Ask him where you can find the patriarch, and ask him which faction he belongs too, and if there are any other factions awake and operating in the city. Can you remember all that?"

Eddie nods, and then stops nodding, so I repeat myself quickly in the hopes he will retain the information this time and with a twinkle in his eye and a solidifying grin, I believe he has.

"Oh, and Eddie?"

"Yeah Gab?" Eddie smiles like a child does on their first Christmas just as they open that first present from the fictional character they'll praise for years and only mourn briefly when they finally discover the truth or have the terrible reality thrust violently upon them.

"You know that you of all people should never wear white underwear."

His expressions sours just like a child's does when they first find out that Santa isn't real, but it doesn't last. It was never about reality, it was about the magic; and within that same thought Eddie and I share, I grab him and shake him, severing the bond.

Eddie can actually feel hands on him, shaking him violently, but they aren't mine because I am part of his dream. They are Shaw's hands, and Eddie comes crashing back to reality, waking from a dream that wasn't just a dream. Hopefully retaining the crucial information, I shared with him because he needs a hand in the right direction, hell, he just needs help in general.

I told you it would get weird...er.

CHAPTER 16

Shaw jams his thumbs under the soft parts of Eddie's clavicle in an attempt to rouse him from his deep sleep. It works.

Eddie returns to consciousness as aware and excited as a resurrected sitcom from the 90's: similarly lost and almost certainly doomed. Eddie returns, gasping for breath and flailing for freedom and the pain to stop.

"What! What the fuck? Relax! I'm up. I'm up. Stop shaking me."

Shaw desists his 'shakening' and returns to his seat, defeated.

"Shaw, I had a dream about Gab…"

"Gab?"

"My dead best friend. But I think it was a vision because he told me things about the guy in my tub."

"He told you things?"

"Yeah, he um, told me I needed to keep him submerged in salt water and that would keep him from becoming… shit what was the word? Incorporeal?"

"Incorporeal."

"Yeah, that, whatever the fuck that means."

"It means he can move through solid objects."

"Fuck, they can do that?"

"Eddie, I don't know."

Shaw pulls his brown hair back from his forehead and jostles it leaving it looking like a broken bush of jagged stems and sticks jutting out every which way.

"Oh, and he said to ask him who the patriarch is. Again, not sure what that means."

"Man, if you spent half the time reading instead of snorting, smoking, popping, and gulping down drugs you would probably know these words. Patriarch means the male head of a family. Like, the oldest male."

"What, like a grandfather?"

"Yeah, like a grandfather."

Shaw puts the car into drive, signals, and then merges with traffic.

"What else did your friend say?"

"He said to ask the guy, Sebastian, if there are any other factions awake in the city."

"Whatever that means... anything else?"

"We need iron bonds like the kind in western movies. Do you know where we can get iron bonds?"

"Yeah, maybe. The evidence locker always has a bunch of weird shit. First though, we need to eat, and you need a shower. And because there is a vampire in your tub, we can go to my place."

Eddie watches the world blurrily pass him by from the passenger seat window, drifting in and out, fighting off the urge to fully sleep. He ponders just how little people know about the world around him and he considers just how nice it would be to be like one of those people again. Strangers passing strangers on the street, on the subway, in a park, and all of them thinking that monsters aren't real. Eddie knows that monsters are real. Some are vampires, some are werewolves, and some are humans. He wonders if there are any other kinds. And then he remembers that file, and that he needs to sit down and read that file that his neighbors made for him.

They pull up to Shaw's flat, a modernized structure that is at least two floors. It looks like a brand-new condo, no more than a couple of years old. Open concept with large windows and skylights, the kind of place that looks cold and unwelcoming but fresh and trendy. Every piece of furniture and appliance line up as symmetrically as possible, optimizing for more space. They enter an underground parking garage, and Eddie begins to wonder how Shaw affords a place like this on a detective's salary—even though Eddie doesn't exactly what detectives make.

They enter an elevator lined with mirrors and Eddie gets to see just how terrible he looks. His eyes are sunken and circled by bags and you can barely see the beautiful green orbs that nest in their sockets. His skin is pale and pulled over his cheekbones and jaw. On his maw is a lawn of dark bristly hair that started as an unkempt five o clock shadow weeks ago, that now looks more like a blotchy a Keanu Reeves beard. He has lost at least ten, maybe even fifteen pounds. His clothes that used to fit comfortably are now hanging loosely off his frame. His hair is greasy and long, starting to go grey at his ear line. He snorts the blood crusted remains around his nostrils, wiping the holes clean with his sleeve, before opening his eyes wide, sighing in discontent.

"Fuck, I look horrible."

Shaw smiles.

"Yeah, you really do. You know, we can get you into a program and get you cleaned up," Shaw says with a resonating sincerity that Eddie didn't expect.

"Yeah, maybe I'll look into that after this is all over," Eddie says, nonchalantly brushing off the offer for help, sweeping it under his rug of shit he needs to do.

The elevator opens and they walk into the main room of the apartment, which looks exactly like Eddie thought it would: mostly empty with perfectly aligned furniture sitting in front of a big screen television. A single glass coffee table sits under it, littered with papers and empty beer bottles.

"Nice place. Live alone?"

"Yeah. I do now," Shaw says coldly, his tone rasps with sadness. "Shower is in the bedroom. Use it, and Eddie?"

"Yeah?"

"Don't do any drugs in my apartment, okay?"

"Come on, who do you think I am, an idiot?"

Shaw looks at Eddie, empty of expression.

"Don't answer that. I won't. Christ."

Eddie stands under a rain shower head while warm water runs down over his body wiping away the filth from the previous week. He closes his eyes and his mind takes him to a place he doesn't want to go, his memories. He remembers his old life, his fully furnished apartment before Jane left him and took the love for life with her. He remembers when they were happy. When they would have friends over for game night or movie night. He remembers the time before I died that took nearly everything from him when I went.

He visits the time when his life was good and his activities involved other things besides bars and bathrooms and bar bathrooms.

He remembers hockey on the pond and hot chocolate on the couch. He recollects and reminisces being healthy and working out. Before the times that came with tasting toilet water night after night, splashing back from his volcanic-like vomit from being sick from too many drugs and alcohol.

He gags, and falls to his knees, shaking his head. Trying to ignore the memories that flow like the hot water from above him. He remembers one thing suddenly and all too well. He recounts just how much he hates being sober and he scatters out of the shower, dripping wet, grabbing for a towel to dry off with.

He goes for his piles of clothes and tears his pants from it, tossing them on the counter top. He looks up at the gigantic fogged mirror in front of him and he can see his silhouette behind the veil.

He is panting, fighting the urge to dig the drugs from his pocket and just go to town on them. He takes a final deep breath and fights the terrible craving that tugs at his very core. He wipes his hand across the mirror and exposes the skeleton that wears his skin, barely recognizing the man that now stares back.

Suddenly, something catches Eddie's attention; someone is standing just behind him slightly out of focus.

He slowly turns around and nearly jumps in place when he sees the person grabbing at the counter behind him with blind hands for balance to help him to stand.

A young woman stands there, naked and wet. Her hair hangs over her face like the girl from the ring and her skin is without pigment like that of a cold corpse.

"Eddie?"

"Fuck! What the fuck? Oh shit. Holy shit!"

In the living room, Shaw sits up, hearing Eddie. He puts down his glass of whiskey and mutes the television.

"Eddie are you alright in there?"

Eddie hears Shaw ignoring him, grabbing for a towel to shield the dead girl from his shriveled and shower-pruned dick.

"Eddie. I'm not here to hurt you. I need your help."

"Are you dead?"

"Yes, Eddie, I am dead."

"Are you a ghost?"

"Yes."

"Holy fuck... ghosts are real, no way..."

"Yes way. Eddie, please."

She takes a step forward, and Eddie jumps on the counter recoiling.

"Your friend Shaw saved a boy from a monster. The boy is in trouble. You have to kill the monster to save the boy. Only quicksilver can kill the beast. You need quicksilver to kill him and then the boy will be saved. Do you understand?"

Eddie goes through his pants, grabs his drugs and tears them out. He opens the bag and snorts deeply, in attempts to calm his nerves because he can't handle sobriety anymore and he definitely can't handle a ghost.

He looks up from the bag and as the drugs hit him, not only breaking the blood brain barrier but knocking it down completely, she vanishes, repeating the same thing about a boy, a monster, and quicksilver. But before she is gone completely, she says a different thing. She says a name: Duncan Cartwright.

Shaw is now banging on the door calling Eddies name.

"Eddie if you don't answer me, I'm going to kick this fucking door down!"

"Shaw, I'm fine." Eddie says wiping the residue from his nose. "I was just taking a really crazy shit, sorry. I'll be out soon."

Shaw takes a deep sigh and then his face cringes and he mouths the word gross before he returns to the living room.

Eddie flushes the toilet and dresses before looking at himself in the mirror. He ponders something: do the drugs chase away the dead? If he sobers up for good, would he always see phantoms? He shakes that thought and exits the washroom.

CHAPTER 17

Eddie stands over his rusty bathtub back at his apartment. Now holding a fifty-pound bag of road salt, he just stares down at Sebastian who hasn't decayed at all. Instead, he looks like he is made of porcelain. Like a giant creepy doll with a broken bat lodged in its chest. Eddie drops the bag on the dirty tiles at his feet and cautiously reaches for the tap, biding his time and retaining the right amount of cautiousness— when dealing with undead that could return to the living at any time—before turning the water on.

He cringes when he realizes he needs to put the rubber stopper in. He looks for it, carefully and non-evasively, and searches blindly for it. After repositioning Sebastian several times, he rescues it, and jams it in the drain. Eddie ponders the temperature of the water and if it matters.

As the tub fills, he sits on the toilet and reads through the dossier his neighbors gave him.

We are calling it Monster 101, for the record.

The file tells him about salt and about the iron but it is all speculation, or I guess it isn't, because now that we all know vampires are real then somebody discovered these weaknesses. So salt, according to Monster 101, was used as a purifier by a vast majority of cultures. A cleanser, if you will. And therefore, at some point, some poor sod discovered it worked against the undead. They used it to either ward against or contain said monstrosities. Also, it makes everything taste great. Win, win.

Okay, now for the iron. As the story goes, a long, long time ago, in this galaxy, not far away at all, iron was considered to be the life force of earth. This was before people knew iron was in our blood because this predates chemistry and outdated medicinal practices. It was also celebrated and worshiped—as far as metal worshiping goes— because it could withstand both fire and cold and you could only find it deep within the earth. So yeah, iron rocks. So according to the past, iron could harm or contain evil spirits because of its natural purity and strength.

Seriously though, did someone accidentally figure these things out? Is it like how we figured out what we could eat and what would kill us? Trial and error, I guess. Two guys are walking through a forest way back when and they come upon tasty looking mushrooms and they're like, rock-paper-scissors to see who might die? Anyway... just a thought.

Eddie feels water at his feet and realizes he let the tub overflow; he tosses the file out of the washroom and scrambles to shut off the water. He cuts open the bag of rock salt and looks at it trying to figure out how much to use. After several moments of careful consideration, he just dumps the whole bag in to be safe.

Better to be safe than have a vampire escape interrogation, am I right?

Eddie giggles uncontrollably because Sebastian bobs up and down like an apple in a barrel. If apples were vampires and barrels, were very dirty tubs.

Eddie cleans up the water on the bathroom floor with dirty laundry before rescuing the file from the kitchen floor.

As he begins to read it again, he is startled by a loud knock at his front door causing him to inadvertently drop the folder and all the loose papers in it.

As they scatter every which way, he panics and chases them at random as the knocking continues. He forgets the papers and closes the bathroom door and goes to answer the door, terrified and sweating right through his clothes.

He pulls it open. "What?"

What starts as a loud and annoying question immediately diffuses when Eddie sees whom it is he is questioning and when he sees them, his tone instantly becomes passive and apologetic within the same breath.

Alexi stands there with her hand resting on her very high hip on her very long and defined leg. She is dressed up and stunningly beautiful, a side of her Eddie has never seen or knew existed.

She looks nothing like a body builder now, instead, she looks like a supermodel. Her blonde silky hair is perfectly straightened, and it sparkles in the shitty hallway light, like gold flakes in a dark stream.

She is wearing a solid white tight dress that leaves absolutely nothing to the imagination because Eddie can see every single bump of her areolas surrounding her diamond hard nipples and he is a deer in her headlights.

"Eddie? Are you going to invite me in?"

Eddie closes his mouth and stutters.

"Alexi...what...what are you doing here?"

She pushes past him effortlessly and that is when Eddie notices Tom Morrow and Chester Day blocking the rest of the hallway with their hulking frames, completely eclipsing the hallway behind them. Not like Eddie would notice because how distracted by Alexi he is.

Eddie goes to talk to them but Alexi cuts him off.

"They will wait where they are. Shut the door."

Eddie obeys her like a trained mutt and shuts the door.

"Alexi, what're you doing here? I mean, it is great seeing you, and I mean great, but this is unexpected."

"Well, Eddie," Alexi starts talking as she looks around the "living room" before continuing.

"To be honest, I was worried. The last time I saw you, you bought a gun and a lot of drugs and then I haven't heard from you since. So, and I mean no offense, I was worried you killed yourself. Bit the bullet, if you will."

Eddie completely floored by Alexi's concern, cracks a small smile and exhales.

"Well color me pink and slap me with a dink, Alexi, that means a lot."

Alexi raises one of her perfectly drawn on eyebrows.

"It's just an expression."

"I've never heard that Eddie. So, tell me, what have you been up to?"

Alexi clip clops across the floor toward Eddie, swaying hypnotically.

"You know, being a big old piece of shit, as per usual."

Alexi frowns, sincerely upset by Eddie's deprecation.

"Eddie, you aren't a bad man. You aren't shit. You're just lost."

Eddie begins to shuffle, growing nervous as Alexi looks around.

"Well thanks Alexi, I appreciate that."

She looks over her shoulder toward the kitchen, bedroom, and bathroom area and Eddie goes cold.

"Eddie, give me the tour of your kingdom, yes?"

She begins to walk into the kitchen but Eddie runs around her and blocks her. In her lightning blue heels, she stands half a foot above Eddie.

"Listen, Alexi, it's not that I'm not super pumped you are here and you cared enough to check on me but now isn't the best time for a chit chat and a grand tour."

"Eddie, just a quick tour, just so I know you're, well, okay?"

She pushes past him, and let's be honest, Eddie probably couldn't stop her if he wanted to.

Eddie watches as she looks about the refuse of his kitchen and his stomach nearly falls out his ass as she looks back and forth, deciding between the washroom and bedroom.

When she chooses her next adventure, which is exactly the one location Eddie doesn't want her to explore—the bathroom— Eddie does something completely unexpected.

Eddie slides in front of Alexi. He slips his hand behind her blonde curtain of hair, gently cradling her head, and he pushes his lips over hers. With his other hand he pulls her at the hip, pulling her into his body, pressing firmly against her frame.

He kisses her like he is feeding a fire. At first, gently adding kindling slowly, letting it breathe, and staving from smothering it the embers that at any minute will transform into flame. Then when the fire is licking ravenously at whatever fuels it, hungry and wanting more, he feeds it. He just feeds it more and more, adding fuel to the flame but in this case instead of wood kindling or gasoline or whatever else you light fires with, this fire is fed by his exuberant and playful tongue.

I think I may have rambled on about the fire comparison to the passionate kiss and I'm sorry, but I can't really undo you reading that, because you have already read it...anyways...Even though now she really just wants the wood. Ha!

After several hot seconds that seem like minutes that feel like hours, he breaks away free.

His and her lips are smudged, stained, and splattered by her bright red lipstick. She gasps deeply, shocked by his actions. And for several seconds, a fear so deep and thick overtakes Eddie. The fear that he has made a terrible mistake. That is until she smiles.

Then a different fear surfaces as her smile turns and she looks like she is going to devour him. She kisses back hard. Her tongue slams into his mouth violently, penetrating his. She takes control and her superior strength shows.

She lifts Eddie up and carries him into his bedroom. She tosses him on his bed and before he can do anything, she grabs his pant legs and rips his pants off.

He scurries backward but she chases after him. She grabs at his underwear, ripping them off too, and his dick bounces out freely and flaccidly.

Eddie is the wrong side of naked and exposed. She leaps on him, clawing at his half hard dick, and when she gets it firmly in her grasp, she hungrily devours it in one moist gulp.

Eddie's head reactively hangs back in ecstasy as Alexi's head bobs up and down. In seconds he is standing at attention and she wastes no time. She pulls her face away, carrying a line of drool that is still connected to his dick like an umbilical cord. She hikes up that tiny dress, exposing her completely bald better half, and with one fluent wipe of her mouth she lubes herself.

She mounts Eddie, violently, crushing him between her horse-like hips. And she rides him full gallop as though she is escaping in a western, heading toward the sunset, with no end in sight to never be seen again just before the credits roll.

She straddles on top of him, pounding down on him repeatedly with the same power of a jackhammer dispersing solid concrete. She is completely in control and to prove it, even though nobody involved is questioning that fact, she shoves her fingers into his mouth, forcing him to suck them.

Eddie is trapped between terror and pleasure. Unsure which one is winning, he just goes with it, and he ignores the truth that at this point he has no choice.

Alexi shines with sweat, like a golden goddess, she glistens. And hypnotically, Eddie gets lost, watching this beauty climax. And just like watching the sun cascade over a blackened night sky, rendered speechless and paralyzed by the sight of it, Eddie explodes.

(Caught you pervert, you turned to the page looking for smut...don't worry about it, we all would. But as it turns out there is no continuous Tess sex scene, but there was already smut here, lucky you...)

CHAPTER 18

Eddie's lids blink open reactively and he squints away the sun that licks at his retreating retinas. He smells something sweet, something floral. He remembers last night as Alexi's blonde hair annoyingly sticks to his stubble as he moves, tickling his lips. He bats it gently off. She moans, waking as her head slides off his chest as he sits up.

"Eddie. That was... well that was fantastic. And honestly, well, unexpected."

Eddie is a shake and bake mix of confused, scared, relieved, and relaxed. He is sober in the way of someone who spent a night partying hard and wakes up still drunk but functional is. That is Eddie right now.

"That was fun, and if we're being honest, overdue. I mean there has always been this tension between us..." Eddie releases his unedited mind in the form of verbal diarrhea.

Alexi sits up, turns to face him, and her hair slowly flows into the sun, blinding him further. But this is a sight that causes his retinas to focus rather than retreat; this is pleasant and welcomed. She slides up smiling, coming face to face with him, and it is captivating.

"Oh, is that so? Eddie have you crushed on me for some time then?"

Her broken English, however comprehended is for the first time, just cute.

"Yeah, but as you say, you must've crushed on me at some point because you immediately reciprocated."

She just smiles, exhaling her morning breath, and Eddie doesn't mind at all. Eddie inhales it welcomingly. He doesn't retreat. He just smiles back. He just stares at her. He gets lost in her eyes and their swirling bright colors and he wonders if have they have always been this beautiful. And he just gets lost in her.

They both remain silent and keep gaze for what would be an uncomfortable amount of time if you were just an observer. But if you were either of them, you wouldn't think of time; you'd just want this moment to keep going, fearing that the other would break it and it would be just a fantasy, but it isn't for them and they both know it is as real as the daylight that breaks through the blackout curtains.

This is one of those moments that unless you're directly a part of you wouldn't understand it, and even if you were in it, you still wouldn't understand it completely, but you know it makes sense in a way that you don't want it to end.

This is what love is. A chemical reaction at first that eventually becomes more and it becomes unexplainable but somehow understood by the people involved.

Look at me trying to explain something I can't and doing a terrible job at it.

"Eddie," Alexi says through ruby red lips that he spends far too long salivating over, remembering what they did and what he wants them to do again.

"Yeah Alexi?" he replies in a hot breath, exasperated and frustrated. Hot and bothered is what the kids call it and you can hear it in his voice.

"I really don't want to leave you but I really need to pee." She rises and he watches the blankets expose her flawless frame and he is hypnotized by her every move as she makes her way to his washroom. She crosses the kitchen gracefully, and with every step she takes it shows him more things he wants to see because he didn't know they existed... however he returns, remembering what lies in his tub...

"NO!" Eddie screams, realizing what waits behind the bathroom door, and he leaps out of bed chasing her with his dick swinging freely like a broken pendulum.

He has her wrist before she reaches the door and he spins her. Face to face, his eyes well apologetically.

"Alexi, please. I'm sincerely ashamed, but my washroom is disgusting."

She smiles wickedly, and in that smile his pendulum freezes to a hard stop.

"I've seen some pretty dirty things darling. Don't worry, after last night, I see you in a different light. I won't judge. I like how dirty you are," she says in a whisper, a very sexy whisper, as she kisses him softly.

He tries to push her away and as he does his pendulum of a cock sadly retracts and starts to shrink exponentially and as it does, it disappears, as does the explanation it once heralded.

"No, I mean..." Eddie drops his gaze, lowering his head in shame before continuing.

"...The toilet. It's backed up and doesn't work... hasn't in a while. And well, it isn't just disgusting... it's fucking horrible. I've been using the neighbors. That is how bad it is."

Eddie watches helplessly as Alexi's expression changes into a familiar one, one that he has seen countless times, and until just now had never bothered him. That expression is one of judgment and sympathy. Alexi has never looked at Eddie the way she did last night and this morning. She usually looks at him, like everyone else does. Pitying him through ocular observance. Seeing only a shell of a man. But the way she looked at him last night and this morning was very different. She looked at him like he was still a human, flawed or not, but still a human and she saw him truly; endeared and willing to see what everyone else ignores. He never cared if she ever saw this in the first place but after she did, everything has changed. He cares now, and worse, he watches her in real time change her opinion back to the way everyone else looks at him and now she shares that sight with them.

"Maybe I should just go."

Eddie, overwhelmed by shame, complies with this outcome and awaits further punishment openly. As much as he wants to see her look at him the way she did last night again, and even more so the way she looked at him this morning, he knows there are bigger things at play behind the bathroom door that he just can't explain right now and he doesn't want to involve her, especially now.

"Yeah, maybe it would be for the best."

Eddie barely gets that sentence out without it feeling like someone kicked him in the balls and punched him in the heart at the same time. He stands, naked and frozen in his kitchen and watches silently as Alexi dresses and goes to leave. She stops at the front door.

"Eddie, I've seen the real you. Last night was… well it was amazing. I really hope that I can see that again," she says without turning around to look at him. She opens the door and Tom Morrow and Chester Day are still there waiting for her. They part, letting her pass, and they close the door as Eddie watches Alexi disappear between familiar sinew and muscle. As though she is gone for good and the only token he has left over is smothered by body odor masked by cheap body spray.

Eddie collapses with his hands firmly grabbing his face, squeezing the blood from it constrictively, and screams angrily in genuine frustration from between closed teeth all the while screaming one word. He does so very, very, very—*can't stress this enough*—extremely loudly.

"FUCK!"

He keeps the scream going until he is interrupted by a knock at his door.

He scrambles across the kitchen and down the hallway toward his front door; still as naked as the day he was born, but with a much bigger dick now. Length times girth, times importance.

Eddie opens the door, hoping Alexi has come back for one last romantic moment. Sadly, she hasn't…

"For the love of fuck Eddie put some pants on, Christ." Shaw shouts while turning away and shielding his eyes from Eddie and his semi-erect birthday suit.

Eddie slams the door, screaming the f-word again while walking toward his room with the intention of dressing. All the while Shaw lets himself in carrying several bags from the police evidence room.

Shaw enters the kitchen, breathes in, and cringes just as Eddie hobbles out of his bedroom pulling on a pair of pants that haven't seen a laundry machine in over a month and probably smell as bad as how wrinkled they are.

"It smells like sex and shame in here." Shaw giggles, trying not to look at the bathroom and what future it holds all while trying not to look at Eddie and his disappearing nude figure.

"Hardy fucking Har... how did the hunt go?"

"As well as it could I guess, there was a lot of shit on this list that was weird as fuck," Shaw replies grimly.

"Great...just great..."

"Hold on to your pathetic package... I got it all."

"Everything?"

"Does all not mean the same thing to you that it means to me? All means everything, does it not?"

"Yeah, yeah, it means the fucking same. I'm just having a rough night... er, morning, whatever the fucking time is... it's rough."

"Well, I'm sorry somebody shit in your corn flakes princess, but we have a job to do. Are you ready?"

CHAPTER 19

Shaw and Eddie slowly make their way to the bathroom. They exchange glances, each waiting for the other to open the door. Shaw insists Eddie opens it and after several reluctant moments, he does. They are first greeted by the sour-sweet smell of rotting meat left out in the sun—*not sure if you've ever left meat in the sun but it smells gnarly*—a strange mixture of red onion and body odor on a bus. They synchronously gag and cover their mouths as they walk in. Shaw opens his bag of goodies, and Eddie scoops up the scattered papers of the Monster 101 file he dropped last night and attempts to organize them. Shaw sits down on the toilet, rooting through his bag before finally dumping its contents on the dirty floor below.

One early 1800's crucifix (*I'm guessing cause it looks old as fuck*), pre-civil war iron shackles from the American mid-West (*don't quote me, I'm not a historian but I've watched a lot of westerns okay?*), two sterling silver rings and a silver diamond studded necklace, and one copy of the bible.

"You got all this stuff from evidence?"

"Yeah, you'd be surprised how much junk they have in there... Oh, one thing: leave the tags on because I have to return them, okay?"

"Gotcha."

The overhead light flickers on and off, exposing the mess Eddie calls a washroom, a mess even before there was a paralyzed undead creature floating in his tub.

The tiles are filthy, coated in what appears to be an inch of dirt and mildew. Whatever color they were, they aren't now. The walls look like they're sweating blood, painted red, but it's just rust from the leaky pipes overhead staining them.

A thin white scum that could be toothpaste, but isn't, coats the mirror above the sink, obscuring all reflections. And the toilet, fuck, don't get me started with the toilet. You ever walk into a truck stop washroom and it's clogged with shit and toilet paper piled up almost to the rim of the seat? Well this toilet looks like that toilet, but much, much worse. Eddie wasn't kidding, this washroom should embarrass him, even before he was hiding a body in it. This is vile. Anyways...

Shaw begins to shackle Sebastian's frozen mitts, linking the chain under the tub before pulling it back up and cuffing the other wrist. All the while Eddie dumps the remaining rock salt into the tub. The two stand up after completing their tasks and exchange nervous glances, inhaling and then exhaling deeply, preparing themselves for what lies next... waking Sebastian up.

Eddie stands stupidly at the end of the tub, holding the crucifix in front of him. He dons the silver necklace and wears the silver rings on the same hand that holds the cross. In his other hand he holds out the bible. Shaw more conventionally has his service weapon out and pressed firmly against the temple of Sebastian while his other hand firmly grips the bat, ready at any moment to tear it free.

"Should we do a count-down?" Eddie chokes out, voice cracking like he just hit puberty.

"What do you mean? Like a count down from 10?"

"I was thinking on 5?"

"Like I pull the bat out after 1?"

"No man, after 0!"

"So, you are going to count down from 5 to 0, and then I pull the bat out?"

"Not after 0, on 0."

"Seriously, Eddie?"

"Okay, after I finish saying 1, you tear that fucker out."

"Alright, after 1."

"Can I get high first man? I'm really sweating here."

"No, you can't get high, I need you on your toes."

"I would be on my toes if I was high. Think about it..."

"Oh for fuck sakes. Fine, but hurry the shit up." Shaw sneers. His brow soaked in sweat, his hands tremble but remain firm. He watches Eddie bounce out of the washroom and disappear into his room. After several loud nasally snorts later Eddie returns extremely focused and committed. White residue litters his nostrils and the stubble of his upper lip, reminding Shaw that this is the worst alliance possible. He considers what's crazier, the situation or teaming up with a junkie? He chooses to ignore the answer.

"You good?" Shaw asks.

"I'm fucking gravy baby. Let's fucking do this."

"Of course, you are."

They both remain still; neither says or does anything until Shaw realizes Eddie has completely forgotten that he was supposed to count him down.

"Eddie!"

Eddie snaps out of whatever zone he wandered off to and shakes himself vigorously before repositioning his weapons.

"Right. Sorry. Ready?"

"Yes. Fuck. Let's go already," Shaw barks back.

Shaw raises the gun, returning the barrel to its former position. In the silence of the washroom you can hear his grip tighten around the bat.

"5..."

Shaw rolls his shoulders back and wipes his brow with his gun hand before realizing what he is doing and jams it back in place.

"4..."

Eddie begins to sway back and forth like a hockey player during a national anthem, which slightly annoys Shaw but he shakes it off and returns his attention to Sebastian's bat.

"3..."

Shaw repositions his legs, readying himself to transition from squat to stand to draw the bat and he imagines the motion in preparation.

"2..."

Eddie is now yelling uncontrollably. His voice ricochets thunderously in the small confides of the bathroom. Shaw hears it loud and clear and almost like time has slowed down.

"1..."

Shaw tightens down on that bat pommel so hard it looks as though he is going to snap it.

"Pull!"

Shaw yanks with his entire centrifugal force, ripping the bat stub free from Sebastian's broken ribcage, and leaps backwards aiming the gun back at his head. Eddie however, inches slightly closer, jamming the weapons of "god" he holds in hand mashing them against Sebastian's reactionless face. Nothing happens. Sebastian doesn't move. Shaw fights nature and ignores the screaming flight response. He jams his weapon harder, trying to get a rise from Sebastian's corpse. His flight response becomes so overwhelming, he begins to shake. His tremors resonate so heavily that he can't even steady the weapon pressed against Sebastian's forehead.

He is all flight, no fight. But he doesn't run.

"Eddie?" he squeaks from the corner of his mouth.

"Wait for it," Eddie replies without breaking focus. Almost like he has some other force assisting his drive, assuring him of his sanity... *oh wait, he does.*

Shaw begins to relax slightly but doesn't move his gun from the target: Sebastian's bloated, decaying head. And as moments pass, and nothing happens still, Shaw's body relaxes more and more.

"Maybe he isn't going to come back this time, I mean, he's been stuck for several days. Maybe, they can't come back after a certain time. Like an expiry date?"

Eddie drops the holy weapons and picks up the file, rifling through the pages in a chaotic search for answers. Suddenly, they hear the splash of water on the floor. They both turn their attention to Sebastian who remains motionless while the water around him moves. Slight ripples on the salty water have formed and smash into the sides of the tub like waves on the shore.

Eddie returns his focus on the pages and Shaw peers over him as he does, both sequestering answers from this makeshift encyclopedia of monsters. Eddie's panic-stricken page turning is interrupted by another splash I n the cesspool. And then, suddenly, all at once, it happens.

It starts with a noise that one can only describe as a blood curdling scream—*if one actually knew what blood curdling sounded like*— and then quickly turns into a sound that doesn't belong to this world at all. A sound from the depths of space never meant to for human ears.

Similar to an underwater scream but instead of muffled its deafeningly load. It attaches to the ear and reverberates deep into the brain like a head trauma causing a concussion; an expression of sheer agony.

Through it, Eddie and Shaw begin to fall to their knees, desperately clutching their ears trying to muffle it out. With them follows the majority of the tub water, exploding out and upward before raining down all over the washroom. But it isn't like a refreshing rainfall, not at all, it burns like acid to the touch, transformed by the body that poisoned it. The acid bath water sears sores on their exposed skin, melts color from their clothes, and peels the aging paint from the walls. It bubbles and hisses on contact with any surface it touches but as soon as it starts, it stops abruptly, settling like calm water; running and pooling away.

Sebastian reanimates, lurching forward before being pulled back by his bonds which burn his skin, sending plumes of smoke from his wrists. His face contorts demonically, morphing from the pleasant attractive male- to something that only can be described as terrifying. From hot to not to no fucking thanks in seconds they can't look away and wouldn't want to because as fast as fuck ugly happens, it reverses, returning to the yes fucking please face he started with.

Sebastian sits up now, conscious and alive as a reanimated monster can be. His chest cavity has regenerated. He seems not only confused but in extreme agony as small plumes of smoke burst from the water, he is submerged in which appears to be boiling around him.

As Eddie and Shaw rise, raising their weapons of choice, Sebastian immediately focuses on them ignoring his apparent agony.

"Who the fuck are you, why the fuck am I here like this, where the fuck am I, and what the fuck do you want from me?"

Eddie chuckles uncontrollably and responds in kind.

"Truly covering the who, why, where, what but forgetting the how and the when, aren't we?"

Shaw elbows him in the chest moving in front of him, stealing his crucifix and raising it up and out in front of his gun.

"Get that shit out of my face. You need to believe in religion for that to work asshole," Sebastian chuckles, laughing at the crucifix.

Shaw looks at it and then tosses it out of the way. Eddie dodges the discarded little cross and takes action. He jumps into the tub, armed with the silver on his fingers and the chunky silver necklace in his palm and jams it on Sebastian.

At this point, they're kind of being scientific in their approach, testing to see what works and what doesn't and it is a surprisingly intelligent plan because let's be honest, they're all virgins at this party.

Sebastian recoils painfully the instant the silver makes contact and begins to seer his skin like a steak on a cast iron pan.

"Stop, fuck! Okay, okay, you've made your point. What do you want?"

Eddie pulls away the silver back but only by inches, still straddling Sebastian ready to reapply. Suddenly Eddie retreats— becoming the smartest action he has taken in awhile—taking a couple steps back because he doesn't know how dangerous Sebastian still is.

"We want to know everything?" Eddie replies tentatively.

Shaw nods at Eddie, permissively, and Eddie returns savagely with the silver. Sebastian pulls back nearly dunking himself completely into the bathwater to escape Eddie and the silver.

"I'll tell you whatever you want, just make this stop, you have no idea how much this hurts," Sebastian cries submissively while flailing what he has left of his hands, waving them in the air as proof. They look like swollen desiccated husks, digit-less. And the wrists that barely hold them up, continue to burn within the iron that binds them. They could be mistaken for used kindling.

Shaw looks at Eddie. Challenging their plan. Eddie looks confused. Shaw sighs loudly and exhaustively before barking orders at Eddie,

"Pull the plug and drain the tub but those cuffs are staying on."

Sebastian, settles, goes still and then slowly allows a seemingly genuine response.

He smiles relieved.

Eddie, however, doesn't move.

"Shaw. According to the manual, he can turn into smoke and escape. I don't think that's a good idea to drain the tub."

"The iron is keeping me here. The salt water is just fucking overkill man, please, please just drain the fucking tub," Sebastian begs.

Eddie looks at Shaw unconvinced, but Shaw insists with his deadpan gaze that Eddie has no choice but to do what he says and not undermine him because Shaw is the cop after all. If looks could speak when it comes to Shaw you better listen.

Eddie —despite ever fabric of his being disagrees with this— reaches under Sebastian and tears the plug free. He steps back, shaking his head.

As soon as the water is completely drained away and swallowed down the drain. Sebastian's wounds heal instantly and instead of the feeble, begging prisoner he just was, he appears reborn. He is ready to break free like Queen wrote the song about him.

Shaw encroaches confidently, pistol raised and powerful. Pushing his way past Eddie. He places the barrel on Sebastian's forehead, before leaning in, and then whispers, "Now you're going to tell me everything I want to know or I'm going to blow your fucking brains out, get it?"

Sebastian smiles through every whispered word. He doesn't flinch when Shaw presses the barrel between his eyes. Instead, that smile just grows, and his eyes never even give Shaw a glance, they have been fixed on Eddie the whole time. Through closed teeth and an ever-expanding smile, he whispers back as slowly as time allows:

"You should've listened to the junkie."

He raises his arms high above his head and then savagely slams his hands down on the rim of tub cutting both shackles clean off, freeing his wrists from the irons and with them the leftovers that were his hands. They blacken and wither before disappearing completely like dust in the wind. His skin becomes transparent and he begins to cackle wildly before the rest of him imitates his hands and begins to fall away.

That is, until Eddie intervenes.

Eddie lassos the silver necklace around Sebastian's neck like he is catching a wild mustang and tugs him back like he is attempting to garrote him instead of tame him and with that, Sebastian's transparency fades and he returns to his sickly white color, trapped in the tub.

Sebastian's eyes bulge out sickly, and he stabs at the chain with his stubs trying to pry himself free, which is futile and he quickly submits as it begins to smolder and smoke.

"Fill the fucking tub back up! There should be some salt left in that bag and if that isn't enough there should be some kosher salt under the sink in the kitchen," Eddie commands as he drops behind Sebastian, fighting to control his flailing movements that weaken after every passing moment.

Shaw does as he is told.

The tub is once again full and diluted by salt (a bit of rock salt and an entire small box of kosher salt). The iron shackles again restrain Sebastian but this time they're on his ankles and *insert 80's hair metal band here* drowns out his cries through the speakers of an old boom box sitting just outside the washroom.

"Okay twilight, let's start from the beginning. And tell us everything." Eddie instructs, seething and sharing a new found confidence brought on by Shaw's failures. Shaw sits back, stewing, but never taking his gun off of Sebastian.

"We don't know who the first was but our history tells us the first clean blood was a king in the early..."

"Whoa, whoa... not that far back, fuck. I want you to explain, like, what you guys are up to nowadays. You know, current affairs."

Shaw hangs his head sighing, dismissing Eddie and his absolute disrespect for history.

"Umm... okay, well, what do you..."

Eddie interrupts. "How does no one know you exist? How do you remain secret? Where is your secret base? Who is your leader and if we kill your leader do, we cure everybody?"

Sebastian begins to laugh despite being in serious agony before responding.

"You're so over your head, junkie. You know that? Before I answer anything, I want you to really look at yourself and ask yourself, really ask yourself, if you're ready for this?"

Oh fuck, he is going to try and mind fuck Eddie.

"What do you mean?"

"Addiction dumbass, how is that not apparent? You suffer the same fate we do. That hunger. That ravenous, insatiable, never ending hunger that eats away at you until you get your fix. Everything else is trivial and ignored until you feed. That hunger is so powerful that it consumes you until you are just it. Only it. There is nothing else. And it is so big, so much bigger than you, that you can't even see that you've been replaced by it and it's walking around as you, using you..."

Eddie steps back like he is wounded as this realization dons on him.

"There it is," Sebastian continues. "You know exactly what I'm talking about, don't you? Every time you feed you feel powerful, important, beautiful, unstoppable and righteous and as long as it's still coursing through your veins everything is just fine..."

Eddie tries to fight this reality check: that he is lost and hungry and the only reason he is here is so that he can keep feeding.

"Well," Sebastian starts again, "we do the same thing, but unlike you, we actually benefit from feeding. We do it to survive. It actually keeps us alive. It makes us powerful. It retains our beauty. We are unstoppable and we actually have a reason to keep doing what we're doing because if we don't, we die. What is your excuse? You don't have one, do you? If you think about it, you're the real monster here."

Eddie is paralyzed, silent with shock.

He has gotten inside Eddies head, and yes, he may be spot on but he is a vampire and Eddie is just a fuck up. This thing kills to feed his habit, Eddie just burns bridges and loses loved ones to fuel his, which isn't great but it isn't the same, at all.

Shaw is fed up. He steals Eddie's silver and takes control of the situation and shuts Sebastian the fuck up by burying the silver into his throat.

"Answer the questions asshole. How do you stay under the radar?"

"We have rules. We can't feed with our fangs. They're removed." Sebastian opens his mouth, exposing his missing teeth looking like a hillbilly high on meth fornicated with kind of hot recast Vlad the Impaler but Impaler was a euphonism.

"Who removes them?" Shaw probes.

"The patriarch or matriarch, whoever the oldest of the brood is."

Shaw buries the silver again but this time in a different place. Pain flares over Sebastian causing him to gyrate like he is having a seizure.

"What does any of that mean?" Shaw retorts with frustration. "And what is with the fucking straight razors? Is that how you feed?"

"Are you fucking kidding me? Yes, the straight razors are how we feed. We don't have fangs remember? And we stay hidden because all of you are like cattle, buried in your smart devices, completely self involved and unconcerned with the actual world around you. No one connects the dots because everyone is so fucking distracted and self-important. Before social media we could only feed once every couple years and we would have to share but now, fuck now, it's like the old times but without people catching on. We coexist perfectly now and as long as we don't get too greedy and we follow the code, we can flourish again."

Shaw can't believe this, can't comprehend how easy it is.

This can't be as easy as he is making it but the more he reflects on it the more it makes sense.

People are so distracted and so disillusioned that everything he said would be possible as long as they kept to their system and didn't break it. The attention span of our society has changed so heavily that people can barely keep up with everything going on because so much is going on. And now Shaw is in his head, falling back, and not paying attention. He is lost, like Eddie.

Shit, they may not see it but you have to, this fucker is playing them and if you, Eddie, or Shaw had read the Monster 101 file, then you'd know as well as I do that, this is what they fucking do. They play off your mental weaknesses and influence your thoughts. Like a toxic partner, they'll say anything to get their way and if you now see what I see, which of course you do because you are wicked smart. They both folded like a flimsy deck of stacked cards and it shouldn't have been that easy...

Suddenly, Eddie jumps back in and leaps on Sebastian, tearing the silver necklace out of Shaw's hand on the way, before burying it on Sebastian's chest as hard as he possibly can.

"Listen motherfucker. No more games. You're going to tell us exactly what we ask and nothing more. No more speeches. No more personal evaluations. Just answer exactly what we ask, are we clear?"

Sebastian, defeated, painfully nods in agreement, just wanting the end to come sooner that he knows is anywhere but near.

CHAPTER 20

The tub is empty now and so is any trace of Sebastian ever being there, having melted away entirely after his execution. Shaw and Eddie bled him dry of information and then destroyed him. When he, or any of his kind, is truly destroyed, they completely dissolve.

They evaporate just as water does, leaving no trace. Well, almost no trace, they leave behind clothes and anything they carried. But that's it. There is no biological trace left after a vampire is destroyed. Now, I know, why not say killed? Well, genius, you can't kill something that is already dead. Get it? Good. Moving on.

What did they learn?

Sebastian belonged to a particular brood or hive of vampires, one of many to be specific, but this one is the only active hive in the area.

According to Sebastian only one brood is currently awake. Vampires sleep a lot. And I don't mean they nap, no, they hibernate for decades at a time and there is only one active brood at any one time. Like shift work. One at a time, decade-by-decade, one faction functions and feeds and then retires allowing another to rise and flourish for a time. And they have been doing this since vampires were vampires and they needed to be on the down low.

So, the straight razors are personalized to each vampire and identify them as individuals - like birth certificates and social insurance numbers for the undead.

The most important thing they learned is where the brood functions out of, and now Eddie and Shaw have this piss-poor idea that they're going to lay siege to it and eliminate every vampire of this particular brood, disregarding completely that this is only one cell of many. But to them this is, or will be, a win if they succeed in eliminating them.

But all of that has to wait until after Dan Maurier's funeral, because that is today, and they both need to make an appearance... well, Shaw has to because he was his partner. Eddie really should as well, considering at one point in time he was considered family, or at least had spent enough time with them that he *should have* been considered family.

So, after the interrogation Shaw collects himself and catalogues the items, he borrowed from the evidence room— items he stole but intends to return— and dips.

For those who don't know what "dip" means I'll explain... Tony dipped suddenly without saying goodbye. Layman's terms: Tony left suddenly without saying goodbye. Understand? Good.

So now here is Eddie, left all alone—which is always a bad idea—to his devices. He blankly stares at the reflection that stares back at him in the mirror in the washroom that has never been this clean, ever. The mirror image cast back is a youngish looking man draped in a tasteful cobalt blue suit and because everything appears different and unfamiliar, Eddie decides that this is the time for change and he must be present for Dan's funeral. Welcomed or not. He is going to be there. Eddie takes one long inhale, as though he is drawing a deep breath of smoke, and then coughs it out.

As he leaves, bringing with him all the doubt he can't shake like an overloaded suitcase, visibly dragging the weight of it in his step, he looks back at something. Or someone. But no one is there, at least no one he can see.

I am there, watching. I always am. Maybe he'll never see me but I need him to face the grief. Because when you carry that kind of weight, that kind of hurt, it never gets lighter until you face it. Think of grief like a cage sinking in the ocean, surrounded by circling sharks. And the longer you wait to leave the cage and swim up to the surface away from the sharks and away from the darkness and the cold, the harder it gets.

Just look Eddie, acknowledge that this pain reminds you of the one you carry, and face it—me.

Instead, Eddie just walks out the door, locking it behind him and heading to the funeral, which he is certainly already late for.

When Eddie arrives at the cemetery a light rain begins to fall as the clouds darken ominously overhead. The rain is refreshing, cooling his feverish skin. He is coming down and the withdrawals are kicking fiercely. It's late in the afternoon and the ceremony has already begun. He can see Shaw with Dan's family in the distance but he hangs off behind some weeping willows just out of sight. The rain starts to come down harder and he watches in wonder as black umbrellas sprout synchronously like blooming flowers in a sped-up time lapse video. Suddenly, the entire crowd is a field of onyx flowers, encircling a small green patch of grass with a single headstone and a large red stain coffin sinking into its center.

Eddie begins to tremble and he swallows hard. As wet as it is out here, his throat is dry, so he wets it with a flask of whisky he carries in his coat pocket. As he swallows the burning liquid, lightning his nerves like striking a match, and a memory burns out from it. Between the words of the priest, the rain, and the grief, he is reminded of my funeral—yes, my funeral.

We're doing this here? Okay, lets do this. Remember.

Eddie shakes and takes another swig, and then another, chasing away the memory. But each guzzle of the burning liquid only further fans the fire of the memory he attempts to drink away. Instead, it burns bigger, tearing across his thoughts, scorching his mental defense down with it as it goes.

He staggers back, as though slapped with the memory as the heat of it overwhelms him. He hides behind the tree after he screams out his favorite word in a panic and the crowd turns back to look. He slams his back to the tree, hard, hiding away. And he pulls his hair off his eyes and begins to talk himself up. Fighting this all the way, but it isn't enough; it isn't working, no, he needs his medicine—his fucking medicine.

He wipes his hand on his jacket, desperately trying to dry the back of it. He frantically pulls from his pocket a bag filled with his favorite powder, and it isn't much, but it'll do —-or at least he prays that it will. His fingers are wet and he struggles to open it, and when he does, he spills it out onto his hand. But the rain is too heavy, it washes it completely away and as he clumsily smashes his nostril on to his hand to snort it up, it either doesn't move or just smudges away. In his frustration, repeating this pointless attempt, he drops the bag onto the wet sod below and the remaining booger sugar disintegrates between blades of grass every which way.

He lets out a feeble cry, falling to his knees in the mud, and paws at the bag jamming it into his mouth and sucks at it greedily, turning it inside out in hopes he can absorb the remnants orally.

This is just pathetic man; can't you see that? I mean look at yourself dude. This isn't okay.

Eddie looks up through the sleeting rain with tears welling in his eyes, and he looks right at me—well, if I had a physical form and I was visible, which I'm not, he is looking where I would be standing— and he smiles in disbelief.

Holy shit. Can he see me?

He nods, as though he just heard me ask that.

Wait, holy fuck, Eddie? Can you see and hear me?

"Yeah, Gab, I can. It's been along time. How're you man? Well, besides being dead, I mean?"

This isn't possible. The living can't see the dead. They cannot. They can't see us. They can't hear us...

"Gab. I don't know if I'm just coming down harder than the Titanic, but I can see you, and I can hear you, in here." Eddie taps his skull as he hangs his head from the weight of the water falling down. And now, somehow, I can feel the weight of it. It was raining this hard...

"The day you died."

Yeah, the day I died. Fuck me Friday, you really can hear me.

"Yeah, I can Gab. If any of this is real, you, this…" Eddie says, tugging at himself, pointing at me, and then pulling at the grass below him.

"I can't tell what is real anymore. I mean, with all of the crazy shit happening, nothing seems real and I'm too fucked up all the time to be able to tell the difference anyhow. But yeah, it was raining like this the day you died…"

He chokes on his words, holding back the waterworks, like the words are razor blades mutilating their way up his throat and he is just dealing with the pain of them.

"…the day I was supposed to. The day I should've. But you Gab, you just had to take my place…"

He looks like he is holding back vomit now, choking on the words that burn their way up. Words he has been meaning to say for a very, very, very long time. Words that have decayed more in his stomach than I would have had I been buried—I was cremated for the record.

"I should be the ghost. I deserve to be. But even knowing that, truly comprehending that I'm alive, and you're dead, and should be living life to the fullest honoring your memory… your sacrifice. Instead, here I am, at a funeral trying to drink drugs out of the grass. I'm… fuck… I'm so sorry."

And with that, Eddie lets the memory out, and he faces it. And I follow him there and we both get to watch the movie of a memory that went straight to VHS release because of how bad it was.

It rained that day, just like today, and I mean just–like–today, exactly the same. I got home and you were gone.

"Yeah, but I left a note I was sure you wouldn't find until it was far too late."

But I found it almost immediately. However, I get why you thought I wouldn't find it because of how fucked up we both were back then and how we barely ever ate. Looking back, it was a good place if you didn't want it to be found right away. You'd left that fucking sad letter in...

"In the fridge..."

In the fridge...

But that day, unlike the others, I was hungry, and I remember that hunger. Which is weird because for the most part the dead completely forget what it is like to be hungry. But that day I was ravenous. I remember getting in and calling for you because I was worried. I had just heard that Jane had moved out and you weren't answering my calls.

"My cellphone was destroyed because it got too wet."

I knew something was wrong because before I even got to the fridge to hopefully find something to eat, which was a gamble in itself, I saw all of your clothes and your boots just lying in a bundle on the floor. Which normally wouldn't have been weird because the apartment was always a mess, but if you weren't home then what the hell were you wearing on your feet...

And that is what made my Spidey-senses exploded with warning. And I knew something was horribly wrong. But as worried as I was, I was still unbelievably hungry, and so I did the first thing a starving person does and looked to quench that thirst.

I opened the fridge, and there on the only edible morsel of food was a hand written letter...

"What happened next?"

I read that letter as I ate that corner store sandwich.

"And that is how you knew where I was that day..."

Yeah, as soon as I put two and two together, I took that sandwich and hopped into the first cab to get me to you.

"Wait, did you eat that sandwich?"

Of fucking course, I was starving.

"That was old as fuck."

Yeah, well I'm pretty sure that isn't what killed me. You want to tell this part? Fill me in with the parts I'm missing?

"I was standing in the rain, that heavy fucking rain, right on the platform, in socks and tighty-whities and nothing else, holding a flip phone and mumbling to myself. Everything was white, well off-white, but see through all the same. And I was staring down at my feet, watching my toes wiggle away, and I remember the cold and weight of it. But I remember, mostly, that this is it. I was at peace. I was ready to go. People had already started staring at me from the second I arrived.

They had their phones out recording and watching me. Not a single person tried to talk to me, not even one of them tried to contact help. Because they just wanted likes. This was something that could be viral. They didn't realize what I was trying to do. I didn't even. But as time went on and that rain beat down on me, I knew that this was it. But all my audience did was prove that I didn't have a place here anymore. I really just didn't want to live anymore. And I know that is depression. That is reaching rock bottom and then falling under the rock. I'd been living there for far too long and I didn't think after fucking up my life so heavily that I could climb my way back up, and I was just too exhausted and unwilling to try.

So, I did what any unstable, morbidly depressed, mostly naked and ashamed person in my place would've done. Just as the 1:11 train was speeding its way into the station, I jumped in front it..."

Yeah, but you never met it and all of its raw and unbelievably awesome power and force. You never got intimate with it. You never got to be fucked by it like I did, and know for certain, that nothing would ever fuck you like it fucked me because nothing can, and that is why I never got to be buried because all that was left of me wasn't WORTH burying...

"..."

To answer my question for you, no, you won't, and will never try too again.... Period.

I arrived—just in time, if you think my timing was right— on that platform and unlike all those fucking parasites, I did something. I tried to save my friend in his darkest moment from making a mistake he couldn't—fuck that, wouldn't—be able to unmake. Just as you walked off, I dove, pushing you out of the way, just in time to truly experience what it feels like to be obliterated by a train. And that was it. I saved you, and I was gone. Well at least, I don't know what happened immediately after but I know what eventually happened to you.

"Gab, I'm so..."

Eddie, fuck, instead of being sorry do something about it. Obviously, you have a purpose now, and you can't run from it because it is physically here. So, embrace it, and do good, and do the right thing. Be the person I've always loved and sacrificed my life for so you could keep living. Alright?

Eddie stands up, nodding, and for a moment he appears as though he has absorbed and learned from this very fucked up moment. But as quick as he rises, and after a second of standing proudly, he ruins it all by collapsing, landing face first into the wet muck below, and remaining there completely unconscious.

Luckily for him, Shaw somehow finds him there, because he just happens to be walking by at the right time in the right place, and rescues him from the facedown— passed out and drowning in the mud—position and successfully resuscitates him before paramedics arrive to do the rest.

I'm not going to try to even attack the unbelievably thin odds of someone finding him, let alone someone he knows, and that person is the only friend he has now. No, and let's not even try to argue whether this was supposed to happen or he is just really this lucky, dumb, and lucky.

However, at least, I actually feel better knowing that he realizes what happened and admitted it. And that you know the truth about me, and that, just maybe, I can still connect with people even though I'm dead.

CHAPTER 21

Eddie is connected to a machine that instead of quietly monitors his pulse, loudly reminds everyone close by that he still has one. Sadly, the only ones who would be comforted by the tune don't exist. No one is here. Eddie is alone. His emergency contact list consists of two people: one is dead; the other considers him already dead.

Shaw was here earlier but only stayed long enough to be sure he was alive. After that he left, found a bar, and got so drunk he ended up in a home that wasn't his and in a bed that wasn't his own and balls deep in a wife that wasn't the one he was married to. As soon as he came, he fell into a deep sleep, the kind void of dreams, and that is just the kind Shaw needed.

Eddie very slowly tries to move. His joints feel stiff and rusty, as though he is an ancient robot springing to life for the first time in a long time and trying to use his corroded appendages... actually that is just what Eddie is like, except, you know, human.

He gags as he pulls a ventilation tube up his throat and out of his mouth like a gigantic flaccid robot penis. And after he frees it, he laughs at the thought of that despite the pain and doesn't stop, that is, until a voice interrupts him. Someone is in the room.

As soon as he hears the voice every single hair on his body rises to a sharp point. There is something horribly familiar to it even when he wishes more than anything, he could forget it.

"Edward, you have been a nosey boy, have you not?"

Eddie is physically incapable of looking at the speaker, try as hard possible, he can't. He is afraid, and that fear is paralytic. It courses through his entire being. He can only see the person through his peripheral and that is enough to terrify him.

"You've been hunting us Eddie. And we can't have that. How'd you discover us?"

Eddie still can't speak. But he remembers Maple Street and Sebastian. Then suddenly a foreign feeling washes over him. Intrusive and penetrating, it feels like his memories are being forced forward and projected somewhere outside his mind. This strange feeling is so powerful and nauseating, if he could move, he'd puke. But instead, hot bile splashes its way up his throat before falling sickly back down his esophagus causing him to convulse uncontrollably.

"Oh, at a bar. Really? Was Sebastian really that careless? Doesn't surprise me. That's how you discovered our existence huh? Well, thanks for taking care of him but you didn't stop there, did you? The nightclub massacre... That is where you met me..."

Forced into the corner of his memory, Eddie returns to the scene like a cheesy flash back. Eddie watches himself from the shadows as he nearly dies fighting the vampires. He watches himself overcome all odds and then collect their belongings, his rewards, and he follows himself out the door. The pain in his skull gets far worse, as he watches himself face that formless being that tosses him out the window. But he is watching from over its shoulder and he still can't see it. And the more he tries to look at it, in this memory, the more it hurts.

He watches it toss him without touching him, a blurry appendage raised in his direction. And just watching it again brings a deeper fear of it. And then the memory stops. And he is back in the hospital bed.

If you don't remember the club, feel free to go back and reread it.

"I warned you then, but you didn't heed my warning. So, here we are. You now have to deal with the consequence of your actions. We have your friend. The pretty drug dealer..."

It shows Eddie the night they fucked, slowing every moment of their exchange to a stand still. So, he can watch each reactive expression of pure ecstasy and every shimmering, sweaty, glorious position change and alteration of rhythm and hardness before snatching the memory from him and replacing it with bitter darkness.

"You will never see her again. I guarantee this. But you can save her. And I know this is so cliché but your life for hers. Actually, no, you and that cop's life for hers."

Eddie's fear quickly turns to rage, overwhelming the cowardice and forces Eddie's gaze to snap at the stranger.

He looks at the stranger, his gaze burns hot, and his teeth smash into a deep grind. But when he looks, he can only see a blur. The person seems to shift in place. He can't make out any details, only a ghastly shape, moving in and out of what appears to be existence. Like the stranger is there for a second and gone in the next.

"Nod if you understand," it commands.

Eddie can't speak because under all that red-hot anger, he is still horrified. Sober and terrified. This is a strange feeling for Eddie. Even with his current state, he throws his head up and down in a makeshift nod.

"Good boy. We will send you the location. Don't keep us waiting."

The stranger vanishes and doesn't return. And with the stranger's final disappearance, Eddie can move. As though the horrible dread has evacuated his system. Not just emotionally or spiritually, but physically, as the first thing he can do when he moves is puke on his gown. Just as he relaxes slightly, another voice has him nearly leap out of his bed.

"Eddie, how're you feeling? You gave us quite the scare."

A young doctor stands in the doorway, reading over Eddie's chart.

"So, Eddie, why're you killing yourself?"

"Pardon doc?"

"Well, you have a drugstore running through your blood. And healthy people don't have that many toxins destroying their body and mind. If you keep this up, you'll be dead in a month. So Eddie, it might be time to seek help, is that something you're interested in?"

"Doc am I good to go?"

"Well, I'd like to keep you here for observation but you're technically free to go."

"Well how 'bout you give me some pamphlets and I'll consider rehab? But I gotta be somewhere yesterday."

"I really think, and this is in your best interest, that you stay here and get the help you desperately need."

"I appreciate the concern but someone needs me and I'm not going to let her down."

Eddie is already sitting up, shakily, but he has enough energy and drive to get moving.

Eddie runs out of the room dressing as he goes, not bothering to take off the hospital gown. Instead, he just pulls his pants on under, jumping into them one leg at a time through the hospital hallways. As he exits, he tries calling Shaw but his phone keeps going to voicemail. Finally, exhausted, Eddie leaves one long frantic message.

"Shaw, Eddie here. Uh, thanks for taking me to the hospital. Sorry about that. Listen, they have Alexi. The vampires, they said we have to go to them if we want her to live. I'm headed to her apartment right now. Maybe I can find some, I don't know, fucking clues or something. Just meet me there. I'll text you the address..."

Eddie has a brief moment of humanity before hanging up where he wants to warn Shaw, at least to give him the choice of going straight into a trap, but instead just hangs up.

After a short cab ride, Eddie pops out in front of Alexi's apartment. He climbs the stairs and jams the buzzer to her apartment for longer than needed, several seconds longer to be exact. And then he waits. Nothing. He does it again and again. Nothing. *Shit.* He leaps down the stairs and heads around the building looking for a fire escape and he's in luck, an archaic fire escape rigidly runs up the side of the building and leads right to her living room window. After several terribly unsuccessful attempts to jump, he finally catches the collapsing metal ladder and pulls it down as it creaks rust flakes raining down into Eddie's eyes and mouth. He winces and wipes the flakes away and spits them out as he clumsily scales the ladder.

When Eddie finally reaches his destination, Alexi's window, he dives through the opening completely ignoring every possible consequence of plunging head first into the unknown. *Good old Eddie.*

Before Eddie's hands can find a stable place to land and prepare for the rest of his weight to follow, he is halted mid-leap and captured by the throat by just a hand, a very large and strong hand.

Eddie is caught like a weak fly ball at a softball game and tossed effortlessly across Alexi's apartment. But unlike that easily caught softball, he is still in play and more important than ever.

Eddie recovers rapidly from being tossed from Alexi's window by Chester Day. However, Eddie quickly assesses the situation and worries about Tom Morrow and what he is going to do, because he doesn't look like he is all there. Actually, him and Chester both wear that same empty expression entirely. They usually look like pair of towering, throbbing, steroid over-using, under stimulated, meat-headed morons. Only now they look like towering, throbbing, steroid over-using, under stimulated, meat-headed morons with no consciousness.

Tom squeezes Eddie's throat so hard it feels as though his head is going to pop off. Eddie does his Sunday best to fight back, flailing haymakers that land empty and softly on Tom's chin. Tom walks Eddie across the living room and body slams him on that gigantic crystal table Alexi loves so much sending a mushroom cloud of cocaine into the air.

If he had wind left in his lungs, he would've been completely winded, but you know, being choked doesn't leave much. Tom climbs on top of Eddie and begins to press down harder—if it already wasn't hard enough—he squeezes the last little bits of precious oxygen he has left. As the cloud settles, drugs find their way into Eddie's eyes and mouth and nose, and it burns. Eddie's pupils dilate from either drug dosing or absolute oxygen deprivation and with that, his survival instincts—better late than never, I guess—kick in. Eddie's hands scratch across the smooth surface searching for something to use as a weapon. When his hand finds it, an equally gigantic crystal ashtray, he wastes no time and brings it as hard as he can across Tom's head. It shatters explosively raining crystal shards, cigarette butts, roaches, and black ashes across the room. Tom falls on to the couch with a geyser of blood following him from a fresh wound that spans the right side of his skull.

Eddie shoots up, sucking in as much air as he can, like when you burst free of a watery prison after being under for too long. Coughing violently, he tries to move, but he is still very weak. Sadly, he doesn't get time to recover. Tom is replaced almost immediately by Chester. And Eddie barely sees him coming, and before losing oxygen again, Eddie sighs, exhaling a word:

"Fuck."

Chester's speed is uncanny for someone that big and Eddie thinks how unfair that is, and how he has to be using steroids but he reminds himself none of that matters. Too bad for Eddie, but in his weakness and his desperate attempt to recover, he's paralyzed as Chester lands on him from a massive leap. Chester's colossal hand replaces Tom's, assuming its place on Eddie's throat possessively, like he owns it, and now he wants to destroy his property.

As Chester crushes the life from Eddie, Eddie's eyes begin to swell like engorged balloons just before they pop. His lips quiver and smile over with white foam as he desperately attempts to breath but Chester's weight is impossibly heavy, like the gravity of a collapsing star, his weight is a terrible void sucking everything down with it. Just before Eddie blacks out for good in a terrible exit left of life, Shaw interferes by showing up in the "Knick of Time". *I know it's an expression, but who is this Knick and why is he always on time?*

The front door flies open but Eddie doesn't notice. He can barely make out the sounds around him. Everything is muffled and distant like he's under water again. He somehow figures out that the noises are orders. Someone is telling Chester to stop. He doesn't stop. Then there is a very loud bang that rings through Eddie's ears echoing through his skull.

A bullet hungrily eats its way through Chester's elbow, tearing sinew into spaghetti and slurping it up. Chester's arm slingshots with impact, sickly flicking back the wrong way, but immediately and reflexively releasing Eddie from death's horrible embrace. *And again, I know the expression, and let me tell you there is nothing sweet about death "embracing" you. Shove the poetry somewhere else, like maybe your ass cause it certainly doesn't belong here.*

Eddie shoots up greedily sucking in air, lapping it down so quickly it's like he thinks the whole world is running out of air and he wants the last of it for himself.

Meanwhile, Chester creepily hasn't made a sound. Instead, he absentmindedly stares at the mess that is his appendage. Dead-eyed and dopey, he simply turns his attention from his arm, and glances down at Eddie as though he is about to continue his murderous assault. He freezes momentarily from brain inactivity and pauses his actions entirely, as though remote-controlled and awaiting instructions. He rockets from Eddie and turns, so suddenly, and he charges at Shaw—apparently the orders were entered and received—and before Shaw can react the Chester train hits him.

They tumble backward past the shattered door, down into the stairwell into a human ball, head over feet, end over end. In the chaos, Shaw somehow manages to prepare himself for the impact that the bottom of the stairs brings, and braces. Unfortunately for our brute, he isn't thinking, and he goes head first through that plate glass door at the front of the building, knocking him out. His head sticks out of a sharp hole, slicing a crown of tiny cuts around his head that drool blood dribbling down over his filthy maw. Shaw flinches as rises and when he goes to move his arm, he screams as red-hot pain tears from his shoulder down his arm. He knows it is badly dislocated, and he knows what to do, but he doesn't want to do it.

"Eddie!"

Eddie lights a joint he finds on the floor and takes a deep breath as he eyes a large pile of blow, sitting like a little mountain on the edge of the crystal table.

"What?"

"I need your help?"

"With Chester?"

Eddie exhales a plume of smoke deeply from his mouth and nose, like a dragon preparing its oncoming inferno.

"No, it's my shoulder, I need help relocating."

"Ew, no. That's hella gross."

Eddie hits the joint in quick repetition, taking little puffs.

"Eddie. Get your fucking ass down here!"

Eddie greedily climbs that snowy mountain, snorting it all, before rising with a synthetic second wind—hell, more like a second hurricane—before energetically bounding down the stairs to assist Shaw with his wound.

At the base of the stairs, with Shaw's instructions, they barbarically attempt to reset Shaw's shoulder. When they do Shaw makes a noise so alien it thoroughly surprises Eddie. But Shaw and his foreign noise and all its thunder are overshadowed by Chester talking to them. That is because Chester is still so obviously unconscious and the voice that emanates from his vocals isn't his own.

"Eddie, can you get any more predictable?"

Eddie and Shaw, still mid-embrace from resetting his shoulder, just stare down at the unconscious hulk clearly being used as dummy by a distant ventriloquist.

"We are waiting for you at the Devlin heights complex in the central tower. Come soon. We're impatient and hungry and she looks delicious."

Chester goes limp. Returning to the nonconscious dying mass he was moments ago.

"What in the sideways love of fuck was that?" Shaw cries out, shaking Eddie.

"You see the shit I've been dealing with? Shaw…" Eddie feels that humanity coming on and he desperately fights it.

"If you wanna back out now, I get it, but could you at least drop me off?"

Shaw, wide eyed and almost hysterically laughing, gives him another shake like he is a present on Christmas, like when you're not sure of what it is but maybe by shaking it you can get a read on its contents.

Never works.

"Are you fucking kidding me? Naw. We're seeing this out. I can't just back out now. This is all real. I mean, really real. And I'm not crazy, I know that for sure now, and that is good enough for me. I know no one is going to believe this, and it'll take too long to try and convince anyone that it is. And even if we ever could, it would be far too late. But right now. Right now, we can see this through, like it or not, sane or insane; right now, we don't have the time or choice to do anything else but finish this."

Shaw charges out of the building, driven by a purpose Eddie doesn't understand and maybe can't. The very reason Shaw became a cop was to uphold the law, stand for good, and punish evil. This is Shaw's hang up: to do what is right and just. And he truly believes this is it, his call to action. This calling, if you will, is what Shaw has been waiting his whole life for and he'll be damned if he doesn't answer it.

They both stare out at the road ahead and watch the darkness eat the median, gobbling one yellow brick at a time. Then suddenly without warning, the brick becomes one yellow solid line. That line is, as we all know, is something we can't cross. You're stuck in this lane. You can't pass. You're stuck following it. Just like the path Eddie and Shaw are on.

CHAPTER 22

Sense and sanity left behind, Eddie and Shaw arrive at Devlin heights and rush heart first into the mix. This is the non-linear record of that scenario...

Eddie stares up at the ceiling, trying to guess its age by the era of its design, thinking about the changing popularities of ceiling patterns by the decades.

Freshly winded—which seems to be a common thing for Eddie nowadays— from an assault. Eddie, instead of reacting appropriately, as always dissociates cognitively, and hopes for the best. Whenever conflict arises this is his format and he follows it without deviation every time, regardless of the seriousness of the situation.

It doesn't matter if the scenario is life or death or just a mild inconvenience, to him, the reaction is always the same.

However, this time, what caused him to be laid out and winded staring at the ceiling is one of those super serious situations that Eddie needs to take for what it is.

Eddie remains limp as he is lifted from the ground with ease by a female vampire who looks like a European anorexic runway model. Her expression seems frozen in what I can only describe as "exhausted bitch face", her image locked as though continuously and completely unimpressed. Her skin is translucent like skim milk and under its surface courses empty lime green veins that snake throughout her frame hiding some terrible impossible strength. Her eye sockets are dark and hollow, coated in deep purple eyeliner that make the pale whites of her eyes pop, leaving pins for pupils. Her face is boarded by a concealer that blends perfectly with her lactose complexion. As she lifts Eddie, a smile creeps across her scarlet stained lips, emulating only pure joy in his peril.

She raises him high above her head before dropping him spine first onto her jagged and completely unpadded knee. What follows on impact can only be described as a sick popping sound that you can only emulate when you have worked with your hands for your entire life and decide to finally crack your knuckles for the very first time ever. Try to imagine that sound. Like the sound of walking across a bunch of dry empty chitinous remains.

Eddie just grunts, yes, just grunts, ignoring the pain and possible fracture damage he has just sustained. However, it doesn't hurt as bad as it sounded. He just rolls with it. He is so numb and exhausted that pain is on call and probably won't show up until tomorrow, that is, if he'll see tomorrow.

She has been beating on Eddie for the better part of an hour and she actually appears tired, if that is possible, but she is showing signs of exhaustion. Through a bloodied toothy grin Eddie smiles proudly with the idea that he is wearing her down and she is exactly where he wants her to be. She lifts Eddie from the ground, pulling him to her face.

"Alright, enough of this, I don't care that I'm supposed to keep you alive. I'm hungry and no one said that you had to be in one pie..." Eddie interrupts her by spitting a large amount of blood and mucus into her mouth mid-sentence, choking her words off with a gag. Disgusted, she reactively flings him across the room and he sticks into the drywall before crashing down to the floor pulling parts of it with him.

She hacks out his mouth mess onto the ground, coughing, before drawing a deep breath to speak.

"You disgusting piece of shit."

"You are what you eat sugar tits."

"I didn't take you for the self-deprecating type hun," she says wiping her mouth, before charging toward Eddie like a ravenous lioness. She throws her leg like she is swinging an axe at wood, and clips him in the chin. He nearly does a back flip before planking against the wall, finally sliding back to the ground. He spits a tooth out in a thick red saliva pond that lingers like a tiny waterfall against his chin, before staring up at her, smiling through the agony.

"Ok enough of this, I've worked up quite the appetite."

She walks toward her purse, which is an oversized and overpriced satchel. It is the size of a canvas grocery bag but bright red and made of synthetic leather. It bares a logo that Eddie recognizes as designer and he knows it costs about two months' rent which makes no sense whatsoever to him. She digs through it, searching for something. He laughs through a bloody cough sending a crimson cloud painting the tiles beneath his face.

"What's so funny asshat?" she says, not turning away from the expedition within her purse.

"That you're carrying around your medicine cabinet in that overpriced ugly sack. You carry all these things in case you need them, but when you need them, you can't find them because you have too much shit in it. And while you're digging through it looking for the one thing that you need, you have given me enough time to recover..."

She pulls herself away from her search viciously quick and looks at a bloody stain where Eddie was sprawled out a moment ago. As she whips her head around looking for him, her hungry gaze is greeted and immediately and permanently ended by the head of a wooden bat skewered with jagged rusty nails. Eddie is right there, beside her, swinging at her head with such raw torque that he could jump-start a car engine.

The impact of the bat crushes her orbital bones, shattering them, and the nails follow in suit stealing her retinas, blinding her. Both her eyes pop and spew a thick ichor. She lets out a sound that mimics a cat when you step on its tail. *Not that I'm going around stepping on cats' tails or anything...come on...*

Stunned, she drops to her knees and those unpadded caps make the sound of two sticks hitting a pounding drum when they strike the tiles under them. As she goes to scream again, she is squelched by the second and much more vicious strike of the savage weapon. Eddie swings it with such power and precision that upon impact it instantly collapses her septum and takes her upper row of teeth with it. She crumbles, falling face—well, what's left of her face—first into the floor. Her face unfolds like when you pull Plasticine apart, like opening a book, before finally exploding like confetti if confetti was made of bone, teeth, and blood.

Without pause, Eddie continues swinging. He brings the same brutality to the back of her neck—where neck meets skull. He brings that bat down with the force of a thousand frustrated virgins having sex for the first time; unnecessarily precise and uncannily quick. That impact completely obliterates her head leaving no sign that a solid object was once attached to the remaining stringy sinew of her neck trapped by his bat.

Eddie falls backwards, gasping. Exhausted he falls on his tailbone, missing his ass fat to pad his fall completely. And through his panicked gasps, he gets out one word, and I bet you can guess what that word is.

"Fuck."

Except the f dribbles out, and as he gains oxygen he holds onto the u for several seconds before closing the word out hard on the ck.

"I told you that you should just let me by."

An hour ago...

Shaw and Eddie bound up the staircase of one of the abandoned buildings of the Devlin heights projects. Eddie seems like he knows exactly where he is going so Shaw follows closely without question.

The Devlin heights projects were four higher-class condominium buildings erected in a low-income area in hopes to gentrify the area. It was never finished because the company building it overshot their budget, and their investors pulled out. They ended up declaring bankruptcy and the city paid the bill. To this day the city is still trying to finish the contract.

They enter the foyer, a massive empty room, stricken of furniture similar to Eddie's apartment with the exception of a reception desk. Shaw shines his light from side to side, examining the space; his flashlight sits perched and mounted on the end of a brand new m4 tactical shotgun. He has a belt of shells over his shoulder and his trusty sidearm, with several clips on his waste. He wears a tactical vest, which conveniently protects his neck. Eddie just has his trusty duffle bag of home-made weapons: the half baseball bat which now has rusty nails jammed through it. A cross shaped into a stake which likes a wooden knife. A vile of holy water that Eddie had blessed by a priest which is actually holy water Eddie just filled with a water bottle. A bunch of silver necklaces. A carton of salt. And of course, he is wearing his vampire slaying gear—a piss poor combination of hockey, baseball, and football protective gear poorly pieced together.

"Okay Eddie, lead the way."

"I don't know man; your guess is as good as mine."

"Are you fucking kidding me?"

"Well, I mean, I was just following..."

Eddie is interrupted mid-sentence by a single shrill "ding" sound. Both of them turn their attention to its source. Out of the three elevators, one of them opens following that noise. A flickering light illuminates the foyer from its interior, beckoning them.

Eddie smiles, "Looks like the universe has just shown us the way."

"Eddie, seriously? This is for sure a trap," Shaw snaps.

"Oh yeah, obvs. But at least we know where to go now."

Shaw can't speak because he is floored by how laid-back Eddie is being about all of this, instead he just blinks, bows, and extends Eddie the courtesy of going in first.

Eddie walks toward the elevator. Shaw follows shaking his head. He has realized the gravity of Eddie's sheer arrogance and insanity, which, in turn has him questioning his own resolve. But he sheds the doubt because he quickly accepts that he has always known this since the madness began. He knows he can fight the supernatural and defeat it, but he can't win a fight of logic where logic doesn't exist. He leaves the philosophical debates in that empty lobby.

They enter the elevator as cautiously as one can when entering a guaranteed trap. The doors close behind them and the elevator jerks to a start, ascending. A speaker kicks on, shorting in and out, playing Poison's hit song: *Every Rose has its Thorn.*

Eddie pops two painkillers, swallowing them dryly. Shaw begins sweating. Eddie pulls his keys from his pocket and does a very large bump of cocaine from his apartment key, snorting it hungrily.

"Eddie, are you fucking kidding me? I'm still a cop!"

"Dude. We're going to kill a bunch of vampires. Give me a fucking break, alright? I don't have a gun. Wait, can I have a gun?"

"Absolutely-fucking-not."

"Fine…"

Eddie pouts like a child, and Shaw briefly reconsiders his decision, that is until Eddie rubs his gums with leftovers from the end of his key. Shaw cements he has made the right decision.

They stand silent for several moments before breaking the silence, as both of them begin to sing the hit song. The guitar rings out hauntingly before Brett Michaels begins to sing and the two of them join.

"We both lie silently still in the dead of the night…" Shaw.

"Although we both lie close together, we feel miles apart inside…" Eddie.

"Was it something I said, or something I did, did my words not come out right… though I tried not to hurt you… though I tried…" Eddie and Shaw now hold the song synchronously, belting out loudly together coming into the chorus.

"Just like every rose…"

They both immediately stop singing as the elevator stops suddenly, the lights flicker off and on, and the doors lurch slowly open exposing a dimly lit hallway. They both stride out in tandem.

The hallway seems to stretch on endlessly, every few feet a door with a number on it. A number marking an apartment no one is living in, or at least, they shouldn't be living in.

The hallway ends in a common area. The common area was intended for condo owners to share a small space to get to know their neighbors. It was supposed to have a small wishing pool in its center and several lounging couches. Surrounded by greenery: a proposed hydroponic garden where they could have a community grow-op for their vegetables. Instead, replacing it, a graveyard of abandoned plans and lost dreams.

In the middle of the empty room, right in the center of that half constructed wishing pool, sits a single woman on a single chair. She looks like a mannequin: synthetic plastic, waiting to be molded. That is until she robotically springs to life. She looks up, cracking a lazy smile—more of a smirk.

"Mister Red, Mister Calamus. We've been expecting you."

"Okay fuck this." Eddie laughs nervously.

"Stand up slowly and place your hands on your head," Shaw growls.

"Shaw, man, she isn't going to comply," Eddie laughs.

"Shut up Eddie."

She begins to rise, but she does it at a tortoise-like pace, as though standing for the first time in a long time, or for the first time.

"Man, shoot her."

"EDDIE SHUT UP."

"Listen lady, if you don't let us pass, he is going to fuck your dress up with this shotgun, so you should just let us pass."

As Eddie is finishing his sentence, it is halted completely by a very hard kick to his groin. He was trying to say: "let us pass" but it sounds more like "lettuce pass" as the air is forcibly punted from his testicles that now find home in his abdomen.

She moved in the blink of an eye - fuck that, a blink couldn't even catch how fast she made it from where she was just standing to where she is now.

Shaw turns his shotgun toward her and is about to fire but something steals his attention. He hears his ex-wife crying out for him.

Shaw sprints off, leaving Eddie to fend for himself.

Now you're caught up.

Shaw bounds down a hallway, toward his ex-wife's voice. He kicks open a closed door with his shotgun raised.

The door splinters with his weight and he bursts into the room.

The room is dark, actually it is what can only be described as absolute darkness, except for its center. A single overhead light casts down a perfect halo of light into its core where his ex-wife Hannah stands in its middle.

She wears her wedding dress, but the dress is frayed, aged and damaged, only shredded rags remain barely covering her quivering frame. Shaw lowers his shotgun, tears well like ponds in his lids, and his face contorts with sorrow.

"Cal. I'm so scared."

Shaw steps forward, passively. Tears freefall running down the sides of his nose.

"Booboo, it's okay. I'm here. I'm not going anywhere. It's okay. I promise. I won't go anywhere.

Okay. Prepare for a hard, un-lubricated ass-fuckery to the feels. Shaw's wife is dead, very dead, long dead. She died of cancer, like the bad cancer. Like the kind of cancer that has the lowest possible survivability: the pancreatic kind. It spreads so rapidly and withers away its host completely before painfully killing them. The kind of cancer that all other cancers consider too harsh. Yeah, she died of that cancer. Shaw's wife died of the worst possible version of cancer that exists, but it took way too long to kill her. She suffered all the way till her body and soul gave up. But what's worse is that along the way of her impossibly slow and extremely painful demise, Shaw stopped being there. He stopped visiting. He left her to die alone. He isn't proud of it. He hates himself for it. But he couldn't stomach watching her wither away. If you have ever watched someone eaten, consumed and changed to the point where you can't recognize them. Then finally taken by the cancer, but as slowly as time possibly can slow to, then you may sympathize but if you haven't experienced that horror, then and only then can you consider Shaw to be a terrible fucking piece of shit...

"You left me! You left me to die!" she screams.

Shaw stops dead in his tracks, still armed, but completely defenseless mentally. He lowers his weapon but doesn't let it go fully. Somewhere in Shaw's subconscious is screaming that this is a ruse and that whatever is in front of him isn't Hannah and cannot be. But that isn't how the conscious works. Just like cancer, the conscious brain eats away at all your actions and decisions without logic. Your own mind is sometimes your worst enemy. Because even though you know the answer to the problem, you'll do everything to find any other explanation before you accept that what is, is it, especially when you're trying to avoid the pain of losing someone.

"Han, I'm so sorry. I know that doesn't mean much, but I am. I just couldn't do anything. I couldn't watch anymore. There was nothing I could've done."

"YOU SHOULD'VE BEEN THERE!"

The Hannah impersonator shrieks so powerfully that the dress that is barely there obliterates, exposing her decaying, cancer ridden, naked skeletal frame and it also forcefully pushes Shaw back.

What Shaw doesn't see, because a supernatural force is hypnotizing him, is that the person speaking isn't Hannah. It's Tess.

You remember Tess, right? Oh, you don't? Tess was the girl who went down on Eddie at the beginning of the story. The one scene I discontinued due to adult content. The cocksucker. And man, she really is...

And Tess isn't alone. The room is crowded with bodies. Bodies strapped to what look like dairy milking machines, but they aren't extracting milk, they're extracting blood. And attached to the machines are human beings, alive, but drugged. Instead of extracting milk from utters, they're sucking blood from veins via needles placed in the arteries. But for the comatose males, they have an additional extraction point; there are devices attached to their dicks and they are sucking semen from them. The males are being milked like cows.

Semen is blood btw. Look it up.

Shaw can't see any of this. All Shaw can see is his wife, crying and screaming, standing naked; living in the state that she died alone in, in the middle of the room.

"Han. Fuck. I'm so sorry. I just. I just couldn't watch anymore. Hannah, I'm so sorry..."

"You left me. You left me to die alone. Do you have any idea what it's like to be that alone? You just stopped coming one day. No explanation. I would've understood. But you just disappeared. How the fuck do you live with yourself?"

Shaw falls to his knees sobbing, relieving himself of his weapon, and begins to crawl towards what he thinks is his wife. Tess in turn approaches and just before she reaches Shaw, intending to snap his neck, Eddie crashes the party.

Eddie comes in flying and swinging. He crushes Tess's face with his bat in one fluent swing. It eradicates her flawless porcelain perfect face in one hit. Leaving a mess of a maw: her jaw hangs limply, dislocated, and missing most of the perfect teeth it had. Stunned, Tess loses her footing, concentration, and her face, and in-turn the ability to keep the illusion captivating Shaw.

However, Shaw has just seen his dying ex-wife have her jaw cleaved off her face and crumble after the blow. Instantly and appropriately, Shaw goes after Eddie, strangling him, but as the fog of illusion begins to fade and he can see things the way they actually are, he immediately releases him.

Eddie, confused by the entire situation, didn't fight Shaw when he started to choke him, but he does speak as soon as he is granted the air to do so when Shaw lets go.

"Did I just ruin a Hallmark moment?"

Shaw returns to reality and refocuses. He instantly recognizes that Hannah wasn't there, and this was a sick horrible spell cast by whatever the fuck is stumbling in front of him in a room filled with human cattle. He looks for his weapon.

Tess lets out a sound so guttural and alien that it immediately erases the daze Shaw fights to shake from. The sound resembles a tiger's roar: loud and bestial but then it quickly morphs into what sounds like that same tiger roaring as its being slowly fed into a large mechanical meat grinder.

With the change of the sound she releases, she too changes from a beautiful woman into something else entirely. She shakes her broken dangling jaw from side to side. Her chin cracks off and falls, leaving an open void of hanging sinew and flesh. A large boney proboscis-shaped appendage springs forth, unraveling like a fruit rollup before solidifying like an erection. Her shoulders sickly pop, cracking out and upward as her arms seem to split in half and become large leathery wings. Her shirt tears open as she changes, exposing her once perfect perky c-cup borderline d-cup breasts and converting them into something else that now hang sickly, looking like two bags of ground beef shoved inside clear plastic bags. Her short shorts split off as her calves expand and her legs crack, inverting at the knees, before ending at her feet. They split open at her ankles, tearing across her flesh like a fissure on rock before a rockslide, before finally exposing raptor like talons that replace her toes that shred through and shed her shoes.

This creature is like a cross between the mythological harpy that had a terrible one-night stand with a bat and then their offspring fell into the teleportation machine from the movie *The Fly* but instead of being genetically crossbred with a fly, a mosquito got there first and was like: "I got this."

The creature turns its attention on Eddie, who is now bent over vomiting, holding his hands up in the time out motion. Its beady eyes bulge out as though it is shocked by Eddie's actions. It steps back as though recoiling in confusion awaiting an explanation. Shaw looks at his shotgun that is just behind the creature and considers diving for it while this thing is distracted.

"Talk about hiding your true self, get fucked, really cause this takes the cake..." Eddie says through a gag, swallowing the vomit back before continuing. "I mean, really, Tess. This is pushing the hashtag no makeup, all natural, sorry not sorry movement too far. Like come on. You're fucking hideous. And I am hashtag sorry not fucking sorry for saying so."

As Eddie finishes his rant, the creature formally known as Tess, enraged, charges him, but he doesn't flinch, not at all. No, Eddie being Eddie, instead charges toward it. He gets his hands up that are protected by those bulky mismatched hockey gloves, and he catches that spear of a proboscis and he just enjoys the ride. He holds on as the Tess creature smashes into the wall behind him, all the while he holds on for dear life but completely avoids being impaled by it. The Tess creature has lanced the wall, struggling with Eddie attached to her head as she wrenches herself free.

Shaw runs and dives toward his shotgun, avoiding the locomotive charge of the Tess creature completely. Within his dive and slide he rescues his shotgun, and while still sliding turns on his back and releases the entire capacity of the shotgun in several fiery draconic breath-like bursts into the creature's back, shredding its arm-wings' leathery canopy into tattered, hole ridden, bloody ripped denim. He runs out of ammo as he hits the far wall, holding the smoking boom-stick smiling and sweating.

The Tess creature falls to one knee, freeing itself, but it begins to convert to the beautiful girl as it bleeds out heavily. Tess whimpers, wavers, and then falls flat motionlessly. Eddie reaches down lifting her arm before letting it go. It drops instantly. No resistance, just dead weight.

Eddie smiles his "I'm way too okay with what just went down" smile and silently raises his oversized fist before struggling to give a thumbs up to Shaw.

Tess begins to dissolve leaving behind the remaining rags of clothes she had on. And with that, Tess is dead, or rather, destroyed. Eddie reaches down and rescues her belongings: her hello kitty cellphone, crimson red lipstick, a hot-rod red straight razor, a wad of cash, and a single bronze key with a key-tag with the words "The Down" in big bold black font.

CHAPTER 23

Eddie and Shaw herd dozens of dazed and confused freshly freed human cattle in an orderly fashion toward the exits the best they can. Doing their best to keep the chaos and questions to a minimum to hurry their escape. The freshly freed don't argue as somewhere deep down their instincts have taken over and they know that they are in danger as long as they remain, so they follow because that same instinct tells them that these two are leading them away from danger.

We call it a gut feeling but it's more. It's survival instinct that we have forgotten through eons of evolution, and we now ignore it regularly but deep, deep down, it is still there and it is always right when it comes to things being wrong. Try as we might to separate ourselves from animals, when it really counts, we are still just that. We are creatures of instinct, no different from any other animal in that regard. You can't take the animal instinct out of human beings no matter how hard you try. And all things considered, that isn't so bad, is it?

Cheers to instincts, am I right?

After Shaw and Eddie are sure they have freed everyone, watching the last bunch silently thank them from the elevator before the doors close leaving them behind, Eddie breaks the silence.

"They still have Alexi."

"Are you sure?"

"Sure, as shit boss."

"Fuck."

"Damn right, that also means we haven't met the leader. The patriarch or whatever."

"The patriarch?"

"Yeah, according to the file, if we 86 the patriarch... all of them die."

"What file? And 86? The fuck?"

"Shaw catch up, damn. The research file that the team compiled on all things that bump in the night. Our monster manual if you will. And 86 is a term for when you kill something."

Shaw sighs and shrugs off Eddie and his condescending tone and humors him.

"Okay, so where do we find this patriarch and how do we kill it? And if we can kill it, how are we sure that the others will die?"

Eddie looks up to the left, pondering.

"Those are the right questions, none of which I have answers for currently, but I bet my last buck if we search this shit hole, we will at least answer one of them."

"Eddie, this isn't a game. You know that, right? Please tell me you know how fucking serious all of this is?"

"Of course, I know it's not a game. We have to trust the 'intel' though."

Shaw in that moment realizes what he is talking about when he is referring to the "intel" and nearly gets sick, but rage takes over before he can.

"Are you fucking kidding me? You mean the tabletop kids from apartment 3B?"

"Yeah, they put a lot of time and effort compiling this information for us. So, we would know what we were fighting."

"Eddie. For the love of sweet fuck everything. Please tell me you understand that no matter the time and effort they spent that it doesn't for sure mean that everything in that file or-, fuck that, that anything in that file is accurate? Like, please, you understand that they just hunted down stories and that those stories are just that, stories. And that we are in some serious shit and you need to come back to earth right now because we are blind."

"Alright Shaw, I'm not a complete fucking moron. I realize that, but hey, as far as I knew before all this shit, is that this shit wasn't real, and it was all just stories. So now that we know that these aren't just stories, maybe just fucking maybe, those stories are not just stories, right?"

Shaw is speechless. In this moment he realizes that Eddie is making sense. And he just purses his lips and nods his head in recognition of Eddie's point.

"So, Eddie, what do we do?"

"Uh…" Eddie stammers and then suddenly erupts expressively.

Eddie has an idea and Shaw sees him have it, like he has a cartoon light bulb hovering over his head. Eddie reaches into his pocket and opens Tess's cellphone.

Eddie searches her text history microscopically analyzing each one like a jealous psycho boyfriend before stumbling on a single conversation that he obsesses over.

Tess: Are you sure this is a good idea?

Mr. Dreamy: Yes, I'm sure. He's just a lucky bug that knows the web is dangerous. But flies can't say no to shit and she is the shit.

Tess: Wtf are you talking about? Cryptic much?

Mr. Dreamy: You play your part and everything will work out.

Tess: Ok, srsly though, wtf is my part?

Mr. Dreamy: Keep him busy, you're good at that, aren't you? 8-----D 0:

Tess: Fuck you. You didn't ever complain.

Mr. Dreamy: Hello Eddie, you have made it this far. Congratulations.

Tess: Wtf r u talking about?

Mr. Dreamy: I think it's time we met face to face. You probably have Tess's key. Use it in the elevator to reach the floor under the basement. We'll be waiting.

Tess: Who r u talking 2? U r texting me still.

Mr. Dreamy: Goodbye Tess.

Tess: Brb, the cop is here. Ttyl. <3

Eddie closes the phone and begins to hyperventilate. Shaw grabs him by the shoulders lightly trying to comfort him because he is visibly disturbed by what he read.

"Eddie, talk to me?"

"Shaw, we're fucked."

"How so? We made it this far, haven't we? Haven't we always been fucked?"

"No man, this is different."

"How? Don't chicken out now Eddie."

"He, or whatever it is, knows we're coming but it knows we were coming before we were coming."

"What? Eddie. You're making less sense than you usually do."

"It was texting me in a conversation it was having with Tess but before we showed up, like it already knew the outcome. It can see through time..."

"Or Eddie, maybe, just maybe it is presumptuous and it bet on you instead of Tess. Instead of it being all knowing, maybe it just knew that you would prevail and Tess would fail."

Eddie's expression sours to the point where his whole face is completely following his disbelief with a squint, like he is doing a bad impression of Robert De Niro.

That is when Shaw drops a logic bomb on Eddie because he—or at least he thinks he has—worked it all out.

"Eddie. For fuck sakes practice what you preach. Is it that unlikely that a supernatural creature would have the intelligence to bet on you—an unlikely enemy that despite all odds continues to prevail—instead of his minions that have been defeated by the likes of you?"

"Ouch. But I get what you're saying..."

"I hope so. Because what is a more likely scenario?" Shaw takes a couple of just incase inhales to pad his lungs with the air they need to finish a speech.

"Is it that hard to believe that a super intelligent predator who until very fucking recently, we all believed to be only fiction, is in fact very real, and has continued to exist. Probably by playing it super safe and to keeping that illusion. Probably doing so by carefully choosing who knows the truth and who helps continue the species. Which has gone on year by year, decade by decade, generation by generation, until it had to deal with our situation. It is forced to pass that torch to the most available option.

Consider that our generation is almost entirely composed of self-involved, self-depreciating, anti-social, extremely sensitive, attention deficit hyperactive disorder having cannon fodder. Every single one of them blaming everyone else for the way things are instead of taking responsibility for it and trying to change it. All while sharing every waking moment with the world via the internet. Making it choose the best of very bad situation. Therefore, that creature does what it has always done to survive and passes the flame.

And that would make sense...

Or is it more likely, that in our world, a god-like creature exists who can see through time—is all knowing— but still insists on keeping the company of the same fuck ups even though it knows the outcome? And is worried about a fucking junkie and washed up sell out cop exposing it.

What is more likely Eddie? Really?"

Eddie takes the blow. But it doesn't imprint or dig deep. It doesn't go anywhere. This is how addicts work. They are so out of it that even when confronted by the absolute solid truth of just how far gone they are, even if only momentarily, it is immediately deflected and left unrealized because the addiction takes over.

The hunger (addiction) is just that, ravenous, and feeding it further becomes the sole drive. Eddie and his enemy share one common trait, an insatiable hunger that dominates every facet of their being. They both require something to survive and will do anything to satiate that appetite.

But Eddie's hunger is different.

They need blood to survive, I think, they kill to feed and by feeding they survive.

Eddie doesn't need the drugs or the booze. He can live without all that shit.

Eddie has lied, cheated, stolen, and betrayed for his hunger but he has never killed. But he didn't need to do all that other shit.

They may share a hunger that at first glance appears identical in nature but if you get "all philosophical" about it, their needs, although similar in what they'll do to feed them, are in fact— without a doubt— very, so inconceivably different.

One is a creature feeding through killing but does so to survive.

The other is a creature that is willing to do anything to feed that hunger, no matter the cost, but continues to feed even though it knows it doesn't need to, to survive.

Holy fuck... is Eddie the monster?

Tess's phone buzzes with a text message. Eddie nervously removes it from his pocket and looks at it. He nearly crumbles under its sheer capacity. The message is from Mr. Dreamy, and it reads:

"I'm down here waiting... come on down."

The "come on down" vocalizes inside Eddie's head like he is a contestant on a game show, but he actually hears the voice. The voice belongs to the creature that visited him in the hospital, but this time its tone is hauntingly joyful, hungry if you will, and Eddie can feel it.

Eddie looks over at Shaw trying to pocket the phone.

"It's waiting for us."

"Where?"

Eddie just points down.

CHAPTER 24

Eddie and Shaw stand silent in the elevator staring at a button and a keyhole next to it that they somehow overlooked or could swear wasn't there before. Eddie stands motionless with key in hand while Shaw stares at him, waiting for him to do what they both don't want to do. Everything has led to this moment. The moment where they have to face the very evil thing they have been hunting, whether they know it or not, this is the moment that connects all the dots.

Eddie takes in one long deep breath and slides the key in. He seems to hold that breath forever as though he is underwater. Finally, after turning red and just before Shaw says something, releases it, turns the key, and pushes the button marked: "All the way down."

His eyes reflexively close as he does it and when nothing happens, he opens them, confused. He looks at Shaw and just as he says "the fuck?" the elevator steals his breath from his lungs like when you drop and lose all gravity on a rollercoaster. The sheer massive shift in gravity makes it impossible to scream. *You know what I'm talking about.*

The elevator seems to plummet instead of descending and when the boys get to scream, they do, losing all their preparedness in the process, and only fear exists now. The fear tells them that this is their end that this elevator was a death trap and they walked right into it like a bunch of dumb mice in an experiment. As all hope bleeds from their very beings with the acceptance of failure washing over them, they begin to assume the fetal position acknowledging their defeat.

Suddenly, without a possible scientific explanation, they come to a complete stop without any of the jarring powerful inertia that should've followed with that speed of the elevator tossing them airborne.

In disbelief and confusion, they rise, looking at each other for explanation, but before they can form thoughts, let alone sentences, the doors open with a pleasantly soft "ding" exposing a dimly lit hallway. A hallway that looks more like a mining tunnel lit only by torches that lick the dark away and cast shadows down its corridor.

Shaw swings his shotgun in front of himself, ready for battle while Eddie lifts his arms and sucks in air.

"What in the actual fuck?"

He screams into the darkness, his voice travels down it cacophonously, echoing angrily, before returning his question in a different voice, which sends a cold chill up his spine.

Eddie takes a step forward and his foot sends up a cloud of red dust, going from a modern elevator floor to medieval mineshaft. He coughs loudly, a cold layer of sweat glistens on his skin before breaking and falling into beads with his movement. Painting a red dye down his face.

They walk for what seems like forever, unhinged and nervous, jumping at their own shadows. Finally, after what seems like an eternity they arrive at a massive cavern of a room. It is lit worse than the hallway, only a single massive chandelier-like torch sways in the center of the ceiling, rocking light back and forth over the room, exposing its only decoration: a single stone well that sits in the core of its center. Upon further inspection, tubes that connect countless chambers run across the ceiling, like connective heart valves, that seem to all run into this room, and empty whatever they carry into this one well. Just like the valves to a heart.

Shaw raises his shotgun toward the well, gauging it confirming it is ready to fire, before turning on the shotguns mounted flashlight.

As soon as the light hits the well, it flickers chaotically, before inexplicably and incrementally dies out completely. Leaving only the darkness it unsuccessfully fought off from its micro secondary forced sabbatical.

"That isn't good," Eddie whispers, his voice trembles, but doesn't break, as it takes every last iota of bullshit he has—which is already borrowed from credit he as long overdrawn and exhausted just to find another loan he won't pay back and is so much worse just— to hold it together.

"Well, hello gentleman." A voice booms within the emptiness of the room, and it seems like it is coming from everywhere, as though several people are talking at once. The sheer impossibility of that instills a fear that makes them sick.

Somehow, Eddie finds a courage that neither of us knew existed, and he replies without flinching.

"Where is she?"

"My, my...Eddie...Edward Alan Devon Red... I didn't take you of all people for a romantic?"

"Cut the last boss bullshit Mr. Nightmare and keep your word."

"In a world where words mean less and less with every passing day, I'd prefer to keep to, well, mine, and as promised, here it is..."

A strange noise stirs from the well, reminiscent of a shop vacuum suddenly and violently unclogging. Like someone choking, gagging, gasping, and luckily clearing the obstruction; the well mimicking a mouth ejects the obstruction. The well ejects it violently upwards but it isn't food obviously because the well isn't an esophagus, it is a well...

Hold the fuck on sorry, it is nearly the same thing and I don't really know if the well isn't a throat of some larger creature...I am just the messenger and you know what they say, right? Don't swallow the messenger...I know it is don't shoot the messenger. I wish it was swallow the messenger...fuck, I don't know how to handle this...

The "well" clears its air way and the obstruction is the motionless body of Alexi, covered in a goo like substance, rapidly ejected from the vast void of its unknown airway before way to accurately crashing, soggy and lifeless right at Eddie and Shaw's feet.

As naked as the day she was born and seemingly covered in what looks just like amniotic fluid. She looks stillborn.

Eddie drops, immediately trying to cradle and embrace her up his arms protectively but instead of his every noble effort, he fails. She messily falls out greasily, seemingly getting harder to hold after ever attempt. Like picking up Jello constantly being doused in oil. As he doesn't give up and keeps trying to cradle her, he makes it worse, and tries to shake her to consciousness but she doesn't respond, falling and flailing greasily from his grasp.

"You fucking piece of shit, you said our lives for hers."

Shaw shakes his head before the white-hot rage has him screaming through grinding teeth.

"What do you mean our lives for hers, motherfucker? What did you do? You stupid fucking junkie, did you know this was going to happen?"

Shaw drops his scattergun and grabs Eddie by the throat from behind, choking him, as though his primitive rage has taken the wheel altogether going anywhere it fucking damn well pleases.

Shaw begins to strangle Eddie with the entirety of his weight, draining the life from him. The assault continues and Shaw's strength intensifies as he thinks how Eddie has betrayed him. And it gets stronger as he realizes he shouldn't have trusted Eddie to begin with. And he is just about to snap Eddies neck when Alexi moves, begins to cough, taking tiny breaths in to show she's alive before crying loudly, just like a newborn. This causes Shaw to release Eddie and what Eddie says next makes Shaw feel stupid.

"This. Is. What. It. Wants."

In all of Eddie's stupidity, this time, he isn't. He sees through the smokescreen of this entity. How or why, Shaw can't figure, but he is right, this is what this thing wants: to turn them against each other. Eddie, however fucking dumb he can be and usually always is, and no matter that Eddie brought them into a trap, he was doing a job Shaw swore to do. In this moment, Shaw trusts Eddie to do what is right.

Shaw moves just as something rises from the well and transitions from nothing and corporealizes. He unnecessarily somersaults toward his shotgun. Finding it, he turns it on the creature that is now hovering over the well. Without thought, he begins to unload shell after shell at it, but it moves inconceivably fast.

As quick as he can aim and fire at it, it is elsewhere, and with every strafe it gets closer, unscathed. It's seemingly impossible to hit—fuck that—its impossible for him to hit.

When his chamber is empty, he swallows hard, cause when he looks up, it stands before him.

But before he can get a good look at it, Shaw is thrown violently upward with such force he flies across the empty room. Twenty feet up into the air, and across the void; viscously scarping the ceiling of the room.

When the being finally releases him, he is out cold, and without the clothes that covered his back part. Replaced by roof rash and oozing blood. When he makes impact; thrown like ones throws garbage hoping it is going in the right part of the bin but just like that discarded refuse, Shaw winds up in the wrong place, and in his unconsciousness, his broken fingers loosely release and drop the shotgun, and it scatters away, lost.

"Hello Edward."

Eddie swings at the corporeal thing that just threw away Shaw like he was a downtown pamphlet. His makeshift bat never connects because it just passes right through it, like it, this thing, isn't there at all. The phase shifting creature, settles after, and lands, confronting Eddie face—to, well, I mean nothing fits better than to face even when it doesn't have just one—face. And it wears a face he knows so well and will never forget... *My face.*

Eddie's eyes well with tears as he whimpers out a name, "Gab? Gab is that you?"

NO! Of course, it fucking is not. This isn't an M. Night Shyamalan movie. He's playing on Eddie's weakness.

Eddie reaches out to touch the imposter me, and it lets him.

Eddie! Fucking hit him!

The imposter welcomes his touch, and extends his arms, hugging Eddie.

MOTHERFUCKER!

Eddie folds, hugging back, crying... no, not crying, Eddie is sobbing.

"It's not your fault Eddie."

"Shut up."

"It's not your fault."

Eddie tries to push away, to fight this touching moment, before allowing it to happen, but begins to cry harder and hug back like Matt Damon in...

Oh, you know the fucking movie.

Eddie sobs and sobs and this fucking creature just holds him tightly letting him get it out like this fucking thing is the reincarnation of Robin Williams' fucking character.

What in the actual fuck?

What happens next, which I barely notice, and I know for fucking sure—captain, my fucking captain, it doesn't notice— is Eddie's eyes open, and they are clear as fucking crystal, tearless, with pupils like fucking pins. Eddie is fucking sober, and when Eddie is sober, he can see the dead.

Okay, so it's sort of like an M. Night Shyamalan movie I guess, go fuck yourself.

The creature doesn't feel the penetration at first; no one does, not when the object is sharp enough. Or how fast the object is introduced. It is more of a feeling of "oh shit, something isn't right."

You know the one.

Eddie has impaled his bat through the chest of this thing, and it is just realizing it has been skewered or better yet, right fucked by it.

Eddie gives me a wink, because I'm standing right there watching him, and I'm shocked.

The creature, Mr. Dreamy, or as Eddie calls him—or rather called him—Mr. Nightmare, speaks in his own voice which is much so much less intimidating naturally.

"Motherfuck...e...r."

Eddie releases it and it falls, collapsing on its knees but instead of turning to stone instead begins to crack and crumble, turning to dust.

All while this happens, Eddie lights a smoke and watches this transpire through the flame of his zippo torch. In one long inhale he sucks out the flame, and with it, the creature collapses into a cloud of dust like flicking the long ash of a dying cigarette.

It's gone. And with it, its brood. Every single offspring of its evil is released from its curse, or at least, Eddie would like to think so.

Eddie lifts Alexi as she slumbers, covered in whatever sick slime and is hopefully blissfully unaware of the events that have transpired, slumbers. He walks toward Shaw, and starts to push him with his foot, saying:

"Hey, wake up, it's over. Hey. Shaw. Shaw. Shaw. Wake up. WAKE UP!"

Shaw doesn't. So, he sits down, cradling Alexi, covering her with his coat. And waits. Eventually, lights illuminate the tunnel, followed by a legion of cops and the guns they hold, hold flashlights. And all their lights find Eddie. Screaming for him to surrender and comply. He doesn't resist at all. In their minds, he is responsible for Shaw's disappearance. Shaw hasn't shown up for work and he's been gone long enough to be reported missing, and cops protect cops, so they traced his phone and tracked him here. And it doesn't look good for Eddie.

A legion of cops, uniformed, on duty, off duty, and some who appear retired all now flood the room armed and angry, and all direct their fury towards Eddie, completely and totally enthralled by it...blinded by rage.

They rescue Shaw and this unknown lady from Eddie, and drag Eddie like he is the witch in their witch hunt, ignoring everything else.

They get Shaw and Alexi to the medical crew that waits outside the building and drag Eddie, while taking their turn gifting their own version of justice for their "brother".

This "gift" includes several punches, kicks and cheap shots at the bound and silent Eddie that accepts his undeserved beating. He knows protest or explanation of any kind, would fall on deaf and unsympathetic ears, and it would only worsen everything. As they drag the limp Eddie toward a police car, something happens. So intensely that it steals the attention of every ignorant and tunnel eyed member of the blue-blooded, cop lives are more important always-cult that forgets their duty instantly when "one of their own" right or wrong is in duress.

It starts as a tremor, unnoticed completely, but grows. Eddie knows what it is. And just before he is tossed in the back of a police car, he speaks.

"You need to uncuff me."

"Why the fucking sweet hell would I do that?" A random angry cop justified by ignorance questions.

In one of the ambulances, surrounded by caring coworkers, Shaw stirs and regains consciousness. He shoots up, trying to catch up with his new reality, and springs up and heads straight toward to Eddie, screaming something.

Everyone is confused, accept Eddie.

This is a first.

Shaw tries to move through the crowd of his brothers in blue, but doesn't get far, his screams drown out by the celebration of his safety. But Shaw instinctually knows what that rumbling is and as it worsens, he knows it isn't explainable, and what follows is really, really, bad.

He screams an order that isn't heard.

"Let him go."

Eddie, looks at this unnamed cop, just doing his job, and instead of trying charm or bullshit. He just stares at him carrying a look that can't be ignored, honesty through his eyes with a solid seriousness that can't be feigned, and repeats itself unblinking. A look that is microseconds old and is as serious as a still birth. You couldn't ignore it if you tried and you'll never be the same after seeing it.

"You need to let me go right now."

The pavement below the cavalry cracks and then shudders, before breaking into shards. Splintering solid ground into shattering shards beneath every cop car, fire truck, swat vehicle, and first responder, swallowing them whole. Devouring them completely and randomly before they all are consumed entirely. But the tremoring hungry it doesn't stop there, instead it spreads outward. Unbiased it ravenously eats away whole buildings and anything in its unknown path.

Like an earthquake that forgot the scale but everyone above it knows it isn't that, it is something different.

Eddie, doesn't wait for freedom, instead he stands up and moves toward a swat truck as the ground scrambles like eggs on a hot pan before spitting bubbles of pavement upward and begins shattering holes with the stress of it all. The holes widen rapidly and as they do, the begin to eat up the vehicles that rest on their surface. And the void grows wider and wider, eating its way toward the van Eddie disappeared into the back of and just before the ground falls away, like a hungry maw gasping for air before opening completely, sucking everything around it inward like everything else in its path, Eddie walks out casually, carrying something. Within the exact second it is swallowed, Eddie walks away as though he had the supernatural prescience the exact moment it would be consumed.

As everyone else scatters chaotically, trying to escape, as the earth below them is no longer there.

Eddie, somehow, just goes elsewhere every time just before it is devoured. He strolls away from it, never looking back. Cop cars illuminating the night with crimson and azure disappear, abandoned, and erased. Fire trucks, painting the night sky with their scarlet and ivory essence are squelched as they disappear into the nothingness below, their loud cries become death knell whispers as they shrink away in the distance.

The new void hungrily consumes everything and grows outward, like a black hole growing, eating everything caught in its path.

Eddie walks on. Unflinching. He just walks at the same pace. Even though the ground just under his feet, nipping at his heels, continues to fall away. And then he stops, and so does the black holes appetite.

Eddie, freed somehow from his cuffs, puts the thing he carries under one arm and lights a smoke. Still with his back to the void. He takes a long inhale, seemingly endless, watching as the ember just eats away the white of the paper. He visibly is waiting for something or someone to do something.

Well, this sounds all to familiar...

From the void a sound sifts out. At first, barely audible. Like a hidden fart between clenched cheeks buried under heavy sheets, it disappears unheard unless witnessed by the person releasing it. Then the air, stales, and that same sound booms out, echoed, and magnified a hundred times. It is so loud that thunder should reconsider its job.

The thunderous sound—that I did so impossibly dirty by comparing it to a fart, is something so not humors. It is something that can't be defined or compared. This impossible, all attention controlling air-raid like sound—is a voice. And that voice clearly is trying to command. And that command is as crystalline as a prism now. And that command is for Eddie to stop.

A hulking mass of moving flesh and sinew spews upward, like a gore geyser, and it begins to form something. Eddie doesn't move. Doesn't turn. Doesn't flinch.

It begins to form a humanish creature. The sick blob forms a head, arms, chest, and abdomen. It looks like a twisted sick impression of the genie from Aladdin. I'm not talking about it being anything like the late, great, amazing, animated genie that Robin Williams played.

No, I'm talking about the nightmarish CGI Will Smith version. Yeah. That horrendous abomination. Fuck, I'm kidding, it isn't that bad.

You ever watch Akira? It was a fantastic movie. It was an anime, still brilliant, and extremely relevant because that would be the closest and most accurate comparison...don't be a dick and watch it...why do I have to defend awesome stuff...

"Eddie. We are not done."

The abdominal flesh mountain that is the final form of Mr. Nightmare bellows.

Eddie continues to smoke his cigarette. Still hasn't turned to face this abomination or even seem like anything else matters like he wrote that Metallica song.

"I can take your pain away Eddie. You of all people understand hunger. Join us, Eddie. Imagine a world where you are not judged or looked down at. Imagine a world where you are incapable of grief, pain, regret, shame, and most of all, time. Things that have and do consume you completely would be nothing more than a blink; fleeting and immediately forgotten. But you would remember and be witness to an ever-changing world, watching empires rise and fall and be outside of it, entering, and exiting as you please, unchanged. You could indulge as much as you want without consequence. Pure satisfaction. A paragon of pleasure. You were made for this..."

Eddie flicks his cigarette as there is nothing left on it more than a cindering brown butt. As smoke billows from all his face orifices possible of exhaling the carbon monoxide, he turns, but so slowly he seems injured or trapped in some sort of slow-motion movie gimmick. The only thing around Eddie that flows with the proper motion of time, is the thing under his arm, that he now brings to his shoulder. That thing is a functional rocket launcher. Like the kind you see in the movies that the bad guy's fire on the good guys as they fly overhead, and it is always announced with the same identical fear and sounds like this: "RPG!".

Eddie, as still as statue, like the kind of statue that you shouldn't have erected in the first place. Does what statues do, doesn't move. He stays like this for far too long. And just before you start to question that maybe he is now a petrified rock that now will remain until toppled or erodes through the weather of time or by the weather of well, weather.

He coughs and comes alive. He clears his throat and speaks, and it is extremely hard to make out what he actually says because it is drown out by what he does, but I think he said:

"If the only thing I have ever been right about is how wrong I've been, I'll take it."

What in the B-movie dialogue?

The missile starts sluggishly from the only place it has ever know, free falling effortlessly like it as just been shat out like an unwanted turd. Suddenly, ignition, it is expelled forward by a patient inferno that licks its back end coaxing it from its cold womb. This brand-new baby fireball burns a bright and short story behind it as it careens uncontested in its unwavering path towards its target.

Night becomes day briefly as it explodes upon impact like a supernova birthing the next universe from within the creature's chest, resembling fireworks saved for the last fourth of July and if fireworks carried the same destructive concussive force and shrapnel induced collateral damage as a rocket propelled grenade.

The creature is gone, vaporized. Only a crimson shower of bone tick tacks and singed ribbons of blackened sinew remain.

And if you didn't think about what the rain was, it would be quite pleasant. Just saying.

Eddie, being Eddie, just drops the rocket launcher, now covered in gore, and mind you is still wearing one cuff of handcuffs hanging on a bloodied wrist like he is trying to start a trend, acts like nothing happened, and instead roots around his pockets and draws a cigarette. And as he sparks that flame, just before it touches the end of that cigarette, he speaks a sentence loudly as though someone, other than us is listening,

"There is nothing wrong with me."

Eddie says struggling to smile that smile before dropping to his ass and watching; waiting for a new world to unfold from all of this.

Instead, he sits staring at the refuse of the void, trying to find some greater meaning in everything, like something greater or more amazing than what already rose from its vastness will suddenly rise and give him all the answers.

This is finally where it happens. This is where Eddie, having overcome such unbelievable nightmarish circumstances, falls victim to personal demons. This is the moment Eddie has ignored and swept every rational thought under the rug like the mess will clean itself and is no big deal. But it is a big deal, a massive galactic sized fucking deal, and he is finally confronted, and cornered by something much more nefarious; so much darker, and that thing is reality.

Eddie in this moment, is forced too—oh so long fucking overdue—finally, face his real demons. Which are much scarier than the actual infernal spawn he just dispatched.

He sits silently, tears running, finally unable to keep his emotions at bay. The unconfronted grief starts first. Savagely penetrative and unconcerned with lube or warning. He feels the years he lost. He tries to stomach losing her. And he succumbs entirely, ugly crying when he finally accepts that I am dead and that he will never see me—at least physically—again.

He sits, watching the slide show of horror mentally that he has avoided for so long which painfully catches him up from all the excruciating moments he has mentally ninjaed his way out of. He just cries. Slowly experiencing exactly what he has needed to go through, until...

"Eddie?"

Shaw's voice, steals him away.

Eddie wipes away his tears, hiding his sadness, before doing his Sunday best to which is his Monday worst to convince Shaw he wasn't crying.

"You did it man." Shaw shouts.

Eddie, reactively, and immediately listens up.

"Eddie. You did it. Stand up man. Come on. We did it." Shaw screams, lifting Eddie to his feet as the current situation begins to come together.

"Shaw, I need help man, I think I have a problem." Eddie whispers.

Shaw, doesn't hear him, or doesn't have the capacity to hear what he said. Instead starts a chant.

"Eddie. Eddie. Eddie." Shaw repeats until others join him.

Eddie watches and cheers up as his tears dry on his cheeks at this crowd chanting his name. But suddenly Eddie—being the clever fuck that he is—doesn't buy it. This is a far too story book, feel good, fairy tale happily ever after ending, end. Which doesn't happen, ever. This is bullshit. How did he get out of the cuffs? Why did the swat team have a Rocket Launcher? None of this makes any real sense...

This is when Eddie feels the mouth on his neck ravenously gulping his blood. He feels the point of a probiscis like fang acting like a straw. He fully grasps that—even though you and I haven't but now are—that slaying Mr. Nightmare and everything that followed was an illusion.

M. night Shyamalan-ed. What the fuck does the M stand for?

Sorry.

CHAPTER 25

Like a record on repeat, Eddies hand comes to life and constrictively strangles the bat that was just limply hanging in his palm. Before anyone inhuman or human could react, Eddie is quicker. The former baseball bat, now vampire slaying stick is forced through Mr. Nightmares solar plexus driven upwards savagely, obliterating flesh, and displacing organs before penetrating his would-be heart and carrying it violently out his back through his spine.

I know the first time Eddie "killed him" was so romantic and a much better end but that isn't how things work. Please, right now, count on one hand how many times things worked out cleanly like that, like in real life. If you even get one finger up, well, fuck you cause that shit doesn't ever happen and you're probably lying. But if you actually have experienced everything working out that neatly, well, how nice for you and you probably aren't reading this but if you're, fuck you and I'm happy for you, but seriously, get fucked...Wow...I have to stop interrupting.

Mr. Nightmare pulls Eddie close enough to kiss as the broken bat obliterates whatever remaining excuse for a cardia vascular pulmonary artery he had left—what mouth breathers would call a heart—before going limp and slowly and undramatically starts to die and as he does, he gets right up in Eddies ear—which, with the right person, is super sensual and in my opinion isn't done enough, but with this situation and the wrong person, is the worst—and whispers:

"It is only going to get much worse before it might get better."

I shit you not, that is what his...err...its final words were. Really? Some super shitty saying? That's it? Yep.

Eddie, as disappointed as the lot of us is at first, attempts to not let it bother him.

But unlike all of us, the observers, we don't feel what Eddie starts to.

As Mr. Nightmare doesn't instantly turn to ash or disappear but instead dies slowly in Eddie's arms, bleeding out, and gradually takes shorter and shorter breaths while slowly going limp in Eddies embrace. Like a human would. He reaches up, weakly cradling Eddies face with his crimson-soaked hands, and with the very last ounce of his out of this out-worldly fortitude squeezes Eddies sunken jaw and speaks:

"Thank you for freeing me...replacing me more like. I don't have the patience, stomach, or desire for whatever happens next. I'm tired if I'm being honest, and finally ready...actually, I just don't care if I don't have to continue this existence. Be on the outside looking in...

I've seen the rise and fall of several civilizations. I've lived through great wars...which were not only anything but great, but they invented an evil in humanity that made it forget completely that monsters are real...but your species—my food—kept upping the bar on evil and competing amongst yourselves to who could be as bad or worse than Hitler that you just forgot totally. And as much as I enjoyed total immunity, it gets old. It always does. But what you are, what you're about to go through...well, I'm too tired, too old, and uninterested to watch you become me..."

Eddie wants to drop Mr. Nightmare. Wants to jump up and down on its face till there isn't anything left. But he can't. Not because he is under its spell. It's because he is telling the truth. Eddie can feel it coursing through his veins. He knows the change has been taking hold since Edward bit him in the alleyway.

Mr. Nightmare smiles slowly, reveling in Eddie's defeated expression.

"Your hunger is raven...ughhhh."

Mr. Nightmare gags mid word as though about to hurl.

Son of a fucking...

"I've survived because I make you all sick..."

"No, it's the huuuunnngg..."

Eddie laughs uncontrollably.

"The huuuuughhh."

Mr. Nightmare desperately tries to sell this bit.

If you haven't caught on yet, well, maybe read more? It's another illusion.

Eddie isn't released, he is hurled. He hits a support beam just to slow himself down, but he didn't plan this.

Eddie violently coughs up blood as he tries to get to his hands and knees, coming to clear cognition for maybe the first time or maybe this is just another illusion.

He sees Mr. Nightmare, whatever it is. At first it looks like a man, or it did, every other time. But this. This is something that maybe can't be described but Eddie will try. And hell, maybe this is just another mind game, but it can't be because this thing is sick. Not cool sick. Or looking at it makes you ill. But it is vomiting uncontrollably. Throwing up every single millimeter of Eddie's broken brew. His crimson liquid catalogue. Eddie has his chance to destroy the creature. And again, Eddie realizes, this is too easy. Everything is too easy and too soon. How does a predator that everyone believes is fictional and has stayed only legend get defeated by a junkie fuck-up like Eddie, but not just that, by any human? How would any human defeat or overcome a superior predator. I mean, humans as a whole at least according to science got lucky and were the smartest predator earth offered at one time or another.

For fuck sakes our natural defenses were body hair and piss. Without ingenuity and tools and help from an extinction level event we wouldn't be here. And you're telling me, or rather Eddie is supposed to believe that a smarter, stronger, supernatural predator would be defeated by him?

No offense Eddie.

Also, why would it go to all this trouble or give the bad guy speech at all.

We are talking about the personification of easily the top of the food chain. Like a human but so much better, like... so much better.

Which let's be honest, it isn't hard. To be better than a human, it isn't that difficult. Just don't defend yourself when you're so in the wrong. Or pretend that we are special or better than the next best choice for smartest species on this little planet that we think is the center of the universe. We are just band aids on bullet wounds of much larger problem. Pretending nothing is wrong, while actively making everything so much worse, and arguing that we aren't currently dying by are own sick so selfish accord. Convincing ourselves otherwise somehow while completely drinking the full of shit, super apparent, suicide cool aid that we make even more toxic with every passing second. And the saddest part, it is we without a doubt – we truly believe we aren't the problem.

How would someone like Eddie defeat an ancient superior predator being who has outsmarted humanity all this time...

The same way humanity has been the "dominate" species on the planet for as long as we have. Eddie is smart enough to realize what isn't real and not dumb enough to believe that he could possibly defeat something so profoundly superior in everyway and do so this so easily. But Eddie does have this one thing. He is always massively underestimated.

Eddie's eyes drunkenly open, each lid trying way too hard to open. When Eddie breathes in, this is the first real air he has tasted in who knows how long or rather, what knows. This is real. Eddie is finally waking from the dream. As he acclimates to reality, sobering from what feels like a never-ending dream.

It feels like returning from smoking salvia. Not sure if you know what that feels like, but it feels like this. If you have never tried salvia, you should, it is legal...depending on where you live of course, but it is such an intense dissociative and extremely powerful and unimaginably brief high, that you truly question what is real. But it is harmless, I mean, at least as far as I know it is...Whatever...

The first sensation that Eddie is sure is present and very real is the shop vacuum suction sensation of his baby batter being savagely drawn from his confused form fluctuating fuck stick. Eddie sobers like a face plant on pavement, quickly returning, and associating the last thing that makes sense of this terribly awesome yet invasively welcomed experience.

He is being milked. Literally.

Yeah, that is how far back the illusion went. Eddie and Shaw never rescued the cattle from the machines.

Eddie desperately tries to find comprehension.

Its really hard...ha. No, but really, you and Eddie are both trying to figure out just how far back the illusion goes.

Eddie knows instantly when the illusion fuckery began, because he immediately sees where Tess disintegrated and that all the human cattle are still here and now, he is one of them.

Instantly, his mind goes to the most important question...

Where is Shaw now?

He looks around, panic tries to overwhelm his search but is immediately squelched and his superhuman calm instantly replaces it.

Shaw is in his own human "AMS"...

If you need me to fill you in an AMS is an automated milking machine, obviously for cows but now...yeah, if you want to deep dive in automated milking machines look up Rotolactor...

Right next to Eddies.

"That is just lazy." Eddie jokes while trying to figure out how to free himself from his own strange device.

Eddie for the second time in not enough time between occasions pulls a tube from his mouth that helped him live. He then barbarically tears free hypodermic needles that were just in veins far too important to just uncork but he somehow doesn't lose another micro measure of blood. When he reaches his dick whispering mechanical vacuum, he stops.

I can't. Yep. You aren't surprised anymore. I don't have to prepare you.

Eddie lays back and awaits his next extraction.

I am not going to tell you how long he waited...and I am without...just...fucking hell...

Eddie does his best to keep his eyes from rolling back into his head. As Eddie is relieved sexually, mechanically force milked by a machine he was unconsciously attached to by a enemy that intended the machine to drink him dry, killing him. Eddie is unbothered and appreciative.

The only thing that bothers Eddie is he tried to figure out how to free Shaw while ejaculating into his would-be dead machine and it not being weird that he could do both and did.

Eddie pulls the last part from him and does it with such disdain that he really didn't want to.

He disregards his entire environment and talks to himself.

"I mean, if all the ways to go, this would easily be in my top five ways...hell...top three ways I want to go."

He shuffles over to Shaw, inspecting him, and his machine.

He gets right up to Shaw's face, so close that his mouth is touching Shaw's ear. Like so close whispers are deafening winds.

"Shaw, wake up, we are in trouble." Eddies hot breath invades Shaw's ear thunderously.

Shaw doesn't react at all. Shaw is somewhere else completely. Hopefully more dream than nightmare, but so far away.

Eddie slowly and surgically removes the needles that connect his major arteries to the hellish human leech machine, all but one.

Eddie being Eddie waits on one. The dick sucking vacuum. The completely harmless and pleasant part of this terrifying apparatus. But Eddie waits with purpose. Eddie in all his seemingly idiotic methods did have a reason for watching Shaw during his cognitive milking through mechanical attachment. Eddie watched the pattern of this one part of the machine's operation. He knows when it will drain Shaw.

I can't even. You probably know...nope.

Eddie waits, watching Shaw's cycle, and right before Shaw physically and unconsciously signals that he will momentarily release his bad batch. Eddie interrupts him, savagely separating the machine just before Shaw gets to unburden his "load."

Shaw shoots up, conscious, like being shocked back from unconsciousness. Just as confused and in pain as the defibrillation would've been but instead, equally confused, and worse rocking a semen seeping, crying erection, and coming—not coming like ejaculating of course, but coming—face to face with Eddie who as far as you know has just been giving you the most unwanted hand job of your life.

Depending on who you are of course, I don't want to assume that this would be the worst hand jibber of your life cause I for one know that wouldn't make my top three...Normally, that would be funny but no, in this case, it would be the worst...right?

"Eddie...what the fuck...wait...I thought...I mean...wait, what?" Shaw tries to understand the situation.

"I'm going to be the clearest I can be..."

Eddie trails off, just staring at what was once Tess and even though he knows what she was and how every part of their entire interaction was fake and extremely dangerous, at any point could've been fatal. He still somehow grieves her loss.

"Eddie?"

Shaw vocally reminds Eddie that he was just about to explain what the fuck is going on, and that he has a lucy level of explaining to do and he needs to do it a lot faster.

You know with a proper tone in your voice you can say a lot more than you're actually saying. However, not everyone can pick up on it and even when they do they don't understand it properly.

"You need to call for backup. And get these people out of here...again..."

The expression that Eddie makes after finishing that sentence can only be quantified as he might have just short circuited.

"Eddie...I thought...I was sure...we already did this but I know, well, I think I know we didn't... but it feels...I was sure...I don't.."

Shaw begins the hopeless journey of trying to separate fantasy from fiction which is impossible.

I know you're like well how do you know its impossible or why can't Shaw figure it out like Eddie did?

Well, smartass, remember I am the dead guy observing...but then you're intelligently asking... but "Mr. Nightmare" pretended to be you and that was the best ending yet. And I would agree—by the way good for you for having some taste...

But you and I both think we know what is going on because we have both been experiencing this together and I wish it was much simpler than what it actually is.

Is that what you're wondering?

Like why Shaw can't figure it out as "fast", and why does Eddie, a fucking absolutely mess of an almost human see-through Mr. Nightmare's illusion again and again.

If you're thinking what I'm thinking, which you probably aren't but it would be really cool if you were. Is, why can't Shaw, a trained and combat tested officer of the law. A person who regularly endures physical and mental duress through their everyday duty be as effective against this obstacle.

Because Shaw has been coexisting on the same plane of existence as the rest of us, with little to no escape from reality.

While Eddie has been as far away from planet earth as he could possibly get.

I think that is it, Eddie can see through the illusions because he has been chasing a dream that he wouldn't wake up from, and he always does, so he is able to know the difference.

And the only reason he ever comes back to reality is to seek out something to take him back to the fantasy.

His hunger always brings him back. A hunger that he shares with these creatures.

Eddie is just like the enemy, he is hungry. He exists to feed his hunger. Like this superior being that he hasn't defeated yet but might. He knows only what feeds his ravenous hunger and only exists to quench that thirst. Just like that superior predator, Eddie shares that same thing it does. The same thing that prevented vampires from taking over. Vampires and addicts, addicts like Eddie, truly share the same thing.

The conscious acceptance that the pursuit of something that you'll never find and knowing you never will while understanding the futility of that but continuing regardless. The never-ending, unquenched hunger, that is a thoughtless thought and that in itself is paradoxically impossible, but it is the only thing that makes sense somehow while making no sense at the same time. Knowing your very existence is forever tethered to one thing and that one thing will never, ever, and I can't stress this enough, will ever, be enough.

But you're not powerless. No, that yearning swallows you, and replaces everything so perfectly that all that is left is a supernatural creature that exists only to try and satiate a hunger that will never be fulfilled.

That hunger, that addiction, is beyond everything. It is the alpha and the omega. That kind of thirst, unquenchable and unending, is the end.

Hunger. That is, it. Maybe, that is just it. Maybe that is why Eddie is going to defeat Mr. Nightmare. Eddie is hungrier. If both are driven by the urge to feed their addiction, this is where Eddie might be stronger.

"EDDIE!" Shaw screeches into Eddie's face, painting it with saliva.

Eddie snaps back from his pondering, lost somewhere in his mind, daydreaming about this situation.

Or listening to my narration?

"Sorry, what?"

"The calvary is on the way, I'm going to start leading some of these people out of here. Could you please, if you aren't too busy, give me a hand?"

Eddie looks around, watching as several human cattle foggily graze around the room, trying to understand what has happened. Then Eddie notices that some of them have remembered, and are huddle together, whispering to one another.

Pain cascades across Eddies cheek as Shaw slaps him, trying to wake him from whatever spell Shaw believes he is still under.

"Ow."

"Shaw, I'm good, fucking hell that hurt. I woke you up, remember? Listen, keep rallying these people to the exit. Be you, be a cop man, show some authority. They're scared man. Just be strong man, be you. They need you. Get them out of here man. Lead them to safety." Eddie says, genuinely conscious, and completely un-Eddie like.

Shaw just looks at Eddie, stunned momentarily, taking this— whatever this is—in, trying to figure out if this is Eddie sober or just some other Eddieism he has yet to meet. Regardless of what it is, he just smiles, extends his hand to Eddie, Eddie looks at his hand and hesitantly goes to shake it because Eddie is confused by why he wants to shake hands because to Eddie, this isn't a time to shake hands—hell, they don't need to shake hands because they already know each other—but Eddie obliges. They shake hands and continue to for what Eddie feels is an uncomfortably long time and just before Eddie tries to escape the trump-esque hand rape, Shaw sighs painfully, and suddenly; forcibly pulls Eddie into a hug. Shaw holds Eddie, hugging him tightly. Like the kind of hug, you give someone you haven't seen in a long time or know won't see for a long time. Actually, this hug is the kind of hug you give someone you are sure you will never see again.

Shaw slowly releases Eddie and Eddie, despite trying to escape the entire time now lingers in his dissipating embrace because Eddie suddenly understands the purpose of all it.

"Excuse me but can you get us the fuck out of here please."

One of the recently resurrected human cattle pipes up, completely ruining their non-toxic masculine moment.

Shaw and Eddie separate instantly like two dogs being shamed pre-humping one another.

"Good luck Eddie..."

"You too Shaw, not like you..."

Eddie's goodbye is interrupted by a horrific noise that completely squelches all sound instantly.

That terrible noise is a voice. And that that voice clearly calls for Eddie.

Imagine if a thunderclap, loud and distant, but at the same time everywhere as thunder is, but this thunder is clearly calling out for you by name. But not just by name but repeating itself with instructions for you. Just so you, and anyone who may have misheard it, or didn't believe it was calling out for you specifically; well that hurricanic voice, continues repeating itself over and over until disbelief isn't an option and you acknowledge it.

Shaw goes to speak and goes to hand Eddie his shotgun and ammo belt, but Eddie has already started walking away, backwards—doing the worst moonwalk ever—with his arms raised giving the internationally recognized signal for: I don't know what I'm doing, wish me luck.

For the record, I don't know if it is internationally recognized, but I would love to think that it and many more wordless and completely physical expressions exist and carry the same message, understood internationally—or better yet—universally.

Eddie spins in place, disappearing into darkness, lost and now completely alone but ready, finally, for the end...

Well, we are at least...

CHAPTER 26

By now I hope you know what the difference between the narratives, italicized sections, and the rest are?

So why the fuck this far in am I still italicizing when addressing you?

Because, breaking the fourth wall, I need some way of addressing you, the reader...and sometimes I need away to addressing myself like an internal dialogue, or something along those lines...

Regardless of who I am addressing without the italics it would be even more confusing otherwise, right?

Thank you if you agreed, fuck you if you argued, and sorry if you have no idea what the fuck I'm going on about, but if you are still reading...listening...watching...

Thank you.

Let's be honest, I just made everything worse after that, didn't I?

So for the sake of clarification and maybe filler, I will just confirm the difference.

When italicized, I'm talking directly to you, the reader. Or it is a memory, but still, a break in the current, present story.

Now that I have made things even less clear and not followed what I just said, let's dig into something else...

Like, Mr. Nightmare's past...

Imagine for a—pick the biggest measurement time you know—that you were a being like Mr. Nightmare—which you're obviously not—but for imagination's sake, you were. I want you to try to comprehend the frustration of Mr. Nightmare, and that every contingency plan he had in place—which is way too many—and that every actual illusion he fabricated, which is actual magic by the way. Has failed completely. Thwarted by Eddie. Someone who you didn't even consider a thing and now is a threat. If you can imagine frustration and confusion, but amplify it, then maybe you can imagine what it feels like to be Mr. Nightmare.

For the first time in thousands of years, yes, thousands, you are worried.

If you were Mr. Nightmare, obviously, humans can't get that old...I know I don't have to say this but in the off chance that someone thinks that they, a human, could get to a thousand and they find some weird loophole to sue...never mind.

Okay, so stop trying to imagine being an ancient parasitic evil. Done?

Good.

Are you ready for Mr. Nightmares' origin story?

No. Good. Cause this might be all wrong, but here it goes.

Before humans knew how bad they smelt, in some part of the world that doesn't exist anymore, and is called something different and is completely irrelevant, lived a human teenager. Well, a bunch of human teenagers lived nearby, but this is about one. Human adults and children lived there as well, just so you don't get confused.

This human teenager went by the name...

I don't know how to pronounce it, and I won't try because it wasn't a "modern English" name, obviously, asshole, it was a thousand years ago.

Anyhow...

The teenager: let's call them Nomore.

Wasn't like anyone else, ever.

Nomore was extremely unique.

Nomore was shunned and abandoned by his people at birth...

Which was super common back then. Back then they were just throwing out babies all the time. But garbage babies always died, Nomore didn't. Nomore survived harsh elements, predators, and...

Okay, he was a newborn human child that didn't die immediately from being abandoned unlike all the way too late abortions before and after did die.

Nomore, didn't.

Nomore, in his first twenty-four hours of existence killed and consumed a living creature.

As a tiny human baby, he murdered and ate to survive.

How? How is that possible.

Well, obviously, Nomore, wasn't like a super fragile human newborn.

Nomore was something else, something much more horrific. *Cause, you know, humans can be horrific...anyhow.*

A human looking newborn, but was equipped with rows of razor teeth, retractable bladelike nails—more like talons or claws, and leathery armor as skin that had the same durability of the hardest galvanized metal...Oh, and he, more like it, was "born" prematurely, six months after "conception", and ate—we are just going to call Nomore, him for now—his way out of his poor human mother.

The mother, knowing from the first moment that whatever it was that she was carrying, wasn't human, so she chose to exile herself from her other humans. She went as far away as she could. But desperation kept her closer than she should've stayed.

Don't get it twisted, the human mother tried everything to kill the creature growing in her, and nearly died several times in the attempt. Blunt objects, starvation, poison, stairs, hills, and even glutton...nothing worked.

I know you want to know how she got pregnant before I continue...don't worry, you're about to find out.

One fateful evening, the mother, let's call her Terra...

Must be fateful of course. It can't just be one evening...

Terra, young and recently bled, signifying her womanhood—way too young for adult shit—rebelled and went from her village to adventure and explore the nearby forest. The forest, by the way, was a place, to her people, and all humanity at the time was a place that you should avoid because humans would constantly get "lost" a lot and never return, which meant they all died, or actually, were all killed.

Forests were everywhere and super dangerous back then like almost everything back then was. Before we got educated, greedy, and cut them all down. This forest, however, was different, because it wasn't full of life, but it was extremely dangerous, because it was home to something that should never have been in the first place.

I'm not advocating for eliminating untouched nature, I'm just saying...well, you'll see, I mean...you'll read.

Something lived in this forest. This something was the last of its kind because this species ate itself extinct. And truly, this is where our story could've ended—should have ended—but obviously, didn't.

Terra, despite her people's warnings, visited this forbidden section of the forest that she shouldn't go into. So basically, she went into a place she was told not to go to cause it is extremely dangerous and one upped that bad idea by going to a place that was absolutely forbidden to go to.

Doesn't matter how far humans have come since then, being dumb and young always looks the same.

She pushed her way through a dense brush, ignoring the warnings, and found the forbidden pool.

The fiery orange glow of daylight shined behind her, cutting out perfect shadows through the bushes on the still ponds surface, before retreating and letting dusks weak glow replace it.

She quickly shed her only filthy layer, exposing her dirty flesh, and immediately jumped into the forbidden pond without worry.

This was a considerable time before bathing was a thing. So yeah. Being fully submerged in water was a huge deal. It was special in a way we couldn't truly understand nowadays.

Coming up for air, breaking the stillness, cleansed; she just basked in the pond's absolute—until this very moment untouched—tranquility. Terra satisfied and honored that she is the only disruption it has ever experienced, now a part of this place and as she settled became a part of its return to stillness.

It wasn't just the stillness that comforted her.

It was the knowing that nothing came here.

And that comfort was...freeing.

She was safe from everything from her world here.

No forceful men.

She wouldn't be run down and stabbed by their flesh, tearing her places, and wouldn't have to taste their white life or take it and pray that it wouldn't take and force her to bear an unwanted child.

No.

Here, no beasts would devour her flesh, man, or animal.

There was only her.

Nothing but her.

And she was warned never to come here but never told why it was any more dangerous than her village had actually turned out to be for her. And she wasn't warned of those things...

This place had a peace she only dreamed of.

She kicked her feet and went to her back, floating on the surface of the water, staring up through the canopy at the far away stars and wondered if this was the beginning of so many better things.

Terra then started to question the absolute silence.

Everything here was still but lacked so many things that should be here.

No noise. No insects. No fish. No movement. It was completely absent and abandon of anything that is alive and moves. This place was completely absent of life.

Accept her.

In that moment of realization, she became completely paralyzed, and it should've only been momentarily; a direct product from the fear brought on by the unsettling closeness of an unknown presence suddenly penetrating her physical space. No, the paralysis was real and encompassing.

Terra was helpless.

Long fingers from unsee hands breech the still surface, running their impossibly long joints through her tangled hair.

She wants to move but can't. At all.

But she can still feel everything and knows she is about to wish for nothing more than not to be able to.

She feels a body appear from under her as it feels like it is becoming apart of her own. The body that owns those gentle but terrifying hands. She feels its body press into hers, perfectly matching hers, like a shadow finally touching its reflection.

From between her legs, she feels something kiss across her closed lower lips, cutting them open. Even as gently as it does, it feels rougher than any man bone before it, but so much larger, and void; entirely absent of the blood that makes a mans flesh feel like stone. It is harder than bone and so much colder than stone.

She feels lips caress her ear, then teeth, and then words she doesn't know because they're spoken in another language but understands them somehow.

The voice calms her, removing the physical fear, and replacing it with violent hunger she isn't hungry for and can't be, but starving for it all at once.

Never has she wanted anything more than she wants whatever this is and at the same time not to at all.

She has dreamed of others from her village this way, but they were only dreams, and never as powerful as this feeling is.

This feeling, horrible, and phenomenal all at once and even if there will be words for it, this will be the only feeling she will ever truly want again and knows will never feel again. But doesn't care right now.

Suddenly, she can move, and the first thing she does is grab that thing between her legs and forces it in herself.

She becomes something else, not someone. She truly doesn't try to understand it and even if she could, she wouldn't.

All she wants is, now, and always this. Whatever this is.

She guides this experience, savagely as she can, forcing it in and out of her. Recognizing that whatever she is allowing in her, is dying, and she is experiencing it die by the second.

When she feels the shadows flesh snake start to pulsate, she reaches back consciously, and tries to hold it from escaping even though it doesn't move.

When she feels the shadows staff tremble violently, signifying within seconds it will erupt unwanted ink in her. She forces down on it, burying it deeper, instead of taking those important seconds and avoiding the sick white mess of man because that has always been the only time to escape.

As it fills her, she feels whatever it is, become whatever it was.

This was its dying breath and its rebirth all at once.

And it goes flaccid, and with that, it sinks underneath her, disappearing as quick as it came.

Terra, lay there floating, and stayed in the stillness. Slowly feeling the horror that she would never experience that again, and as the time passed away, she would experience true confliction. She never would never willingly choose too to do that again, but forever will want to for every second of every hour of ever day until her last day.

And she did, she would return here, till the very moment Nomore, the first of its kind, ate its way out of her. And despite dying in such a horrible fashion, her last thoughts were of the experience that she had just once. Despite the obvious horrible consequences of it and that it was the worst thing to ever happen to her was the only thing she cared did.

She no longer had the capability to see just how bad it was. Not even when the demonic offspring conceived by that one experience—the one she wasted every moment after, literally, every single second of everyday obsessing about—tore its way up and out of her womb, and immediately left her brutalized, suffering in unimaginable agony for far too long. Alone in a field, Terra slowly bled out. That field was just far enough away from the people who exiled her; her entire family, and all facets of the life she lost because of that experience, but close enough to hear them be massacred by the very thing created by that moment.

In my dead mind, this is the birth of addiction, or at least a manifestation of it. Imagine, if that is how things worked. If we could excuse our behavior, guiltless, because there was an entity responsible for it. Oh wait, I think we tried that, and I believe we called it Christianity... shots fired.

"Cool story...What...do you think now that I know it, it'll change my mind about murdering you? Destroying...Err, whatevering you."

Eddie walks into the strange open space of a room he's seen before but hasn't.

He walks blind, because unless he can see in the absence of light, he's blind aesthetically, but somehow he navigates it flawlessly, avoiding the abyss that consumes its epicenter.

Mr. Nightmare tries to get into his mind, weaving waking dreams of things Eddie would be enthralled by, but hard as he tries, they fail.

Eddie somehow shuts him out now.

Eddie suddenly can

But he can't change that suddenly...

but he has.

Eddie is different and Mr. Nightmare doesn't know just how different, or how he is able to be this different.

But he is, of course, he is.

But not in the way a person grows positively. Like, in every story, the hero changes throughout the book, becoming a better version of themselves.

No.

This whole time Eddie has been changing so much differently and Mr. Nightmare just now realizes it.

Fuck. I just did too. Did you?

Mr. Nightmare reactively tries something so alien before the overlooked realization is even finished being accepted. That is how fast he moves.

Not fast enough though.

Mr. Nightmare, foreign to using his supernatural speed, arrives where Eddie just was.

How? I mean, I'll let you off and won't make you feel bad. But I'm not going to explain it.

Mr. Nightmare, for the first time—possibly ever—feels the sick, molasses stillness of fear.

He is kicked violently into the wall, pinned, and as hard as he tries can't force himself to freedom.

Eddie holds him there, smiling that fucking smile, but that smile is completely different because now it isn't just bravado flavored by misplaced mentally malnourished illness convinced of invincibility, Eddie is cashing cheques his body can afford.

Eddie is no longer demented; Eddie actually is just as impenetrable physically and mentally as he used to just believe he was.

Sebastian's first taste of Eddie started this, and it just took longer for Eddie to get here.

You didn't notice, I didn't notice, hell the one who apparently started this whole thing didn't notice because...well...Eddie.

" If I kill you, does it reverse everything?"

"Wha..."

Before Mr. Nightmare has a chance, Eddie hurls him across the wide expanse of the room, and he hits so hard, if he had air in his lungs, he would've lost it.

He shoots up supernaturally fast, but again, like a person who hasn't used their muscles, they don't work as they are supposed to.

"If I destroy you, kill you, absolutely annihilate you. Would everyone become human again?"

Eddie doesn't wait for him to reply and catches him by the throat, or at least the area where a throat should be.

"I...don't...know..."

Mr. Nightmare struggles to breathe out the words because he too needs air to speak, surprisingly.

"Well, only one way to find out."

Eddie effortlessly lifts Mr. Nightmare up and over his head. His other hand catches one his legs and he begins to pull him in two different ways repeating what he did to his childhood toy. Using every atom of his old and new strength, Eddie tries to pull Mr. Nightmare apart. However, with a whispered word, he stops completely.

"What did you say?"

"Alexi."

CHAPTER 27

Eddie stops pulling Mr. Nightmare apart with the mention of Alexis' name.

"You think the mere mention of her name is going to stop me from ending you? Aren't you were supposed to be the smart one?"

Eddie brings Mr. Nightmare's face to his own, whisper close, and Eddie takes his time speaking this sentence:

"You would think with your ever-changing mask and countless number of years beyond me... your expertise in the subject of survival...that you, of all people, would know that she is just away I've survived by.

Alexi just helped me feed what kept me going.

Hell, maybe at one point, maybe, I believed that she was more than just a meal ticket.

But she wasn't anything more, no matter how much I wanted her to be.

I couldn't invent a fantasy where everything would ever be okay, happily ever after, if I could only be with the right person.

I have known this entire time, deep down, admit or not, I am fucked and have been doing everything in my power, intentionally or unintentionally to end my existence while you have been doing the opposite.

You may have been alive or dead or whatever the fuck you are and have been here longer than I've been. And found a way to survive. Rationing that hunger. Controlling that sickness that you spread. Comprehending that the moment you lose control; your existence is extinct.

Which is what you don't want.

Unlike me, my existence has been spent trying to end it and the only reason I became an addict for anything was just because I can't stand existing.

So, if your only bargaining chip is my drug habit fueling fuck friend connecting me to a world, I wanted to leave a long time ago...then I'm sorry, so not fucking sorry...you're about to see the world through my eyes. Unforgiving and uninterested.

Well Mr. Nightmare, or should I call you by what Terra was going to..."

FUCK! Eddie, Stop!

Eddie stops talking and looks for my voice that interrupted his train of thought...

This is where I step in. And I can't believe that this is happening right now. I just now realized that Mr. Nightmares back story started with when he was a "human" teenager but immediately focused on his creation and never got back to that part.

"Shut up." Eddie whispers.

Wait is he talking...

"Shut the fuck up, this is another illusion and thank you, but I just got it... Gabe is dead, and I killed him. But he is dead, so dead, and no matter how much I wish wasn't, is dead. communicate with me, hasn't been, it has been you. Asshole. Really cold. He is dead...the whole time. It is just us...And honestly, I don't know why me, but you are him and I don't understand."

Well here comes the M. Night Shyamalan or however he spells it, yes, oh, what a twist.

Eddie stops his assault because he knows yet again, it is pointless.

I am, and have always been Mr. Nightmare, Dreamy, or whatever we didn't settle on calling me. Truly, doesn't matter. And don't feel cheated. Because why the fuck would anyone, at all, good or bad, natural or supernatural, live or dead; spend this much time focused this entirely on person if they weren't completely tethered to. Well? Do you have a reason instantly? No? Then. There you have it. It makes sense...

"It doesn't make sense and sense never had anything to do with it and I don't know why you're trying this. This is yet another fucking illusion. Another extension of you trying to perpetuate your destruction."

Gabe here, real Gabe, not fake Gabe. Back in control. Eddie, as always, somehow sees through it. Mr. Whatever the fuck—you, Eddie, or I—want to refer to him as.

"This is just another façade. And yes, now I'm losing the ability to recognize what is real and what isn't but let's be honest, I've been doing that for so long that I can recognize the difference between under the influence and your whatever the fuck this is..."

Eddie is cut off mid-sentence as he takes a shot to his body, mid-center, and is sent soaring backward. The illusion unravels like the thread of your favorite overworn sweater; way too fast while losing too much, somehow all the while holding itself together still.

The room where Eddie had not been giving Mr. Nightmare the not actually successful business, if you will, dissipates, revealing the actual room where Eddie has been the entire time since he got there, the one where he was just another pacified cattle for Mr. Nightmares fun feed himself farm.

Eddie's vampiric supernatural strength, obviously never existing in the first place, is gone, and he is humbled—by the wall that breaks his journey after being thrown into it—returning to reality and assuming the lowest form of human—his form. Back to the worst possible person for the job of dispatching this one-of-a-kind super apex predator and saving countless lives if successful.

Totally no pressure Eddie, just kidding, it is all the pressure, imagine the entire pressure of the ocean trying to get into your little submarine of a mind that is currently trapped under all of it. That is how much pressure it is.

Eddie, if you can hear me, this, this is the moment you have to take seriously. You have to realize the gravity of this immediate situa...

"Gabe, shut the fuck up." Eddie screams as he lifts himself from the wall, coughing blood from somewhere internally he shouldn't be bleeding from.

"I have been dealing with all of this, this, this absolutely impossible situation now, and every unimaginable situation before this, and look, here I am, still..."

Mr. Nightmare grabs Eddie, cutting his next words off, and tosses him all the way across the room to the very far away wall. And Eddie hits this wall harder than the last. He mumbles something, gasping for air at first, forming words between the visceral vocal reactive grunts to injury. He forms coherent sentences despite more blood and broken bones that try to silence him. And as he says his next several statements, he is staring at where I would be, if I was physically here, and he addresses me as though I am.

"Gabe, I know you have always wanted to protect me, but I am still here, and you would be too if you had only trusted that I knew what I was doing. If you would've trusted me that day, you would still fucking be alive. But here you aren't, but are, er whatever, you know what I mean...So protect me now. Show us how you died.

What?

Show us, just like this-insert clever insult- has been "showing" us everything else...

I don't, wait...

Do I have to spell this out for you? Gabe, you have been doing the same thing while haunting me, you have been projecting things this entire time. You can do what it has been doing man, trust me, just fucking try."

Mr. Nightmare, moves the distance of the entire room, not in a blink of an eye, but as you're mid blink. But even within the same blink of an eye speed, it isn't fast enough for him to get to Eddie this time. Because you know what moves at the same speed of a blink of an eye?

A train travelling 120/mph an hour. Listen, I'm not a mathematician, but if Mr. Nightmare moves the distance of the room in 1/3 of a second and a train moving 120/mph moves at 53.463 meters a second then 1/3 of that is...doesn't matter, Mr. Nightmare is now seeing my illusion, and there is a very fast train involved...satisfied?

Mr. Nightmare isn't.

Eddie has a brief opportunity to experience the sensation of hope. Mr. Nightmare pauses just long enough for Eddie to believe that showing our origin death story, the one I promised, and never shared because I genuinely forgot about...That it would somehow lead to him defeating or whatever you call killing Mr. Nightmare, well it doesn't work.

Eddie tastes his own tongue as his teeth are forced into nearly severing it, erasing that smile, as Mr. Nightmare is again trying to beat Eddie to Death. Before Eddie can humanly react, Mr. Nightmare throws another rib cracking, lung collapsing blow to Eddies chest, and before physics move Eddie, Mr. Nightmare headbutts Eddie downward, cracking Eddies skull and sending Eddie through the floor.

Eddie doesn't feel the impact, because Eddie is unconscious, and nearly dead before his lifeless body is forced through the floor and lands in shambles on the level beneath. The room is darkness within darkness, and the only light is from the Eddie shaped hole, and now he lies in the center of the light.

Mr. Nightmare floats down weightlessly like the most horrible balloon, before touching down, straddling my lifeless best friend.

As he lifts Eddies unconscious frame, what seems like he is waiting for Eddie to gain consciousness. Through Eddie waking up it would add living lead to the broken pencil that is his flaccid dead goose like neck. Just so Eddie can be here consciously, just long enough, so he can experience being dealt a killing blow from Mr. Nightmares patient fist.

Shit. Mr. Nightmare is stalling, intentionally or not, he is, he needs Eddie to see he has lost. Which is fucked, because he could've killed Eddie so many times, but didn't or fuck, maybe he can't. Just like I didn't show the story that might've prevented Mr. Nightmare from beating Eddie too death, I needed to see what would happen. Surprise, surprise, he is still here. And I still haven't told you how I died.

The train that I didn't intentionally take and had I just listened to Eddie I would still be here.

Eddie comes to consciousness, bleeding from every orifice, and I mean every orifice.

"You would still be here…"

Mr. Nightmare winds back cartoonishly, but instead of decapitating Eddie, waits.

What is he waiting for?

"I agree."

No, you don't not get to deal with this. You don't get to keep "Eddieing" *your way through life and for fuck sakes, how, how are you still here?"*

"Don't…know… it should've been me though…" Eddie attempts his stupid smile through a dislocated jaw and broken teeth, blood oozes out between breathes inking over his bottom busted lip and drippling down his swollen chin.

Mr. Nightmare lets out a sound that interrupts everything, sucking all the ambient sound from the world around, and replaces it all with his voice.

"Show me how you died." He whispers, hauntingly as he directly stares at me.

I oblige. Roll the flash back footage, sit tight, and enjoy…viewer discretion is advised.

Instead of the room in the dark hellish hideout we were just in, we three—Mr. Nightmare, the incapacitated Eddie, and the ghost formally known as Gabriel— now stand on the tracks of the Bank Street station, looking up at the platform at my past corporeal, very alive self, and a younger, less haggard version of Eddie. Who are yelling down at someone also on the tracks to our right. In synchronously, all three of us dumbly glance over to look at who they're talking to. Tess is kneeling in the middle of the tracks, crying clumps of onyx mascara into several streams that fork down across her porcelain cheeks. Tess, as you know, eventually becomes one of Mr. Nightmares vampiric puppets, just in case you're confused.

"Tess, please, get the fuck off the tracks…" Eddie barks.

Past Gabriel gives him a swift smack upside the head, and stares daggers at him.

"What? This is fucking stupid." Eddie rubs his head, staring at me, wounded and betrayed by the assault.

"Tess, honey, let's talk about this. I can explain. Please just come here."

Tess, sniffling, goes to speak, but something swiftly interrupts her.

A shrill thunderous horn in the distance blares breaking the dead silence of the barren station echoing off and into the night. Immediately followed by a prerecorded voice signifying that a train is about to arrive, the last train of the night. All present and past viewers of this scene look down at the tracks in the same direction, at the same time, and like all good flashbacks, time seems to slow down.

The train speeds around the corner coming into view, barreling towards the station.

You might be wondering, why are they the only ones at this station? Why hasn't anyone else intervened?

That is because this is the very last train of the night, or rather, the last train before service stops and it is three in the morning. Not to pull from the very dramatic flashback but all three of them didn't realize that there was still a train running.

Tess goes to stand and move from the tracks but trips and stumbles forward, crashing down painfully, barely catching her fall.

Past me is already leaping off the platform and is fully sprinting for her and Eddie follows on my heels. Just as they reach her the train operator sees them and their training kicks in and they immediately pull the emergency brake.

Now, this would normally cease forward momentum violently, slowing the train almost to a complete halt, serving its purpose flawlessly. Unluckily for all of us this emergency brake completely fails because these trains were bought second hand from a foreign country and never intended to operate in our climate at all. A failure of our city's poor transportation planning. Something that could've been completely avoided, but, hell, maybe we are all just really unfucking lucky. The train continues, unimpeded, and the operator, overwhelmed with panic, fails to brake for the station trying for the emergency brake again and again.

We have Tess up on her feet and the both of us, lift her on to the platform, and as we both go to jump up and completely avoid the train that barrels toward us at full speed, something equally fucking unlucky happens. My foot gets stuck. Yeah, my fucking boot gets lodged between the tracks. So, I am pulled back mid-jump, falling on my ass, and I quickly get back to my feet trying to tear myself free. Eddie, jumps back down, and violently tries to help me.

The train lights are blinding us now. The train horn deafens us. And this is when seconds start to feel like minutes. As Eddie drops down, pulling at the laces of my boot, desperately trying to undo knots that just tighten the more he pulls at them. I find clarity and know instantly what I must do. Eddie pulls a knife from his pocket and flicks it open and hacks at my laces. But I feel the trains mass just behind me as all the air is pulled toward it. I supernaturally lift Eddie with the strength of a thousand mothers lifting a car from their trapped child and shotput him up and on to the platform to safety. Eddie lands and looks up helplessly in horror, just with enough time to lock eyes with me for what will be the last time, and I watch a piece of him die as I disappear in a crimson blur as the train concussively frees me from life.

And that folks, is how I died, thanks for your patience, hopefully my death lives up to your expectations...End of flashback.

Mr. Nightmare wears an expression that reads: "Well that was a waste of time" returning his attention to Eddie, who is now full-on ugly crying, and winds back with his massive hand that now has blades for finger nails, which I assume is for decapitating Eddie, but just as he is about to swing his coup-de-grace, he realizes that "the waste of time" gave someone the opportunity they needed to get back into the fight.

The gauge of Shaw's fully loaded shotgun is music to everyone other than Mr. Nightmare, and in my opinion, is an absolute banger and should be on the top one hundred hits of the summer only succeeded by the sound of it going off repeatedly as Shaw walks toward Mr. Nightmare unloading the scattergun completely, trying to decapitate Mr. Nightmare.

Eddie falls free, as Mr. Nightmare is pushed back with every fiery blast, forced concussively closer and closer to the edge by a very dedicated shotgun wielding Shaw. Parts of Mr. Nightmare fly off in different directions at every blast, as Shaw empties the entire load of his shotgun, screaming at the top of his lungs as he presses forward.

The worst song ever heard is the sound of an empty gun just before Mr. Nightmare is sent hurdling backward into the abyss, he calls home.

Shaw stops empty just as Mr. Nightmares heels touch the edge of the void, and instead of falling off, he begins to reconstitute everything he just lost, and gains his balance and steps forward as he regenerates, looking more annoyed than injured.

Shaw lets the gun fall to his side, defeated, while letting free a single word, exasperated.

"Fuck."

Before Mr. Nightmare can move on Shaw, Eddie with his famous bat in hand, flies at him, burying it into his chest, spearing him backward, knocking him off his feet, and they both fall into the void.

CHAPTER 28

I would love to describe what happens next is a parallel of the cinematic masterpiece battle between Gandalf and Balrog from Peter Jacksons wonderful interpretation of Lord of the Rings. Like how as they fell, they epically and endlessly trade blows, plummeting into the seemingly unending nothingness. And I would be so fucking happy, if it was in anyway close in comparison to how that scene unfolds, but it isn't. I wish, I could explain how my Gandalf (Eddie obviously) similarly, somehow survives, and rejoins his friends stronger than he left them. It would be the best if I didn't have to tell you what happens, and we could just all move on, never knowing what happened to the Balrog. No, I don't get to do that, these two situations are nothing alike, but I wish they were, but they aren't, and I know I didn't need to do this, but at least, for moment, we both thought about a much cooler turn out and we both got to relive that amazing cinematic wonder—sort of.

Here is what actually happens...

The second Eddie hit Mr. Nightmare, driving his broken bat, impaling Mr. Nightmares vital organs and driving them out his back they begin to free fall into the depths of what can only be described as his lair, a chain reaction starts. Mr. Nightmare, turns to stone, just like Sebastian did, but this time, Eddie is trapped in his grasp, locked in for the ride and this ride has one stop called: you're fucked.

Falling rapidly down the well from every horror movie ever, Eddie tries to free himself without removing the infamous bat from Mr. Nightmares chest and reviving him, he panickily scans every direction. plummeting meteorically down the shaft in the middle of a high-rise building, floor after floor, amassing a velocity that certainly will kill Eddie upon impact. Eddie closes his eyes, accepting this, this is the end, but an end to not just him but hopefully the end of all of the horror Mr. Nightmare was, and will never be again.

Eddie accepts this entirely and a serenity washes over him, consuming him, cauterizing his fears, regrets, and pain completely, replacing them with a oneness and doneness. A peace never known before, or possibly imagined, but fitting for the last feeling he will ever have.

Too bad it won't last...

Meteorically they crash into a large pool of stagnating liquid sending a plum of it upward like an angry geyser and begin to sink rapidly because Mr. Nightmares is a cement block. Eddie frantically tries to free himself from Mr. Nightmares' grasp, but he is completely locked in without any leverage. Eddie tries to open his eyes, but this isn't water, it's something very viscous and oozy, and it stings his eyes in an all too familiar way. Eddie plants his feet into Mr. Nightmare and tugs with all the force he has left as they continue to sink. Pointless. He is fused in Mr. Nightmares' grasp. He begins to fight the urge to inhale as his lungs scream for oxygen, but they will find only horrible thick liquid that Eddie now tastes and recognizes as blood. He panics, heaving erratically to free himself. He knows that the only way he's getting free is if he removes the bat. But that would free Mr. Nightmare. Eddie slows his attempt to escape. Giving up the pointless struggle bit by bit, searching for that peace he found before he was about to drown in a bloody pool attached to a petrified monster. He goes still. And he calms.

On the surface, shown in the light from the floors above. A single bubble forms like on its still surface, before popping, releasing Eddie's escaping final breathes, and before dissipating into the crimson stillness of the blood pit.

Eddie?

Shaw all the while has been making his way down, sprinting down the stairs, nearly falling floor by floor, trying to find where Eddie fell.

I can't summarize the pain that I feel but somehow, it's smothered by pride. Eddie sacrificed himself. He chose to end this nightmare, instead of saving himself, he chose to drown in the dark depths of blood-filled pit, locked eternally to the personification of evil. He gave his own life because he knew this was the only way to stop Mr. Nightmare from spreading like a plague and using humankind as cattle. Fuck. Eddie. You're a hero...

The pool raptures violently as Eddie gasps hungrily for air.

God damn it Eddie...

He swipes blood clumsily, smearing it from his eyes, one hand firmly gripping the bat, he is treading blood, swimming aimlessly, blindly searching for a shore.

"Fuck. Heugh. Fuck. Heugh. Fuck. Heugh." Disgusted, he vomits blood, between fucks.

He tiredly drags himself out of the pool, reaching in the dark for solid ground, but instead his hand finds flesh. He recoils when it moves, but he returns his hand gently, examining it cautiously. He hears a whimper, soft, and weak. He recognizes the flesh as a ankle, and he traces up it, finding the calf. Suddenly, he feels pain, and sees light in his eyelids, as the foot it is attached to finds his nose, violently kicking him back.

"No more..." a voice pleads, in a thick foreign accent.

"Alexi!" Eddie scrambles toward her, fumbling to get his zippo out, trying to clear it of blood to light it and illuminate the darkness...

Obviously.

"Alexi...I came to get you outta here, it's me, it's Eddie." He rambles, groping at her in the dark, while still trying to ignite his blood flooded zippo.

She doesn't register what he says or maybe she can't instead she just weakly crawls away from him, still reeling from whatever horror she endured.

Eddie gives her space, as he slowly crawls up next to her, remaining as non-threatening as possible. In the softest, kindest, and completely foreign voice from Eddie's normal extra tone he whispers:

"Alexi, look at me darling." He strikes his thumb over and over on the wheel of his zippo, at first just sound in the darkness, but then a small spark, and after several rolls over the flint a spark becomes a hungry flame illuminating that famous smile.

Alexi looks up, squinting, seeing light for the first time in a long time and she cries out in joy as she recognizes his dumb face, before she lunges at him, wrapping her arms around his neck, sobbing into his chest. He pulls her in, cradling her in comfort.

"Darling, we have to get out of here before..."

You know those times where you should just never say anything because you're totally going to jinx it, well yeah, this is one of those times.

The surface of the blood pool shutters, before rippling violently, and a bubble loudly explodes from its surface followed by thousands of smaller bubbles announcing the arrival of something horrible coming. Eddie begins to lift Alexis naked frame, still cradling her, and he slowly rises—probably because he struggles to lift her—and he turns looking for an exit. He turns in place, raising his flame, exposing this horrible chamber in its totality. He looks at the pool and fear begins to crawl under his skin, shifting him to naturally walk backwards, as the blood pools looks like its in a full rolling boil. From the darkness a hand reaches out and grabs his shoulder pulling him back and he nearly drops Alexi.

"Eddie, it's time to fucking leave."

"Shit, fuck, god dammit Shaw. You scared the shit out of me. Alexi. This is Shaw. Shaw, Alexi. You're introduced, now can we please get the fuck out of here."

"Nice to meet you." Alexi mumbles.

"Yeah, you too. Now lets fucking go!" Shaw pulls them backward into the darkness which leads to a strange door into an even stranger tunnel filled with what appears to be kegs. Just as they start moving down it, the pool explodes upward in a cartoonish geyser of blood as something very large flies—yes flies—out of it. It superhero lands at the precipice of the should be exit to the tunnel they're trying to escape out of.

Fuck, right, I never explained what Mr. Nightmare looked like and looks even less like now. Sorry. I'll explain the before and after. Pre-blood bath, Mr. Nightmare was a very muscular androgynous human looking creature. Perfectly cut, almost like he was made from the stone he became when skewered. But he still looked like a man. But now, fuck, now he looks like a roid raged veiny human like creature with gigantic leathery wings. I'll let your mind see what it wants to see, and trust me, whatever you can imagine, it is so much more terrifying.

Shaw's shotgun mounted flashlight fully exposes what the new and improved Mr. Nightmare looks like an when it hits him, Mr. Nightmares milky eyes reflexively roll back to an onyx black, just like a great white shark's eyes do before it falls upon its prey.

"Oh come on..." Eddies voice cracks before he turns and starts sprinting the other direction, trying not to drop Alexi who slips from his grasp with every step.

Shaw heroically stands his ground and lifts his shotgun to fire. With a dry empty click all of the heroism leaves his body at once and instinct takes over. He immediately turns, and starts sprinting, easily passing Eddie and Alexi.

Just a horrible thought, but you don't have to be faster than whatever is chasing you, you just have to be faster than the other person running from it. Sorry Eddie and Alexi.

Mr. Nightmare lets out a horrible primal noise which sounds like a lion roar if the lion was vomiting blood as he—fuck it, it—it powerfully thrusts forward from a stand still into the air, going after them.

Eddie sprints as fast as his failing frame allows, especially carrying the very in shape and heavier than she looks Alexi, but he doesn't drop her, and he keeps pushing himself to run as fast as he can. Shaw gets his head on right finally, conquering his instinct, and fighting it, and slows, allowing Eddie and Alexi past and he starts grabbing at the strange kegs, tossing them backward in a meager attempt to slow the flying monstrosity.

Mr. Nightmare soars overhead, just behind them, as they reach what appears to be an exit that Eddie doesn't slow down to inspect, instead he turns slightly, and spears into it shoulder first. Eddie barrels through the double doors into the welcome kiss of the outside air but loses his balance instantly because of momentum and he and Alexi tumble across cold, wet, asphalt. Eddie quickly pulls Alexi to him, covering her like a blanket. Shaw trips over Eddie and falls head over feet several times before curling up defensively. Mr. Nightmare lands in front of them, his wings stretch out, blocking their escape any further and now he is all scimitar fangs, sword like talons, and ravenous rage, and he goes in for the kill, but something stops him, light cuts through the darkness just behind him.

One single beam hits his peripherals, then another shines through his left wing, and then another streams through his veiny reverse demonic legs. Instantly these lights are followed by another and another, now a dozen different beams of halogen light expose his horrific form. He spins in place, facing the lights that expose him completely, and he postures his magnificent and terrifying true form.

"Open fire!"

From dead silence to a deafening symphony, Mr. Nightmare is greeted by the pure force of the future that his food source produced in his absence. The very first-five-five-six caliber round that cuts into Mr. Nightmare and hydrostatically shatters what you would call his orbital bone and decimates the hellish dead black pool ball sized thing you would call his eye; he realizes that he has severally underestimated his prey. With every destructive round he comes apart and it is already too late to move because the damage is done. His horrendous skull fleshly explodes into chunks as his supernatural healing can't respond fast enough to hold it together. His neck, once as wide as a tree trunk is sheered to that of a stringy sinew branch. His chest is punched out in a nearly flawless marksmen grouping, whittling away the bone, and shredding whatever organs were hidden beyond into ground beef consistency. He is stripped away from top to bottom by a storm of high caliber heat, falling away like ash from a cigarette. As the firing squad that is the tactical response team of the police force, one by one, empties their entire magazine. It sounds like an orchestra ending their climatic song all at once, accept one musician is off time and plays late. That is what the last round sounds like.

Eddie, Alexi, and Shaw unfurl and look up at the mutilated husk that falls to its knees, falling apart sickly like brisket meat being pulled into strands. Behind it, the tactical team cautiously moves forward, encircling this abomination.

"Detective Shaw?" The acting commander calls out as he keeps his weapon trained on the creature.

"I'm here." As Shaw goes to stand, he holds his badge in plain sight above his head, cautiously trying not to startle the heavily armed and very confused officers that aggressively close in. The husk speaks.

All the officers step back defensively, immediately training the weapons on this thing that can't comprehend, and their hungry fingers salivate across the triggers of their freshly reloaded weapons awaiting the order to disintegrate whatever is left of this thing.

When it speaks, it doesn't move at all, as though the sound isn't created by its tongue or vocal cords. It does resonate from it but where or how isn't clear. Neither is what it says, because it forms sounds that mimic words, but it isn't a language anyone here understands, at least it appears that way at first. When it stops "speaking" finally, it topples lifelessly, as though it was never alive at all to begin with and as soon as it hits the asphalt, Alexi instantly cries out in agony.

She pushes away from Eddie, chaotically prodding and painfully clutching her abdomen, and the sound she makes is so horribly loud that it immediately damages her vocal cords, silencing her completely. Her eyes bulge from her skull and she gasps like she is drowning. Eddie tries to help her, but she flails powerfully, as though she is having a seizure. And just as the medics run in to assist her, Eddie sees something stirring, pushing up from inside her before disappearing.

"Alexi! Look at me, Alexi!"

Eddie cries out trying to get to her, but the medics push him back like every cliché scene in the movie where they're trying to do their job and a concerned loved one reactively panics and tries to console them because they're truly helpless to help.

Eddie is pulled back by the police and as they speak to him, he can't hear them, their words are muffled and distant because he can only see her.

When he doesn't stop trying to get to her, they begin to assert unnecessary force, tackling him to the ground and pushing his head into the cold pavement.

He powerlessly watches as they wheel her away just as he feels the cold kiss of metal restrain his wrists constrictively. Eddie goes limp as they lift him and drag him through a nearby audience that loudly protests his treatment. Some are documenting through their phones, while others are the very same people, he helped liberate from the human milking machines. They throw him into the back of a large, armored vehicle, face first and he slides to a painful stop at very familiar footwear.

"Well, I didn't see this coming." Shaw says, helping Eddie up, his hands cuffed as well but obviously not behind his back like Eddie.

"Wait. Hold on. How the fuck did they find us? Did you call in back up? And more importantly, why the fuck did they arrest us?"

"Do you want the answers in order?" Shaw chuckles uncomfortably, badly feigning his true state which is worry.

"Shaw..."

"Short answer, procedure, or better yet, the complete disregard for it."

"Shaw, pretend for a second, that none of this crazy shit happened and keep pretending that you aren't still pretending that you aren't freaking the fuck out about all of it. Now, stop, and elab-the fuck-orate."

Shaw inhales, shivering, and listens briefly to the pandemonium just outside the truck before turning back and looking at Eddie.

"Eddie. Nobody has heard from me since Dan's funeral. I stopped going to work. Which raised a bunch of red flags, especially cause my partner was murdered and then I go completely silent. So, I became a missing person, but more than that, I became a missing cop. You putting this together? They tracked my phone. Which led them here. And when they found all these missing people, they brought an army. So, yeah, this is how we are here..."

"Fuck." Eddie shakes his head, visibly realizing what all of this must look like, and then visibly looks like he is trying to figure out just what all this looks like.

"Eddie. We are in deep shit. Do you understand that?"

"It just dawned on me right now, yeah, but Shaw, in the grand scheme of things, the law is the very least of my worries right now dick-tective."

"Fuck sakes Eddie, do you ever take anything seriously?"

"Alexi."

"What?"

"Alexi is the only thing I care about right now. Followed closely by was that the end of this? Did we win? Is Mr. Nightmare destroyed? What happens next? Are there more of those places and more things like Mr. Nightmare?"

"Eddie. I don't fucking know. But what I do know is that we have to get on the same page."

"What?"

"What is our story?"

"The truth, that's our story."

"Yeah, Eddie, what even is that story?"

"Fuck. Good point."

CHAPTER 29

If you were to tell this story, yeah, this one, the one you have been reading that you're almost certain is just a work of fiction when in truth you really don't know for sure, for sure is just a work of fiction. So imagine more than you have already been doing that you had to tell this story to the police and not appear completely fucking mental, how would you do it?

Shaw stands on the right side of two-way glass, watching Eddies interrogation or what it should be properly named the attempted interrogation of Eddie Read.

"Mr. Read, you have to give us something. Can you at least corroborate Detectives Shaw account of what happened?"

"Can I please, please, what is your name?"

"Detective Adalay, but you can call me Rebekah."

"Rebekah, please, please can I have a cigarette, I'm fucking dying."

Eddie isn't acting, he not only is "nicking" for a smoke, but he is also in substance withdrawal. He is soaked in sweat and shivering.

She looks at the mirror, and after a knock, she pulls out a pack and extends one.

Eddie, still in chains, tries to smile as he inches his lips, pursuing them to accept the beige spotted end of a fresh cigarette. She pushes it between his lips, and he catches it roughly in his teeth.

"Little help?"

She lights his smoke, and he sits back, sucking back deeply, before exhaling two streams of thick smoke.

"Rebekah, can I call you Becca? Becca, the last couple of days have been a fucking blur. I know this may shock you, but I wasn't quite in the right state of mind. Too much of a good thing, am I right?"

"You're honestly going to sit here and tell me that you don't remember leading detective Shaw to that horrible building? Or helping him freeing a bunch of hostages from machines that were milking them like cattle? Or how about Being attacked by what I can only describe from the statements as a..."

She looks down at the file.

"Demon?"

"Becca. I can't sugar coat this anymore. I have a drug problem. There. I said it. What I do remember is asking for help to find my girlfriend, which, and I'm being honest, you guys have been super insensitive at withholding how she is doing. I remember, the detective, Slaw or whatever taking my statement before I got text from an unknown number with a location saying that she was there. It seemed super sketchy, worried, I immediately went to the location and the detective, who was off duty at the time if I remember, followed me because it is his like civil duty. And then the drugs kicked in and everything gets really fucked up and I didn't know what was going on. Luckily, for Alexi and myself, Detective Slaw was there. That man is a hero, I want that on the record..."

Eddie stops ranting abruptly and signals for her to take the smoke from his lips as he goes pale. She immediately knows that look. She scatters for a bucket, just in time to catch the majority of his sick, however not quick enough to move her hand from its spray.

"Fucking hell."

"I'm so, so sorry Becca." Eddie says through gagging.

"It's Detective Adalay."

"Awe..huuugh." Eddie returns to vomiting.

Behind the glass, Shaw shakes his head, rubbing his eyes before turning to face his boss.

"So Cal, that is really how it all happened? You just stumbled upon this guy looking for his girlfriend and ended up taking down a human trafficking ring and barely escaping whatever the fuck that thing was? And at no time did you ever think to call for help?"

"Bill. As I said. I was drinking. Hell Bill, I was shit-housed. After Dan, I just broke. And I don't know why I fucking tried to help this guy but I was the furthest thing from ready for anything that followed."

"But you had enough time to arm yourself to the fucking teeth but not enough time to call it in? Cal, why, why are you sticking to this bullshit story? Forget all the disregard for textbook basic police procedure. This whole thing is an absolute shit show. I know you know what is going on and for some reason that I can't figure out, is you're choosing to be as vague and detached as possible despite what this could do for you, hell, if it is what it looks like and turns out to be, could do to the world..."

"And what is that, Bill?"

"What it looks like, however bat shit this sounds, it looks like you two went to slay a monster."

Shaw looks back at Eddie completely ignoring everything his superior, the chief of police, and long-term family friend William Scott just said and instead askes:

"What is going to happen to him?"

"Calamus?"

"Chief, what is going to happen to him?"

"We are going to charge him with possession of a schedule A narcotic with intent to traffic and several misdemeanors. But considering the media support and your testimony which I assume you're going to give, he will get a very reduced sentence, if he gets any time served at all. Calamus, you need to talk to me after this cools down. I'm sure you know you're suspended indefinitely pending investigation."

"Yeah, I figured Bill."

Bill sighs, painfully, and turns to leave and as he grabs the doorknob, Shaw pipes up.

"Bill, I'll tell you everything when I can."

Shaw turns back and watches Eddie being taken from the interrogation room or actually, he watches Eddie being dragged out of it.

This is normally when the narrator would take you back and show you the conversation that lead to this story, but as you probably can guess, this story and I are anything but normal. So, no, I'm not going to show you the ride to the police station where Shaw told Eddie the story that they went with and I'm definitely not going to explain Shaw's justification for it.

THE END

I'm just kidding, I'm going to explain it, or at least a part of it that you need to see...err...read.

"Why don't we just tell them everything?" He bangs his head against the metal in frustration.

"Because, for the last time, because we are fucking out of time. We don't know enough. We barely know anything. We know slightly more about what is actually going on than the people who are about to grill us endlessly and if we give them the truth, it will fall on deaf ears, and then we both will be locked up powerless to change anything. But what I don't know, I know for sure…"

"What the fuck does that even mean?"

"I know that this isn't over. Even if that fuck bag blood sucking parasite is destroyed. We aren't done. I know that there is something just as bad as him sitting in prison, waiting to get out, and he will get out if we don't stop him. So, the only way to make sure he doesn't get out is if you go in and destroy him."

"Wait, what?"

"Eddie you are going to prison to kill a werewolf."

THE END

Or to be continued, whatever…

THE PAGE TO WRITE SOMETHING NICE